An Improbable Scheme

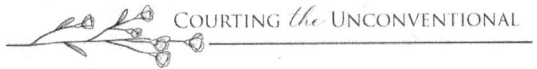

COURTING *the* UNCONVENTIONAL

LAURA BEERS

1

England, 1813

Lady Elsbeth Caldwell tightened her grip on the pistol, her gloved hands steady despite the chill that seeped through her wool coat. She sat atop her restless mare, hidden among the shadows of the dense trees lining the winding country road. Her breath misted in the cold night air as she waited, her heart pounding in anticipation. Tonight, she would uncover the truth, or so she fervently hoped.

Her stepfather, Mr. Alfred Stockton, was a merchant—a wealthy merchant, but a merchant, nonetheless. On the surface, he was polished, polite, even charming, but Elsbeth's instincts screamed otherwise. Her mother, the once Countess of Bedford, dismissed her suspicions as nonsense, blinded by the stability he had brought into their lives after her father's death left them with very little. Now, they were forced to live at her stepfather's country estate in Polperro. It may be grand, but it felt like a gilded cage to her. The life she had known growing up was over.

But Elsbeth could not shake the feeling that something was

amiss. Her stepfather's locked desk drawers and secretive behavior confirmed it. If only her mother would listen.

The faint rattle of carriage wheels reached her ears, and she adjusted her black mask, the fabric itchy against her skin. The image of her stepfather's polished smile flashed in her mind, spurring her resolve. She could not falter now. If she could obtain the key he kept in his jacket pocket, she could unlock his secrets.

A coach came into view, lanterns glowing faintly in the foggy darkness. Elsbeth clicked her tongue, urging her horse forward. She rode into the middle of the road and leveled her pistol at the driver, who pulled the reins with a startled shout.

"Highwayman!" the driver bellowed, his voice carrying through the still night.

Elsbeth summoned the deepest voice she could muster. "Stand and deliver!"

A moment later, the coach door opened and a tall, broad-shouldered man stepped out. The glow of the lanterns revealed his sharp features. He had a square jaw, dark hair neatly brushed forward, and long sideburns. His posture was confident, his expression mildly curious rather than alarmed.

He was not her stepfather.

Drat.

Elsbeth's heart sank. She had stopped the wrong coach. This was a waste of time. She lowered the pistol slightly, irritated with herself. Why had she not taken more care to ensure it had been her stepfather's coach?

"You may go," she muttered.

The man raised a brow, stepping forward. "I beg your pardon?"

"I said, you may go." She tried to maintain her commanding tone, though the encounter was already spiraling into absurdity.

"Are you not here to rob me?" he asked, incredulous.

Elsbeth shook her head. "Not today."

The man took a step closer to her. "Why did you stop and inconvenience us then if you have no intention of robbing us?"

He did make a valid point. She had never tried to rob someone before. It might look suspicious if she did not try to take something from him. "Fine. Give me your pocket watch."

The man hesitated before removing a gleaming gold pocket watch from his waistcoat. "This has been in my family for generations."

Feeling sympathy for the man's plight, Elsbeth said, "Then keep it and give me something else. Something worthless. A trinket, perhaps."

The man studied her for a long moment before smirking. "You are not a very convincing highwayman."

"I am," Elsbeth declared.

The man did not look convinced. "For starters, you are a woman."

"Women can be highwaymen," she argued.

"It is rare," he said. "Almost as rare as a young woman wearing trousers and sitting astride on a horse."

Elsbeth felt her frustration starting to grow. "I do not have time to argue with you on the merits of highwaywomen. I am growing tired of this conversation. If you are not nice, I will demand your pocket watch as payment for you to continue on this road."

"That is fine," the man said with a slight shrug. "It is a trinket that I picked up when I was at the market. It is worth nothing."

"You lied to me?" she asked, trying to ignore the irony of her question.

The man chuckled. "Says the woman in trousers who is trying to rob me."

Elsbeth pointed the pistol at the man. "You, Sir, have just

lost your pocket watch. Bring it to me and you can be on your way."

"Very well, but you could at least tell me where you live," the man said as he slowly approached her.

"And why would I be foolish enough to do that?"

The man stopped next to her horse and extended the pocket watch. "So I may know where to retrieve my pocket watch."

"Where I live is not important."

The man's lips curled into a smile. "I disagree. A lady highwayman is quite rare."

Elsbeth grew tense. "I never said I was a lady."

"You did not have to," the man said. "It is in the manner in which you speak and how you sit atop your horse that makes me wonder why you have turned to a life of crime."

"I did not turn to a life of crime," Elsbeth stated, growing defensive. The unmitigated gall of this man. He did not know her. He did not know why she was doing this.

The man held the pocket watch up higher. "Take it, my lady highwayman."

Keeping the pistol trained on him, Elsbeth reached with her other hand for the pocket watch. "Thank you, Sir."

"Just in case you are wondering, my name is Niles Drayton, the Earl of Westcott," he informed her with a slight bow.

"I was not wondering."

His smile grew. "Pity. I find that I very much want to know your name."

"Well, you shall leave disappointed, then." Elsbeth glanced down the road and wondered if she had missed her stepfather's coach this evening. Either way, her time was short, and she didn't have time to converse with this infuriating earl.

She urged her horse to back up. "Good evening, my lord."

"Do you want anything else?" Lord Westcott asked. "I have

coins. Lots of coins. Perhaps I could remove our trunks, and you could sort through what you would wish to steal."

Elsbeth furrowed her brow. Surely this was not normal behavior. Why was this earl offering to give her more than what she was asking for? "No, I do not need—or want—your money. Or whatever it is that you have in your trunks."

"Just my pocket watch."

Looking down at the pocket watch in her hand, Elsbeth said, "I do not want this either."

"Then why did you take it from me?"

"You left me little choice," Elsbeth said, holding it out. "Take it back."

Lord Westcott made no attempt to retrieve the pocket watch. "No, you can have it. I want you to have something to remember me by."

Elsbeth let out a slight huff. "You flatter yourself, my lord. I do not want to remember you."

Cocking his head, Lord Westcott said, "You are truly the worst highwaywoman ever. Would you care for some pointers?"

"No, I would not," she replied. "I would prefer if you kept your opinions to yourself."

Ignoring her words, Lord Westcott's eyes flashed with amusement. "Is this how you envisioned your robbery to go?"

"I think it is going fairly well," she lied.

Lord Westcott chuckled, the noise grating on her nerves. "I hate to tell you this, but you would be wrong. In fact, everything you are doing is wrong."

"And how would you know this?" she asked. "Have you ever robbed a coach before?"

"No, I have not."

"Then how can you speak with such certainty?" Elsbeth asked.

Lord Westcott held his hands up in surrender. "I am merely pointing out that you are a truly awful highwaywoman."

Just then, Elsbeth saw the driver reaching for something under his seat. She swung her pistol towards him. "Stop that, or I will shoot!"

"Do as she says, Parker. Let her go," Lord Westcott ordered. His tone brooked no argument.

The driver stilled, muttering under his breath, and Elsbeth seized her chance. She turned her horse sharply and galloped into the dark woodland, her heart pounding in her chest. The cold wind bit at her face as she raced towards her stepfather's estate, the familiar path of the woodlands calming her nerves.

Niles Drayton, Earl of Westcott, watched as the highwaywoman disappeared into the dense cover of the trees. Instead of anger or frustration at being robbed, he felt something far more inconvenient: curiosity. Who was this brazen woman? The encounter had felt oddly halfhearted, almost as if she had not truly meant to rob them.

He turned and stepped into the coach, shutting the door firmly behind him. The conveyance jolted forward again, creaking as it resumed its journey. His sister Eugenie sat across from him, her keen blue eyes studying him intently.

"Why on earth did you give that highway*woman* your pocket watch?" Eugenie asked.

Niles shrugged, leaning back into the worn leather seat. "I had little choice in the matter."

"That is utter nonsense. She tried to return it to you, and you refused. Do not tell me that Father's pocket watch means so little to you."

"It means a great deal," he replied. "I simply have every intention of getting it back."

"How, pray tell, do you plan to do that?"

Niles's lips curved into a faint smile. "By uncovering the identity of that highwaywoman. Surely there are not too many genteel women in Polperro riding about in trousers and wielding pistols."

Eugenie adjusted the thick wool blanket draped over her lap, fixing him with a skeptical look. "And what will you do when you find her? Will you turn her over to the constable?"

"That depends," Niles said.

"On what?"

Niles gave his sister a knowing look. "On whether or not she gives me back my pocket watch."

Eugenie shook her head. "We are here to visit Aunt Margaret, not to embark on a search for a highwaywoman."

"I can do both."

Turning her attention towards the window, Eugenie said, "This entire conversation is absurd, as is your obsession with her."

Niles chuckled. "Where is your sense of adventure? We were just robbed by a highwaywoman. That is not exactly an everyday occurrence."

Eugenie brought her gaze back to meet his. "I wouldn't call that a robbery. Besides, it might have been exciting if you had not ordered me to stay in the coach like a helpless child."

Not feeling the least apologetic for his actions, he replied, "I was trying to keep you safe."

"You were being overbearing," she shot back. "And, for the record, I would have loved the opportunity to exchange words with our peculiar thief."

"I will remember that for next time."

Eugenie gave him an exasperated look. "I think it best if we do not speak again until we reach Aunt Margaret's. Your voice is beginning to grate on my ears."

Niles grinned. "You are being quite pleasant this evening."

"I'm tired," she muttered. "We have been on this infernal

journey for days, and all I want is a warm bath and some peace."

He could hardly fault her for that. The journey had left him weary as well. Still, the memory of the highwaywoman played in his mind, finding the mystery of it all to be that much more intriguing. Closing his eyes, he settled in to wait for their arrival.

A short while later, the coach came to a jerking stop before a grand white-brick manor. The footman hurried to set the step down and opened the door, bowing as Niles stepped out. He turned to assist Eugenie, but she batted his hand away with a look that she'd had enough of his hovering.

The main door of the manor swung open, and a tall, thin woman with silver hair and a radiant smile stood waiting. "You are here!" Aunt Margaret exclaimed, her voice ringing with genuine delight.

Eugenie rushed forward, embracing their aunt warmly. "Oh, Aunt Margaret, it is so good to see you. It has been far too long."

"Yes, it has been," her aunt confirmed.

Niles lingered at the edge of the steps, feeling awkward and out of place. Physical affection had never come naturally to him, even among family. But Aunt Margaret would have none of it.

She descended the stairs swiftly, pulling him into a firm hug. "Niles," she murmured, holding him close.

He hesitated before tentatively patting her back. "Aunt Margaret."

She stepped back, her smile intact. "Thank you for indulging me. I know you are not fond of hugs, but I will take one from you any day."

"For you, Aunt Margaret, always," Niles replied.

"You are so much like your father," she said, studying him with a wistful expression. Then gesturing to the open doorway, she added, "Come inside, both of you. You must be famished after your travels."

"I could always eat," Eugenie admitted as they stepped into the warmth of the manor.

"I thought you wanted a bath," Niles teased.

Eugenie shot him a mock glare. "Food first, then a bath."

"You shall have both," Aunt Margaret said as she signaled to a plump butler. "Turpin, inform Mrs. McLeod to prepare some trays for their rooms. They must be exhausted."

"Thank you, Aunt Margaret," Eugenie said, looping her arm through her aunt's. "You will never guess what happened to us on the way here."

Aunt Margaret gave Eugenie an expectant look. "Well, do not leave me in suspense. I am an old woman and could die at any moment," she quipped.

In a low voice, Eugenie said, "We were robbed... by a highway*woman*."

"A woman?" Aunt Margaret repeated back in surprise. "Are you certain?"

Niles interjected. "Quite certain."

Aunt Margaret's face turned grave. "This is serious. We must alert the constable at once. We cannot have a highwaywoman terrorizing the citizens of this village."

Eugenie smirked. "Niles seemed rather taken with her."

Their aunt's eyes widened. "There is nothing romantic about being robbed by a highwaywoman."

"I never said that there was," Niles said, feeling defensive. "I merely found the whole thing to be intriguing."

"I daresay that you need more excitement in your life," Aunt Margaret declared. "Perhaps you need a wife."

Niles stiffened. "I do not need a wife... at least, right now."

"You are almost thirty. If you do not marry soon, people might begin to suspect something is wrong with you."

Eugenie laughed. "Oh, there is definitely something wrong with my brother."

"Thank you, Sister," Niles muttered dryly. "Your support is overwhelming."

"Was I supposed to help?" Eugenie asked with an innocent expression.

Niles glanced at the staircase, longing for an escape. "I think it might be best if I retire for the evening and end this line of harassment."

But Aunt Margaret was not one to let him slip away so easily. "You can't go yet," she insisted. "I want to know how the Season went. I even heard a rumor that Niles offered for a young woman. Are you engaged?"

Eugenie put a hand up in front of her mouth and whispered, "She turned him down."

He frowned. "Must we speak about this?"

"It is not as if you were in love with her," Eugenie replied, lowering her hand. "You only wanted to marry her because she was the diamond of the Season."

Aunt Margaret's eyes gleamed with interest. "Ah, the elusive diamond. It matters not, because I found the perfect young woman for you."

Niles resisted the urge to groan. "You do not need to play matchmaker for me."

His aunt waved off his protest as though it were inconsequential. "Nonsense. What else am I supposed to do with my time? Her name is Lady Elsbeth Caldwell, and she resides at a country estate not far from here. A rare beauty, I assure you."

"I am sure you mean well, but I can find my own wife," Niles replied.

Before Aunt Margaret could press the matter further, the butler reappeared in the entry hall. "Trays are being sent to their bedchambers, my lady."

Aunt Margaret's head bobbed in acknowledgment. "Very

good, Turpin." She turned back to them, her determination undiminished. "Allow me to show you to your bedchambers."

Niles hoped this would mark the end of the conversation, but he knew his aunt better than that.

As they walked up the stairs, Aunt Margaret continued. "We shall call upon Lady Elsbeth tomorrow, assuming you have no objections."

"I have many objections," Niles stated bluntly.

Aunt Margaret dismissed his words with a flick of her wrist. "You say that now, but you have not seen the lovely Lady Elsbeth. She is truly stunning."

"I do not doubt she is pretty enough, but I do not need you to meddle in my affairs," Niles said.

Eugenie huffed from behind him. "What affairs? You spend all your time locked away in your study, reviewing the accounts."

"What else should I be doing?" Niles asked. "I know I eventually need a wife, but I am perfectly fine with ensuring you are settled first."

"I have no intention of getting married," Eugenie declared. "I would rather remain a spinster like Aunt Margaret."

Coming to a stop in front of a door, Aunt Margaret said, "We can discuss this further at a later time." She opened the door. "Eugenie, this is your bedchamber."

Eugenie disappeared into the room with a playful wave, leaving Niles to follow his aunt down the corridor.

When they reached his door, Aunt Margaret lingered, her expression unusually serious.

"Is something the matter?" he asked, his hand on the polished doorknob.

His aunt sighed, her worry evident. "Is Eugenie in earnest about not wanting to marry?"

"I'm afraid so."

"We must make her change her mind," Aunt Margaret said

firmly. "Being a spinster is a lonely life, and I do not wish that for her."

Placing a reassuring hand on her shoulder, he replied, "She is young. She has only had one Season. Give her time and she might change her mind."

Aunt Margaret gave him a small, reluctant smile. "I hope you are right. Goodnight, Niles."

"Goodnight," he replied, watching as she disappeared down the corridor.

As he entered his room, he found Wiley, his ever-efficient valet, unpacking his trunks. "I am almost done, my lord," he informed Niles.

Niles sank onto the settee, grateful to be off his feet. It had been a long day. "Wiley, how long have you been married?"

"Ten years now," Wiley replied, a note of pride in his voice.

"That is a long time."

"Not long enough," Wiley said with a chuckle. "If you ask me, it is just the beginning."

Niles leaned his head back, his thoughts drifting to the highwaywoman who had stopped his coach. There was something about her, something that intrigued him.

Why did he feel as though meeting her had changed everything? And why did he have the distinct impression that their paths would cross again?

2

E lsbeth entered the dining room and paused just inside the doorway, her eyes falling on her stepfather seated at the head of the long, rectangular table. Her blonde-haired mother sat to his right, daintily slicing into a boiled egg. Her mother always ate the same thing every morning: one boiled egg and two pieces of buttered toast. The sight should have been comforting. Familiar. But today it only stirred frustration in Elsbeth.

Her dark-haired stepfather looked up from the newssheets, offering a smile. "Good morning, Elsbeth," he greeted, his tone warm. Too warm.

"Good morning," she replied.

Her mother glanced up. "I trust that you slept well last night?"

"I did," Elsbeth lied. She wouldn't admit she had barely closed her eyes, haunted by the memory of her encounter with Lord Westcott the night before. The replay of their interaction had consumed her, and she felt sure she had appeared utterly absurd to him.

Her mother smiled. "That is good. Come, join us," she said, gesturing towards the chair to her left.

Elsbeth's feet felt like lead as she approached the table. She did not want to eat breakfast with her stepfather. The man was a charlatan in her eyes, though she couldn't yet prove it.

As she settled into her chair, Alfred folded his newssheets and set them neatly aside, his attention now fully on her. "Your mother and I are planning to visit the village today," he said. "I thought perhaps you might like to join us. There are a few shops worth browsing, and I believe you could use a new hat."

The words hit their mark. Alfred was reminding her, subtly but effectively, that without his money, she could not afford the simplest of luxuries. But two could play at this game.

She met his gaze, her expression carefully composed. "How thoughtful of you. I would love a new hat. You are most considerate."

Alfred's smile broadened, clearly pleased with her response. "I know how much women enjoy pretty things," he said with a loving glance at his wife.

"Men seem to enjoy them just as much," Elsbeth remarked, her tone edged with a challenge.

Her mother stiffened, sending her a warning look, but Alfred only laughed. "Guilty as charged, Elsbeth. I find your mother extraordinarily beautiful, and I count myself lucky to have her."

"That is kind of you to say," her mother said, leaning in for a brief kiss.

Elsbeth turned her attention to her cup of chocolate, taking a slow sip to avoid rolling her eyes. She couldn't fathom her mother's infatuation with this man. Her mother had adored Elsbeth's father and had been devastated by his death. How had she moved on so quickly? And with a man so vastly beneath her station?

Her mother broke the silence, her tone brisk. "We mustn't

linger in the village too long. Lady Margaret will be calling on us later."

Elsbeth's mood lifted slightly at the mention of Lady Margaret. "Perhaps we should forgo shopping altogether."

"Nonsense," her mother replied, smoothing a hand over the linen napkin in her lap. "We will have time for both, provided we are efficient."

"I do not truly need another hat," Elsbeth said.

Her stepfather chuckled. "I have never known a lady to think she has too many hats."

"It is rare, but it happens," she said. "Besides, my *father* ensured my mother and I had an abundance of hats. There is no need to buy us any more."

Her mother frowned. "That is enough, Elsbeth."

Alfred, however, seemed unruffled, offering her an apologetic look. "I did not mean to offend."

Of course, he hadn't. The man was a master of manipulation. Playing the victim now, as if her comments had been unwarranted. But she knew better.

Pushing back his chair, Alfred rose. "If you will excuse me, I have a few matters to attend to before we leave." He gave his wife a private smile before departing the room.

As soon as the door closed behind him, her mother turned a stern gaze on her. "Whatever has come over you, Child?"

"Alfred is not who he claims to be."

Her mother exhaled sharply, exasperation etched onto her features. "Not this again. Why are you so determined to malign him?"

"Why does Alfred want to buy us a hat so badly?" Elsbeth pressed. "I daresay that he is trying to buy our love."

"Or perhaps he is simply being kind. Did you consider that?" her mother retorted.

"No, he is playing a game," Elsbeth insisted.

Her mother shoved back her chair, rising to her feet. "I have had enough of this nonsense. Alfred is a good, honorable man and you should be grateful to have him in your life."

"How can you be so blind?" Elsbeth demanded, her voice rising. "He is manipulating us... manipulating *you*."

Her mother's tone hardened. "I think it might be best if you don't accompany us to the village, after all."

"Mother..."

She raised a hand, stilling Elsbeth's words. "Not another word. Alfred is my husband, and I love him."

Elsbeth leaned back in her chair, her arms crossed. "How could you move on so quickly after Father's death?"

Her mother's eyes widened with indignation. "How dare you say such a thing? I mourned your father properly, as was expected of me."

"And then you married Alfred at the first opportunity."

"Yes, and I do not regret it," her mother declared. "Marrying Alfred got us out of that miserable dower house and into a far better situation."

Elsbeth tossed her hands up. "We are worse off. You married beneath you, and you lost your place in Society, despite being the daughter of an earl. We were shunned for it."

"No," her mother said sharply. "We were shunned because of your father's gambling debts and rakish reputation."

"And what of me?" Elsbeth asked. "Did you even consider my opinion or my future when you married Alfred?"

Her mother crossed her arms over her chest. "I did this for us."

"Well, I never asked you to," Elsbeth snapped.

"Would you have preferred to stay in the dower house, scraping by and watching our servants leave one by one because we couldn't afford to pay them?"

Elsbeth pressed her lips together. "Cousin Charles would have helped us."

"Charles was busy managing a bankrupt estate," her

mother insisted. "He cared very little about what we did, much less about what *we* needed."

"I disagree," Elsbeth said. "Regardless, why does Alfred lock his desk drawers if he has nothing to hide?"

Her mother lifted her brow. "Perhaps because his step-daughter has been rummaging through his things."

"He doesn't know that."

With a shake of her head, her mother replied, "Alfred is much smarter than you give him credit for."

Elsbeth reached for a piece of bread from the center of the table. "I do not want to live here. It is cold and miserable. This estate feels like a cage."

"This is our home now," her mother said firmly. "It has been six months since I married Alfred. You'd best get used to it."

Without another word, she left the dining room, leaving Elsbeth to stew in her frustration.

Reaching for a knife, Elsbeth began to butter her bread. She knew she might appear ungrateful, but she couldn't bring herself to pretend that all was well. Something about her stepfather and their current circumstances felt off, and she was determined to uncover the truth, no matter how long it took.

As she chewed her bread, the butler stepped into the room. He gave a small bow before announcing, "Lady Margaret has arrived with her niece, Lady Eugenie, and her nephew, Lord Westcott."

Elsbeth's hand froze, her slice of bread hovering above her plate. "Did you say 'Lord Westcott'?" she asked as she attempted to keep the dread out of her voice.

"I did, my lady," the butler confirmed.

Drat.

What was she to do now? She couldn't turn Lady Margaret away, not when the woman was one of the few members of Society still willing to call on their household. But the thought of meeting Lord Westcott again made her stomach churn. What if he recognized her?

No.

That was impossible. She had worn a mask and tried to conceal her voice. He had no way of knowing it had been her as the highwaywoman.

Placing the bread down onto her plate, Elsbeth said, "Please inform my mother that we have guests to attend to."

Rising from her seat, Elsbeth smoothed her pale blue gown, hoping it would mask the unease threatening to overwhelm her. Lord Westcott was just another guest. Nothing more. So why was her heart racing at the thought of seeing him? Surely it had nothing to do with his piercing eyes, chiseled jaw, or how impossibly handsome he had appeared even under the moonlight.

Pushing her thoughts aside, she headed towards the drawing room. She stepped inside and was immediately greeted by Lady Margaret's warm, familiar smile.

Elsbeth rushed forward and embraced her. "Lady Margaret," she said brightly. "What a pleasant surprise."

"Isn't it, though?" Lady Margaret responded as she took a step back. "We were on our way to the village for some shopping but I thought it best to call upon you first."

"I am so glad that you did," Elsbeth said. Despite her apprehension, Lady Margaret's presence was always a comfort.

Turning towards a blonde-haired young woman, Lady Margaret provided the introductions. "Allow me to introduce you to my niece, Lady Eugenie. She has just completed her first Season."

Elsbeth offered a polite smile, though her heart gave a slight pang. "How fortunate you are," she said. At twenty years old, she had missed her chance to enjoy a Season, the opportunity snatched away by her father's death and their subsequent fall from Society.

Lady Eugenie's eyes held a twinkle of merriment. "Yes, though according to my brother, I failed miserably since I did not secure a husband."

Gesturing towards Lord Westcott, his disinterest evident in his posture, Lady Margaret said, "And this is my nephew, Lord Westcott."

He bowed. "My lady."

Elsbeth knew what was expected of her and dropped into a curtsy. "My lord," she murmured.

He gave her the faintest of smiles, one that barely reached his eyes, as though even that small effort taxed him. "It is a pleasure to meet you," he said, the words sounding more like an obligation than genuine sentiment.

"Likewise," Elsbeth said.

Lady Margaret glanced at the doorway. "I was hoping your mother would be available to receive us."

"She will be along shortly," Elsbeth assured her. "May I get everyone a cup of tea while we wait?"

Lady Eugenie nodded. "That would be lovely. Thank you."

After settling her guests on the settee, Elsbeth reached for the teapot and began pouring. Her movements were deliberate, but her hands trembled slightly as she handed Lord Westcott his cup. Their gloved fingers brushed briefly, and she felt a sharp jolt shoot up her arm, leaving her momentarily breathless.

Good heavens. What was wrong with her? She had met handsome men before, but there was something about Lord Westcott that unsettled her, something that kept her ill at ease. Perhaps it was the nagging fear that he might somehow see through her mask of propriety and uncover her secret. She had stolen his pocket watch, after all. If he ever found out, her family would be ruined beyond repair.

She forced herself to meet his gaze, hoping to find some clue to his thoughts. His dark eyes were unreadable, his expression calm but distant. Did he know? Could he suspect? Or was she simply imagining the weight of his scrutiny?

———————— ~——~ ————————

Niles shifted in his chair as he attempted to conceal his growing irritation. Social calls like these were not his preference, but Aunt Margaret had insisted they visit Lady Elsbeth, and here he was. He would rather be anywhere else. It was always the same: young women batting their eyelashes and feigning interest in him, all because he was an earl. They saw the title, not the man.

Lady Elsbeth was undeniably beautiful. Her olive-toned skin gave her an unusual elegance, and her straight nose and high cheekbones added to her striking appearance. Chestnut brown hair framed her face in soft curls, and the rest was swept up neatly. She seemed at ease, laughing lightly at something Aunt Margaret had said, but Niles suspected it was all a ruse.

His gaze lingered a moment too long, and Lady Elsbeth turned her head, catching him staring. He expected a coy smile or a flutter of lashes, but instead, she studied him with an almost detached curiosity.

"Is your tea not to your liking, my lord?" she asked, her voice oddly polite.

"My tea is perfectly fine," he replied.

She seemed satisfied by his response and returned to her conversation with Eugenie and Aunt Margaret, dismissing him as if he were a mere inconvenience.

It was unexpected. Refreshing, even. But puzzling. Surely she knew he was an earl. Women like her were usually keen on securing such a match. He leaned back in his seat, trying to figure out her true intentions.

Regardless, Lady Elsbeth was not a suitable match for him.

Her family's reputation was in tatters, thanks to her late father's reckless gambling. Her mother's marriage to a lowly merchant had only added to their fall from grace. Not that he thought he was better than her, but he had his own family's reputation to think about. His sister's future depended on it.

A burst of laughter from Lady Elsbeth broke through his thoughts. The sound was light and genuine, and it struck him unexpectedly. Feeling like an interloper, he decided to join the conversation rather than sit there, stewing in his own thoughts. Clearing his throat, he drew the attention of all three ladies, their expectant gazes turning to him.

"It is a fine day we are having," Niles said, inwardly cringing the moment the words left his mouth.

Eugenie gave him a bemused look. "It is raining, Brother."

"Is it?" he asked, feigning ignorance.

Aunt Margaret offered him a sympathetic smile. "How terribly rude of us. We have been ignoring you, Niles. What would you care to discuss?"

Caught off guard, he fumbled for a topic. "I... uh... find that I am curious about Lady Elsbeth." Why did he say that? He cared little about learning more about Lady Elsbeth.

Lady Elsbeth's lips pressed into a thin line, her expression one of mild annoyance rather than flattery. "What do you wish to know, my lord?"

Botheration.

What could he ask that wouldn't make him sound like a complete muttonhead? "Do you ride?"

"I do," she replied simply.

"That is good," he muttered. What was wrong with him? He had never had an issue conversing with a beautiful young woman before.

Turning away from him, Lady Elsbeth addressed Eugenie. "Do you ride?"

His sister grew visibly tense. "I haven't ridden since my accident."

"I'm sorry," Lady Elsbeth said, her voice tinged with sincerity. "I didn't know."

"No harm done," Eugenie replied. "I do not speak of it often."

Without hesitation, Lady Elsbeth leaned forward and placed her hand gently over Eugenie's. "Then we won't speak of it."

"Thank you," Eugenie said.

Niles observed the exchange with a mixture of admiration and unease. Lady Elsbeth's concern seemed to be genuine, and that surprised him. She didn't seem to be playing any game, at least not one that he could discern.

The entrance of a blonde-haired, matronly woman interrupted his thoughts. Her bright smile was directed at Aunt Margaret. "What a pleasant surprise," she greeted. "I hadn't expected you until later."

Aunt Margaret rose and embraced the woman. "We thought it was best to visit before heading to the village for shopping."

"Well, you are always welcome in our home," the woman replied, taking a seat beside Lady Elsbeth.

Aunt Margaret gestured towards them. "Allow me to introduce my niece, Lady Eugenie, and my nephew, Lord Westcott."

The woman smiled graciously. "Welcome, I am Lady Isabella Stockton. I trust that your journey to our quaint village was uneventful."

Eugenie interjected. "We were robbed by a highway*woman*."

"A highwaywoman?" Lady Isabella repeated, her brows lifting in surprise. "How unusual."

Lady Elsbeth suddenly picked up a plate of biscuits. "Would anyone care for a biscuit?" Her voice was loud. Too loud.

Niles leaned forward and retrieved a biscuit, his interest

piqued by Lady Elsbeth's abrupt attempt to redirect the conversation.

His sister, with a gleam in her eyes, continued. "She made off with Niles's pocket watch. It belonged to our father."

"Your father's?" Lady Elsbeth asked, glancing at Niles as she placed the plate down onto the tray.

"Yes," Niles replied. "It was handed down to me after his passing."

Lady Elsbeth gasped, bringing her hand up to cover her mouth. "I'm sorry," she said softly. "I didn't know."

Niles placed his cup and saucer down on the table. "I appreciate your concern, but you have no reason to apologize."

"Yes, of course, I know that. But I would imagine that particular family heirloom means a great deal to you," Lady Elsbeth said.

"It does," Niles admitted.

Lady Elsbeth bit her lower lip, her gaze flickering to the tea tray before returning to him. "I hope you are able to get your pocket watch back in a timely fashion."

"I doubt Niles will ever see it again," Eugenie declared, her tone more practical than hopeful. "The highwaywoman might have already sold it to the highest bidder."

"I doubt someone would part with something so valuable so quickly," Lady Elsbeth contended.

Niles offered her a brief smile, touched by her concern. "What's done is done," he said. "I would prefer not to dwell on it."

Lady Elsbeth nodded, but her expression remained conflicted, as though there were more she wanted to say.

Niles didn't know how—or when—but he would get that pocket watch back. He had to. But first, he needed to discover the identity of the highwaywoman. Leaning back in his seat, a thought struck him—could Lady Elsbeth be the culprit? The idea seemed preposterous. Why would a genteel daughter of an earl turn to a life of crime?

But no. He quickly dismissed the thought. Lady Elsbeth's reaction to his plight was far too empathetic to belong to a common thief.

Aunt Margaret's voice broke through his musings. "Oh, dear. It might not be the best day to go shopping," she remarked as she gazed at the rain pounding against the glass.

"I must agree," Lady Isabella chimed in.

Niles stole a glance at Lady Elsbeth. Her eyes were downcast, and there was a line between her brows. Was she troubled by the conversation? Or was it something else entirely?

But before he could say anything, Aunt Margaret rose. "We do not want to take up too much of your time."

"Nonsense," Lady Isabella contended. "I always cherish the visits I receive from you."

Aunt Margaret smiled. "In that case, I would like to invite you and your family to dine with us this evening."

"We would be delighted," Lady Isabella promptly responded.

"Wonderful," Aunt Margaret said. "We shall see you this evening, then."

As Niles followed the ladies out of the room, Lady Elsbeth called out to him. "My lord, might I have a word, please?"

Here it was.

Niles resisted the urge to sigh. He knew what was coming. The inevitable flirtation. It always came to this. Women were so predictable.

He turned, keeping his expression guarded. "Yes, Lady Elsbeth?" he asked, not bothering to hide the annoyance from his voice.

She stepped closer and her voice dropped to a near whisper. "I do not think we should associate with one another."

Niles blinked, caught completely off guard. Of all the things she could have said, this was the last he had expected. "And why is that?"

She hesitated before saying, "I am sure you have heard the rumors about my family. I do not want to besmirch your family's name—or Lady Eugenie's—by association."

"How thoughtful of you," he muttered, his words laced with sarcasm.

Lady Elsbeth held her ground. "That is all I wanted to say, my lord."

Niles should have left it at that. He should have turned and walked away. But something about her made him pause. Against his better judgment, he took a step closer, matching her low tone. "You do not need to concern yourself with my family's reputation."

"I was only trying—"

He cut her off. "Did you truly think that this scheme would work?"

Her brow furrowed. "What scheme?"

"Women throw themselves at me all the time," Niles said. "You may think you are convincing, but I see through it."

Lady Elsbeth's eyes flashed with irritation. "And what, pray tell, am I doing?"

"You believe that warning me away will endear me to you," he accused. "But it won't work."

Her cheeks flushed, her voice growing defensive. "That is not what I was doing."

She was good. He had to admit that. But he knew better. With a smirk on his lips, he said, "You could have a career in the theater with such a performance."

Lady Elsbeth's eyes narrowed. "I daresay you are so full of yourself, I am surprised your head does not float away."

"Resorting to insults, are we?" he asked, arching a brow.

She took a step back, her chin held high. "And to think, I actually felt sorry for you."

Niles's smirk faltered as he leaned in, his voice dropping to a near growl. "I think we are in agreement, then. The less time we spend together, the better."

"Oh, trust me, my lord, I plan to spend as little time with you as possible," Lady Elsbeth retorted, brushing past him.

Good.

That is precisely what he wanted.

As Niles stood there, his sister appeared in the doorway. Eugenie's brows were drawn together in an expression that was half-disapproval, half-exasperation. "What did you say to Lady Elsbeth?"

"Nothing that didn't need to be said," Niles replied.

Eugenie cocked her head, her blonde curls swaying with the motion. "Oh, really? Because she looked rather irritated. Will you please stop being you for once and at least attempt to be cordial?"

"I don't know what you are referring to," Niles said.

Closing the distance between them, Eugenie lowered her voice. "Aunt Margaret adores Lady Elsbeth. Do try to remember that."

"Aunt Margaret has always been a poor judge of character."

"And yet she likes you," Eugenie shot back, her lips curling in a wry smile.

Niles couldn't help but chuckle under his breath. "Point taken. But that doesn't mean I trust Lady Elsbeth."

Eugenie gave him a pointed look. "Why is that? Is she too nice? Too beautiful?"

His jaw tightened, and he looked away towards the window where the rain continued to fall in relentless sheets. "I do not want to discuss this."

"You never do," Eugenie replied.

Offering his arm, Niles said, "In my position, suspicion isn't a choice. It is a necessity. I must be pragmatic about people's motives."

Eugenie slipped her arm through his. "That is a sad way to live, Brother. Always expecting the worst in others."

"Perhaps, but it is a luxury you can afford to ignore. I cannot."

Eugenie's voice softened, though her words remained firm. "I prefer to believe the best in everyone. It is what Father would have wanted."

Niles pursed his lips. His father's memory was a sore subject, one he was not prepared to confront at this moment.

"You know," Eugenie continued, "not every woman you meet is trying to entrap you. Maybe Lady Elsbeth isn't the conniving young woman you conjured up in your mind."

"I will reserve judgment... for now," Niles replied.

He knew how jaded he sounded as he led his sister out of the drawing room. But there was something about Lady Elsbeth that gnawed at the edges of his thoughts, and that left him uneasy.

3

Elsbeth sat stiffly in the darkened coach as it rumbled down the uneven road towards Lady Margaret's manor. Across from her, her mother and stepfather sat in animated conversation, their voices low but cheerful. Elsbeth, however, was far from cheerful. Her arms were crossed tightly over her chest, and she fixed her gaze out the window. She was not looking forward to seeing Lord Westcott again. The man was infuriatingly arrogant.

Her stepfather's voice broke through her thoughts. "You two are looking rather lovely this evening."

Elsbeth resisted the urge to roll her eyes. Why was Alfred trying so hard to win her approval? But her mother had no such reservations about the compliment.

"Thank you, my love," her mother said.

My love?

Elsbeth nearly groaned aloud. How could her mother say such a thing with sincerity? How could she be so blind to Alfred's true nature? It was maddening. At times, she felt like the only sane one.

She turned her head to the window, letting the rhythmic

clatter of the coach wheels serve as a distraction. She missed her old life in Town. Her friends. Her independence. But all of it had vanished when her father died. Her so-called friends had turned their backs on her family, leaving them to weather the storm of scandal alone.

Her mother spoke up. "Lord Westcott is rather handsome, don't you think?"

Elsbeth snapped her head around, her expression incredulous. "Handsome? Perhaps, but he is also unbearably arrogant."

"He didn't strike me as such," her mother replied.

"That is because you didn't hear our conversation," Elsbeth shot back. "We both agreed it would be best if we avoided each other altogether."

Her mother looked disappointed. "That is most unfortunate."

Elsbeth pressed her lips together. "What did you think would happen, Mother? That we would meet and fall madly, irrevocably in love?"

"And why not?" her mother countered.

She let out a humorless laugh. "Because we are ruined. Completely and utterly."

"You still are the daughter of an earl and have a dowry of fifteen thousand pounds," her mother countered.

"Oh, wonderful," Elsbeth said dryly. "At least I will attract a fortune hunter."

Alfred cleared his throat, the sound irritating her further. She didn't want his opinion, but she knew it was coming.

"I do believe you are selling yourself short," he said.

She had been right.

Why did he insist on having an opinion on everything? Elsbeth knew she was going to regret asking, but she did so anyway. "And why is that?"

"You are a beautiful young woman with much to offer the

right man," Alfred said with a smile, no doubt in an attempt to disarm her.

"The right man?" Elsbeth repeated, her voice tinged with disbelief. "In Town, I was mingling with lords and ladies. Now, I am the subject of village gossip and the pity of spinsters. Where exactly am I supposed to meet this so-called 'right man'?"

Her mother sighed. "I know this has been an adjustment for you—"

"An adjustment?" Elsbeth cut her off, her voice rising. "No, it has been an utter nightmare."

"Let's try to make the best out of it," her mother attempted, her words edged with warning.

Fortunately, before Elsbeth could respond, the coach came to a stop in front of Lady Margaret's grand whitewashed manor. The conversation was over... for now.

Once inside the manor, Elsbeth quickly slipped into the drawing room and spotted Lady Eugenie sitting on the settee, engrossed in a book.

Not wanting to linger near her stepfather or mother, Elsbeth rushed to Eugenie's side and sat down.

Without looking up, Eugenie raised a finger. "One moment, please."

After a long moment, Eugenie closed the book with a satisfied sigh and placed it in her lap. "I do apologize, but I hate leaving a section unfinished."

"May I ask what you are reading?"

"*Common Sense* by Thomas Paine," Eugenie replied.

Elsbeth's brows rose in surprise. "Your brother allows you to read such a book?"

Eugenie looked amused by her question. "My *brother* doesn't allow or disallow anything. I read what I like."

"Are you not afraid of being labeled a bluestocking?"

"That is the goal, actually," Eugenie replied with a twinkle in her eyes. "Following the *ton's* rules is dreadfully boring."

Elsbeth glanced over her shoulder, making sure her mother was out of earshot. Lowering her voice, she asked, "Do you not wish to marry?"

"I am not opposed to the thought of marriage, but I refuse to change who I am to do so," Eugenie said, leaning back in her seat. "What do you read?"

"I hardly read," Elsbeth admitted.

Eugenie gasped. "How do you occupy your time?"

"The usual pursuits, I suppose."

"How disappointing. I doubt we can be friends," Eugenie teased. "I require all my friends to read a book a day."

"A book a day?" Elsbeth repeated. "Is that even possible?"

"It is entirely possible, but you must commit to it," Eugenie said, handing her the book. "Start with this."

Elsbeth put her hands up. "I couldn't. Perhaps I should start small and read another, less controversial book."

Eugenie placed the book down onto the table. "Very well. Pick a book, but we will discuss it afterward."

"I am not a very fast reader," Elsbeth admitted.

"I promise you will be if you find a book that draws you in and consumes you, body, mind, and soul."

Their conversation was interrupted as Lady Margaret entered the room. "You are looking lovely this evening," she said, her gaze landing on Elsbeth.

"Thank you, my lady," Elsbeth responded.

Turning her attention to Lady Isabella and Alfred, Lady Margaret greeted them warmly, pulling them into a conversation.

Eugenie leaned closer to Elsbeth, her voice dropping to a whisper. "I apologize for whatever my brother said to you earlier. He has been dreadfully unhappy these days."

"Aren't we all?"

"I would not give him—or his words—much heed."

Elsbeth forced a smile to her lips. "I assure you that I do not think of your brother at all."

"I am pleased to hear that."

As if their words had conjured up Lord Westcott, he entered the room with purposeful strides. His brown hair was brushed forward and his sideburns were neatly trimmed. It was a shame that he was so handsome but entirely disagreeable.

Their eyes met and Elsbeth saw Lord Westcott's eyes flash with annoyance. Not that she cared. If anything, she found the level of disdain he had for her amusing. It was almost entertaining to witness how thoroughly she could unsettle him simply by existing.

As he approached, she braced herself, preparing for yet another tiresome conversation with the insufferable man. Life would undoubtedly be simpler if they could agree never to speak again.

Lord Westcott came to a stop next to the settee, inclining his head in polite acknowledgment. "Sister. Lady Elsbeth."

Elsbeth returned his gesture with a curt nod. "My lord."

He stood in silence for a moment, their gazes locked as though engaging in an unspoken battle of wills. Elsbeth tried to pinpoint precisely what it was about him that vexed her. His arrogance? His rigid demeanor? His irritating habit of looking at her as though she were a particularly troublesome insect? Quite frankly, she loathed everything about him. His clothing. His face. She loathed it all.

Turning towards Eugenie, Elsbeth muttered, "Excuse me." She stood up and brushed past Lord Westcott. She had no desire to be around him, even for a moment.

She had barely taken a few steps towards her mother when Lord Westcott's voice called out behind her, "Would you care to take a turn around the room with me?"

No.

Absolutely not!

That was the worst idea imaginable. But she could hardly voice that thought aloud.

Turning slowly, she met his gaze and worked to keep her voice polite. "Do you truly think that is a good idea, my lord?"

"I do," he replied. "There are a few matters I wish to discuss."

"Wonderful," Elsbeth muttered. "I am not certain I wish to hear what those matters are."

Ignoring her protests, Lord Westcott offered his arm, his expression unwavering. "All I require is a moment of your time."

Elsbeth hesitated, glancing down at his proffered arm. If she refused, it would be considered rude, and while she cared little for his opinion, she did care for Lady Margaret. Reluctantly, she placed her hand on his arm. "Very well."

As Lord Westcott started leading her around the room, he glanced at her. "I wanted to apologize for my words earlier."

Her feet faltered slightly. She had not expected that.

"Thank you," Elsbeth said. Perhaps he wasn't truly as terrible as she thought.

"I should have not insinuated that you were like the other young women who blatantly seek my attention," he continued. "However, I still believe it would be best if we spent as little time together as possible."

Now that was something that they could both agree on. "I wholeheartedly agree."

"Good."

Elsbeth nodded. "Yes, good."

But then he abruptly stopped walking and dropped his arm. His next words drained any goodwill she might have mustered. "And this should go without saying, but I must also ask that you stay away from my sister. I do not wish for her to be influenced by you."

Her spine stiffened. "My influence?"

He waved a hand dismissively in her direction. "Yes, every-thing about you—the way you speak, the way you carry your-self—is the opposite of how I would wish Eugenie to behave."

And she was back to loathing him.

The audacity of this man! Stepping closer, she fixed him with a glare. "And everything about you, my lord, is offensive to me."

His jaw clenched. "I am merely speaking the truth."

"As am I."

Lord Westcott's lips thinned into a line. "You resort to insults rather quickly."

Elsbeth shook her head. "You are impossible," she declared before turning on her heel and leaving him to stand alone.

Lady Margaret spoke up, drawing everyone's attention. "I was informed that dinner is ready to be served."

As Elsbeth walked towards the dining room, Eugenie appeared next to her, matching her stride. "What did my brother say to you?"

Elsbeth saw no reason not to tell Eugenie the truth. "He doesn't want me to spend time with you for fear of my bad influence."

Eugenie rolled her eyes. "What an idiotic thing to say."

Elsbeth felt herself relax. "I thought so, too."

Looping arms with her, Eugenie said, "Regardless of what my brother says, I think we should be friends."

"Your brother will hate that."

Eugenie shrugged. "So, do you agree?"

A genuine smile spread across Elsbeth's face, the first she had worn all evening. "I do."

"Wonderful!" Eugenie exclaimed. "We shall have such fun together!"

Niles tried to mask his irritation as he sat at the head of the long dining table, the lively hum of conversation swirling around him. Lady Elsbeth's laugh rang out as she spoke with Eugenie, and his jaw clenched. How had it come to this? Hadn't he made it abundantly clear that Lady Elsbeth should stay away from Eugenie? And yet, here she was, seated among them as if her family's reputation weren't hanging by a thread.

He caught Aunt Margaret's watchful gaze from across the table. She gave him a knowing look, one that seemed to suggest she had perceived his thoughts. Botheration. The last thing he needed was for his aunt to think he had any interest in Lady Elsbeth. That would be a disaster.

Lady Elsbeth's laughter again drew his attention, much to his chagrin. Why did her laughter grate on his very last nerve?

Eugenie turned to him, a knowing smile playing on her lips. "Why are you stewing, Brother?"

"I am not stewing," he replied, reaching for his glass.

Aunt Margaret cleared her throat. "Perhaps we should steer the conversation towards something more pleasant than analyzing Niles's expressions?"

Eugenie dabbed at her lips with her white linen napkin. "Very well. I read the most interesting book recently—"

Niles groaned inwardly. "Is it suitable for discussion at the dinner table?"

"That depends on who you ask," Eugenie replied. "It is *Common Sense* by Thomas Paine—"

Aunt Margaret interjected swiftly. "Perhaps we should discuss something less controversial, my dear."

Eugenie merely shrugged. "At least I attempted to introduce an interesting topic."

Turning her attention towards Lady Elsbeth, Aunt Margaret asked, "Are you still making clothes for the children in workhouses?"

"I am," Lady Elsbeth confirmed.

Aunt Margaret met Niles's gaze with a pointed smile. "Lady Elsbeth has started a sewing circle for the orphans in workhouses. A noble endeavor, wouldn't you say?"

Niles hesitated, his dislike for Lady Elsbeth clashing with his reluctant admiration for her work. "That is commendable," he muttered, hoping to end his part in the conversation.

"Unfortunately, it is just me now," Lady Elsbeth shared. "My friends abandoned me after my father's death."

The quiet honesty in her words struck him unexpectedly, but he said nothing.

Aunt Margaret continued. "Eugenie and I would love to assist. It sounds like a most worthy cause."

Lady Elsbeth's eyes lit up. "I would be delighted."

Eugenie chimed in, "We could call it the Bluestocking Book Circle, and we could discuss books while we sew."

"That is a terrible name for a club," Niles remarked.

"Could you do better?" Eugenie challenged.

Lady Isabella spoke up. "I would like to help, as well."

"Wonderful," Lady Elsbeth said. "The more, the merrier."

Mr. Stockton, seated beside his wife, placed his fork down. "I will procure as much fabric as necessary."

Lady Isabella cast her husband a loving look. "That is most generous of you."

"It is the least I can do for such a worthy cause," Mr. Stockton responded.

Niles noticed a flicker of disdain cross Lady Elsbeth's face before she quickly composed herself. Interesting. Perhaps she didn't hold her stepfather in the high regard her mother did. He decided to probe further.

Turning to Mr. Stockton, Niles asked, "Where do you hail from?"

Mr. Stockton smiled pleasantly. "From a coastal village in Sussex."

Lady Elsbeth furrowed her brow. "Which one?"

"Worthing," Mr. Stockton replied, exchanging a glance with Lady Isabella.

"I don't understand," Lady Elsbeth said as she addressed her mother. "You both grew up in Worthing?"

Lady Isabella pressed her lips together into a thin line. "We did. Alfred's father owned the bakery in the village. We knew each other in passing."

"What does that mean?" Lady Elsbeth pressed.

With a glance around the table, Lady Isabella said, "It might be best if we discuss this later."

"No," Lady Elsbeth countered. "I think we should discuss it now."

Lady Isabella reached for her husband's hand. "Alfred and I struck up a friendship of sorts when we were younger. But it ended when I went to Town for the Season. I met your father and the rest is history."

But Elsbeth wasn't done with her line of questioning. "How exactly did you two reconnect? Or did you two ever stop being friends?"

"I do not know what you are implying—" Lady Isabella started.

Lady Elsbeth tossed her white napkin onto the table. "You know precisely what I am implying. Did you and Alfred stay friends when you were married to Father?"

Lady Isabella sighed. "We exchanged letters occasionally, but it was entirely innocent. I was faithful to your father."

"And yet, you couldn't wait to marry Alfred," Lady Elsbeth said, rising abruptly. "Excuse me for a moment."

The room fell into an uncomfortable silence as Lady Elsbeth swept out. Niles felt a pang of guilt, knowing his line of questioning had ignited the confrontation.

Lady Isabella's voice broke the tension. "I apologize for ruining this evening."

"Nonsense. This evening is still reparable," Aunt Margaret

said, pushing back her chair. "I will go speak to Elsbeth, and we will get this sorted out."

But Niles stood. "Allow me."

Eugenie shook her head vehemently. "That is a terrible idea. You two can't stand each other."

"I don't hate her," he said, though he tripped over his words. He didn't quite know what he felt for Elsbeth.

With a knowing look, Eugenie asked, "What is it when two people have an immense dislike for one another?"

"I will admit that Lady Elsbeth and I do not see eye to eye, but I think I can get through to her," he pressed.

Aunt Margaret relented with a small nod. "I will give you five minutes. Try not to make things worse."

Niles strode from the room, hoping he could undo some of the damage he had caused. Or, at the very least, attempt to understand the young woman who never failed to rattle him.

Once he stepped out into the corridor, he saw Lady Elsbeth sitting on a chair, her shoulders hunched as she wiped away the tears streaming down her face. Her vulnerability struck him like a physical blow. This wasn't the composed, sharp-tongued woman who had sparred with him earlier.

Softening his voice, he called out, "Lady Elsbeth."

She glanced up, her tear-filled eyes narrowing with irritation. "What do you want, my lord?" she asked, her words curt.

What did he want?

For a moment, he hesitated, considering his options. He could leave her to her misery and return to the dining room. But his mother had raised him to be a gentleman, and that meant he always helped a lady in distress.

He approached her, his footsteps deliberate, and he came to a stop next to her. "Are you all right?" he asked, his voice low with concern.

She met his gaze, her eyes red-rimmed but defiant. "Why do you care?"

It was a fair question. Niles wasn't entirely sure why he had come out here or why he was trying to console a woman who, truthfully, irritated him to no end. But his sense of duty overrode his dislike.

He grabbed a nearby chair and positioned it next to her before sitting down. "I'm sorry," he said simply.

"For what?" she asked. "You did nothing wrong."

He sighed, running a hand through his hair. "I was the one who started all of this."

Lady Elsbeth pursed her lips as she turned her gaze forward. "You couldn't have known about my mother and Alfred's... past." Her voice cracked slightly, betraying the hurt she tried to mask. "I can't believe they didn't tell me."

"Would it have made a difference?" Niles asked gently. "You don't seem to think very highly of your stepfather."

Elsbeth's eyes hardened. "My mother married Alfred the very day she came out of mourning," she stated. "I'm not sure what is worse—how quickly she moved on or the fact that she expects me to be grateful for him."

"That must have been rather difficult for you."

"Difficult? My mother believes I should be thankful for a man who has exiled us to the countryside, far from Society. But what is there to be thankful for? No one wants anything to do with us anymore. We are ruined."

"You are angry," he observed.

Lady Elsbeth huffed. "How very astute of you, my lord."

He gave her a small smile, undeterred by her annoyance. "I was angry too when my parents died. For a long time, I let the anger consume me. It drove away every ounce of joy I had left."

"What changed?"

Niles leaned back slightly, letting out a slow breath. "I realized that I couldn't go on as I had been. Not for myself and not for Eugenie. I had to find a purpose, something greater than myself."

Lady Elsbeth's eyes drew downcast. "I don't think I can do that."

He reached into his jacket and pulled out a handkerchief, holding it out to her. "You can. It is not easy, but it is possible."

She stared at the handkerchief for a moment before taking it with tentative fingers. "Thank you," she murmured, dabbing at her cheeks. "Perhaps you are not as insufferable as I thought."

Niles put a finger up to his lips. "Shh. Do not say anything. I have an image that I must maintain."

To his surprise, a soft laugh escaped her lips, and her face brightened momentarily. "Your secret is safe with me."

He heard Aunt Margaret's voice echoing from the doorway. "Elsbeth? Is everything all right?"

Lady Elsbeth glanced at Niles briefly before replying, "It is."

"Wonderful," Aunt Margaret said with visible relief. "Would you care to join us for some pudding?"

Niles rose, extending a hand to Lady Elsbeth. She placed her hand in his, allowing him to help her up. Once standing, she withdrew her hand quickly and clasped it with the other in front of her.

As they walked back towards the dining room, Niles said, "I do think it is quite extraordinary of you to make clothes for the orphans."

She gave a dismissive wave. "It is a small contribution. I only wish I could enact real change."

"I am backing a bill in Parliament that is proposing major reforms for workhouse conditions," he informed her.

"It won't pass. They never do."

Niles lifted his brow. "That doesn't mean we stop trying," he countered. "Real change takes persistence."

They entered the dining room, where Lady Isabella rose from her seat, her face etched with worry. "Elsbeth..."

"It is all right, Mother," Lady Elsbeth interrupted, holding up a hand. "Let's not discuss it any further."

Relief washed over Lady Isabella's features, and she resumed her seat. Niles moved to pull out a chair for Elsbeth, and she murmured, "Thank you."

"You are welcome," he replied.

She smiled for the first time at him, and he almost had to look away, as if he had no right to witness something so beautiful.

Shaking off the thought, he returned to his seat, reminding himself that nothing had truly changed. Lady Elsbeth was still the maddening woman who vexed him at every turn.

At least, that is what he told himself.

4

Elsbeth lay in her bed, staring up at the ceiling as shadows from the early morning light danced across her room. Lord Westcott's words replayed endlessly in her mind, as if taunting her. He had seen her anger, felt it, even. It was as if he had stripped her bare, leaving her defenses exposed. But what else was she supposed to feel? How else could she respond when her life had been ripped from her?

She wanted her old life back. The grand balls. The invitations. The respect her family once commanded. All of it had vanished with her father's death, leaving her stranded in a provincial existence alongside a stepfather she was convinced wasn't who he claimed to be. Until she uncovered Alfred's secrets, she couldn't move on. That was her purpose. For now.

A soft knock interrupted her thoughts, and the door creaked open, revealing her lady's maid, Clara. "Good morning, my lady," she greeted, her tone entirely too cheerful for the early morning hour.

Elsbeth groaned, grabbing a pillow and pressing it over her face. "I am still sleeping. Leave me be."

"No, you aren't," Clara replied. "Your mother has requested

your presence at breakfast. We should get you dressed for the day."

Pulling the pillow away, Elsbeth sat up in bed. "Do you think I am angry?"

"Right now?" Clara teased, moving to the wardrobe.

"No, in general."

Clara pulled out a pale blue gown, holding it up appraisingly. "You have seemed rather unhappy since you left Town, but that is to be expected, given the circumstances."

"I am unhappy," Elsbeth admitted, swinging her legs over the side of the bed. "I don't want to be here."

Walking over to the settee, Clara draped the gown over the back. "And yet, here you are. Unfortunately, you have little choice in the matter."

"I know, and that is what is so infuriating."

Clara gestured towards the chair by the dressing table. "If you want any sympathy, you won't find it here. You are beautiful and rich. Meanwhile, I scrape by to send most of my wages to my mother. Not that I am complaining..."

Elsbeth cut her off with a faint smile. "You are not, and I would never accuse you of such a thing. You know I want you to speak freely around me."

Clara returned her smile. "Then sit, my lady. Let me work my magic."

She complied, settling into the chair. As Clara began brushing her hair, Elsbeth said, "I need my stepfather's key to his desk drawers. Once I have it, I can uncover his secrets and expose him to my mother."

"And then what?" Clara asked, pausing mid-brush.

"Then I will be proven right."

Clara resumed her work, her movements steady. "Pardon me for saying so, but your mother seems blissfully happy with Mr. Stockton. Do you truly want to ruin that?"

"What else am I to do?" Elsbeth countered. "I know my

stepfather is hiding things. Why else would he lock his desk drawers?"

"To keep you out of them," Clara replied.

"I am careful," Elsbeth insisted. "He doesn't know what I am up to."

Clara pinned her hair with precision, then stepped around to face her. "What if your mother told him? She is completely devoted to him."

Elsbeth had to concede that Clara had a point. Her mother was so besotted with Alfred that she might betray Elsbeth's confidence. "You are right. I will have to be more careful about what I share with her."

"And more secrets are the answer?" Clara pressed.

"What choice do I have?"

Clara sighed. "You could choose to live your life and give Mr. Stockton the benefit of the doubt."

"I can't."

Clara's disappointment was palpable. "This highwaywoman scheme could get you in trouble—or worse."

"My pistol isn't even loaded."

"That doesn't matter," Clara said. "No one knows your intentions when you point it at them."

Elsbeth rose from the chair and removed her dressing gown. "I just need that key. Once I have it, all of this will end."

"I beg of you to reconsider," Clara said. "You should be in bed at the late hour, not robbing coaches by gunpoint. You were lucky with Lord Westcott. Don't risk it."

As Elsbeth dressed, she grew silent, retreating into her thoughts. Clara's words weighed heavily on her, but how could she stop now? If Alfred was hiding something, she had to know. He was the one in the wrong, not her.

Clara fastened the last button on the back of Elsbeth's gown and took a step back. "You have grown quiet, my lady."

"I was thinking."

Coming around to face her, Clara's knowing look softened. "Whatever you decide, I will support you. Always."

"Thank you."

Clara's lips twitched. "Now, hurry. If you don't get to breakfast soon, your mother will scold us both."

Elsbeth departed from her bedchamber and headed down the grand staircase. As she went to turn down the corridor, she heard raised voices. She slowed, curiosity pulling her closer.

"That is unacceptable!" Alfred bellowed. "You need to dig deeper."

A muffled voice responded, but she couldn't hear what was said.

Finding herself curious, Elsbeth slowly walked towards the study, mindful to avoid the creaking floorboards. It would do no good if someone discovered that she was eavesdropping.

Pressing herself against the wall, she peeked through the partially open door. Alfred sat at his desk, his face red with fury, while a tall, blond-haired man stood before him.

"You expect me to believe that?" Alfred snapped. "Of course, Lord Bedford had enemies. A man doesn't reach his position by making friends."

"Sir, if I may—" the man started.

"No!" Alfred cut him off. "You have one job, and no one can know that I am looking into this."

The man tipped his head. "I can be discreet."

"Good. That is what I am paying you for," Alfred said, dismissing him with a wave of his hand.

As the man turned towards the door, Elsbeth's heart leapt into her throat. She darted into the nearby parlor, pressing herself against the wall. Her mind raced. What was Alfred looking into? Why the secrecy?

The questions piled up, but the answers remained maddeningly out of reach.

Elsbeth waited in the parlor, holding her breath, until the

sound of the man's booted footsteps faded into the distance. With a quick glance towards the study, she slipped out into the corridor, only to come face-to-face with Alfred. She quickly schooled her expression into one of innocent surprise.

"Alfred!" Elsbeth exclaimed, her voice slightly higher than usual.

His brow arched as he regarded her. "What were you doing in the parlor?"

She hesitated, searching her mind for a plausible excuse. "I thought I had left a book in there," she said after a moment, "but I must have returned it to the library."

"Ah," Alfred said. "Shall we go to breakfast?"

Elsbeth stared back at her stepfather. That was it? She was surprised that he was going to take her at her word. "Yes, I think that is a grand idea."

He gestured for her to walk ahead of him, his hand extending with an elegant flourish. "After you."

Elsbeth started towards the dining room, her stepfather falling into step beside her. She tried to keep her movements casual, though her mind raced with questions about the conversation that she had overheard.

"I trust that you slept well," Alfred said, breaking the silence.

"I did," she replied. "And you?"

He smiled, but it didn't quite reach his eyes. "I did indeed."

The air between them felt stifling, and Elsbeth struggled to think of something to say that wouldn't betray her suspicions.

Before she could speak, Alfred continued. "How do you intend to occupy your day?"

"Lady Eugenie invited me to accompany her and Lady Margaret to the village," Elsbeth replied. "I might acquire a new hat."

"Wonderful," he said.

Thankfully, the dining room doors came into view, sparing her from further awkward conversation.

As they stepped inside, her mother looked up from her tea, surprise evident in her features. "I had not expected you two to arrive together."

Alfred moved to give his wife a kiss on the cheek. "Elsbeth and I had a most pleasant conversation."

"Did you, now?" her mother asked, her tone tinged with incredulity as her eyes flickered between them.

Elsbeth moved to sit down and placed a napkin onto her lap. "Yes, we determined we both slept well last night."

"Well, that is a start," her mother responded.

Alfred took his place at the head of the table. "I have business that I need to attend to in the next village over today," he announced. "But I should be home late this evening."

Her mother frowned, her teacup pausing midway to her lips. "You know I do not like you traveling the roads at night, especially not with that highwaywoman terrorizing travelers."

Her stepfather chuckled softly, his demeanor as calm as ever. "You need not fear for my safety, my dear. I have been traveling these roads for many years. They are perfectly safe."

"Still, do be careful," her mother pressed. "I couldn't bear it if something happened to you."

Alfred smiled at his wife reassuringly. "You have my word."

Elsbeth felt a bitter twist in her stomach. The man was hiding something, and her mother, blinded in her adoration, couldn't see it. How could her mother be so oblivious?

Elsbeth knew precisely what she had to do. She would rob her stepfather's coach tonight and retrieve the key.

Her mother's voice broke through her thoughts. "I am going to the dressmaker's shop today. Would you care to join me?"

"I would, but Lady Eugenie invited me to accompany her and Lady Margaret to the village for some shopping," Elsbeth replied.

"How wonderful!" her mother exclaimed. "You will have such fun. Will Lord Westcott be joining you?"

She hoped not.

"I doubt it," Elsbeth replied. "I imagine he has much more pressing matters to attend to than shopping at a haberdashery."

"You make a good point. He doesn't strike me as the sort who would concern himself with ribbons and fabric."

A footman approached, carefully setting a plate of food before Elsbeth. As she ate, she truly hoped that Lord Westcott wouldn't make a nuisance of himself by joining their outing. Surely as an earl, he had far more important matters to tend to.

Niles sat stiffly in the haberdashery, suppressing the urge to groan aloud. Of all the ways he could spend his time, watching Eugenie select ribbons was not at the top of his list. She stood at the counter, holding up an assortment of ribbons, each seemingly identical to his untrained eye. He had never quite understood women's fascination with such fripperies.

His gaze drifted towards Lady Elsbeth, who was admiring herself in a straw hat adorned with a poppy. His thoughts unexpectedly wandered to their conversation the night before, a rare moment when they had both let their guards down. Vulnerability wasn't something Niles was accustomed to showing. It was far easier—and safer—to keep people at a distance. Yet something about Lady Elsbeth's candidness had unsettled him.

Eugenie approached him and lowered her voice. "Must you glare at Lady Elsbeth like that, Brother?"

"I wasn't glaring," he muttered, shifting his focus to his sister. "And why do you insist on being her friend?"

"Perhaps it is my nefarious attempt to make you go mad," Eugenie replied with a mischievous smile.

He glanced at the stack of ribbons in her hands. "Did you buy out the entire shop?"

"Why not?" she asked. "You are rich."

"Being rich doesn't mean I should squander money on frivolities."

Eugenie held up the ribbons. "These are not frivolous. They make excellent bookmarks."

"Scraps of paper work just as well."

"But these are far prettier," she countered, a playful note in her voice.

Niles rose from his seat. "At least your logic is sound."

Eugenie smirked. "Be careful, or I might buy a hat. Or two."

"Please don't," Niles said. "I have had just about enough of this shop."

"Then why did you come along?"

Niles cast a fleeting glance at Lady Elsbeth, who was trying on another hat. "Because Aunt Margaret wasn't feeling well, and I did not want you to be left alone with her."

"There is nothing wrong with Lady Elsbeth," Eugenie said pointedly. "But I am beginning to suspect there is something wrong with *you*."

"I can't fathom why our aunt is so friendly with Lady Elsbeth," Niles stated.

Eugenie shook her head. "Lady Elsbeth is a delight, and I find it amusing how much she vexes you."

"It is not amusing."

"It is... just a little," Eugenie said with a grin.

"Can we just please go home now?"

Before Eugenie could reply, Lady Elsbeth joined them. "Oh, Eugenie, those ribbons are quite lovely," she praised.

"Thank you," Eugenie replied. "Did you decide on a hat?"

Lady Elsbeth bobbed her head. "Yes, the straw hat with the poppy on it. They are boxing it up and will deliver it to the manor."

"A fine choice," Eugenie said approvingly.

Turning to address Niles, Lady Elsbeth asked, "And did anything catch your eye, my lord?"

"No," he said.

His curt response didn't deter Lady Elsbeth. Her lips twitched with barely concealed mirth. "What a shame. I spotted a hat with an ostrich feather that would suit you perfectly."

Eugenie giggled. "Could you imagine my brother wearing such a hat?"

But Niles was not amused. "Can we go now?"

"Yes, I am ready to leave," Lady Elsbeth replied.

"Thank you for stating the obvious," Niles muttered.

Lady Elsbeth gave him an amused look. "You are welcome," she said. "I am walking to the door now."

Niles sighed and looked heavenward as Lady Elsbeth exaggerated every step, narrating her actions. Could that woman be any more vexing?

As she opened the door, Lady Elsbeth informed him, "I am now stepping outside onto the pavement."

Eugenie leaned closer to her brother. "You did thank her for stating the obvious."

Niles offered his arm. "The sooner this outing is over, the better."

"That is the spirit, Brother," Eugenie said, slipping her hand through his arm.

Outside, Lady Elsbeth was speaking with her maid when she glanced over at him. "I am now talking to my maid," she announced, her eyes twinkling with humor.

Before Niles could retort, a sudden noise drew his attention. He looked up to see a large barrel tumbling down the cobblestone street, picking up speed. It was headed straight for Lady Elsbeth.

Without hesitation, Niles lunged forward and grabbed Lady

Elsbeth, pulling her out of harm's way just as the barrel hurtled past. He held her tightly, his heart pounding as he felt her trembling against him.

Eugenie's voice broke the tension. "You can let go of Lady Elsbeth now, Brother."

Niles knew that his sister was right, but a part of him was forced to acknowledge how Lady Elsbeth fit perfectly in his arms. Reluctantly, he released her and stepped back. "Are you all right?" he asked, the gentleness in his voice surprising even himself.

Lady Elsbeth wrapped her arms around herself. "Yes. Thanks to you."

"It was nothing," he said, brushing off her gratitude.

In a soft voice, she replied, "You saved my life."

"As I said, it was nothing," Niles stated.

A large, bald man in a brown apron rushed towards them, his face pale. "Is everyone all right?" he asked in between breaths.

"We are," Niles responded tersely.

The man wrung his hands. "I don't know what happened. I thought I had secured that barrel. I am so sorry."

"Well, you clearly didn't," Niles said, his voice sharp. "Be more careful in the future."

The man nodded hastily and scurried away.

Niles did the one thing he thought he would never do. He offered his arm to Lady Elsbeth. "May I escort you to the coach?"

Lady Elsbeth hesitated before placing her hand on his arm. Her uncharacteristic silence unnerved him. Offering his other arm to Eugenie, he led them both to the waiting coach, helping them inside before taking his seat next to his sister. As the coach rolled away, Niles couldn't shake the protective surge he had felt for Lady Elsbeth.

Fortunately, his thoughts were interrupted by his sister's concerned voice. "Elsbeth, are you all right?"

Lady Elsbeth winced, her voice trembling as she replied, "I don't know. I'm sorry—"

Eugenie spoke over her. "You have nothing to apologize for. You can feel however you need to feel in this moment. No explanations are required."

Lady Elsbeth's eyes shimmered with unshed tears, but she managed a faint smile. "Thank you," she said, her voice barely above a whisper.

Turning towards her brother, Eugenie said, "Niles, I don't think I have ever seen you move that fast before... unless food was involved."

Niles recognized his sister's tactic immediately. Eugenie was trying to distract Lady Elsbeth and lighten the mood. He decided to play along. He chuckled softly. "I can be remarkably swift when the situation warrants it."

"Well, I am impressed," Eugenie said.

"I didn't think it was so easy to impress you," Niles quipped.

Lady Elsbeth met his gaze. "I am truly grateful for you saving my life, my lord."

The sincerity in her eyes held Niles transfixed. "It was my pleasure, my lady. But please, you really must stop thanking me. It was nothing."

"I don't think I have ever been so frightened before..." Lady Elsbeth said, her words trailing off.

Eugenie leaned forward and reached for Lady Elsbeth's hand. "What you experienced would frighten anyone. You are not alone in feeling that way."

Lady Elsbeth gave a small, appreciative nod.

"Why don't we talk about something else?" Eugenie suggested, her voice bright. "We could discuss the weather."

Lady Elsbeth made a face. "Please, no."

Eugenie laughed as she leaned back. "All right. No discussion on the weather," she said. "How about I regale you with a story about Niles? I have plenty."

Niles groaned in mock protest. "Why does the story have to be about me?"

"Because your stories are far more entertaining."

"More so than when you mistook a badger for a cat?" Niles asked with mirth in his voice.

Eugenie waved a hand dismissively. "It was an honest mistake."

"And yet, I have never heard of another person making that mistake," Niles said.

"But I learned from my mistakes, and I have never tried to bring home a badger again," Eugenie responded.

"You say that as if it is an accomplishment," Niles teased.

Eugenie shrugged. "In my defense, I was only eight. I did ask you to come with me, but you said you were too busy."

"Because I had just returned from Eton," Niles said. "I had no desire to traipse through the woods with my little sister."

"And that," Eugenie said, holding up a finger triumphantly, "was your mistake. You underestimated how much I wanted a pet."

Niles chuckled. "Father did give in and get you a cat after that debacle."

"Exactly the outcome I wanted," Eugenie declared.

"Surely there was an easier way to convince Father to get you a cat?" Niles asked, his tone dry.

Ignoring his question, Eugenie turned to Lady Elsbeth. "Did you ever want a pet?"

"No, my mother is allergic to cats and dogs," Lady Elsbeth responded.

"To both?" Eugenie asked.

Lady Elsbeth nodded. "Yes, her eyes water and she sneezes incessantly. My grandmother had a cat, and every visit was miserable for her."

"That is awful," Eugenie said. "Well, I suggest you avoid getting a black animal with a white stripe down the length of it."

For the first time since the incident, Lady Elsbeth smiled. "I do think I will heed your advice."

Niles watched as the tension eased from Lady Elsbeth's shoulders. Eugenie's plan had worked. He felt a strange sense of gratitude towards his sister for her ability to comfort and distract, a skill he clearly lacked.

Eugenie spoke up again. "You simply must visit our country estate someday. My cat, Shadow, is a delightful companion. Niles just adores him."

Niles let out a disbelieving huff. "Adore? Hardly. I hate that cat."

"That is a shame because Shadow absolutely adores you," Eugenie said with a playful smile.

Niles turned to Lady Elsbeth to explain. "Shadow doesn't adore me. He lies in wait like a predator. He watches for the moment I let my guard down and then leaps out to attack me in the corridor."

"Shadow is merely playing with you," Eugenie said.

"One day, that cat will be the death of me."

Eugenie laughed. "You are being utterly ridiculous. He is just a cat."

Lady Elsbeth interjected. "I think I would very much like to meet this cat."

"No, you wouldn't," Niles replied. "You must trust me on this."

As he spoke, the coach slowed before coming to an abrupt halt in front of Lady Elsbeth's manor. Niles shifted instinctively, preparing to assist her out of the coach. Lady Elsbeth reached for the door, but he held up a hand. "Allow me, my lady."

He stepped out first, extending his hand to her. The moment her gloved fingers brushed against his, he felt a surprising spark of awareness. It was an unnerving but not entirely unpleasant sensation. Once her feet were firmly on the ground, she withdrew her hand and took a step back.

"Thank you, my lord. For everything," she said.

He tilted his head, offering her a half-smile. "Can we move past this newfound civility and return to barely tolerating one another?"

Lady Elsbeth's lips curved into a smile. It was so radiant and unguarded that it briefly stunned him. "I think that is a wise course of action."

"Then it is settled," Niles said. "We will return to the way things were before our trip to the village."

Lady Elsbeth nodded. "Good day, my lord."

He stood there, rooted in place, watching her with an inexplicable sense of reluctance. Returning to the way things had been before seemed almost impossible now, not after the day's events. Not after holding her in his arms.

Just as she reached the door, she paused and turned, a gesture so unexpected that it caught him off guard. She lifted a hand in a small wave, and he, without hesitation, raised his own to return it.

And in that quiet, unremarkable moment, Niles realized something unsettling but undeniable: he no longer despised Lady Elsbeth.

5

_____

Elsbeth sat atop her horse, hidden within the dense shadows of trees lining the road, her heart pounding as she waited for her stepfather's coach. She clenched the reins tightly, her breath visible in the chilly night air. The weight of her mission pressed heavily on her shoulders. She needed that key. The secrets it guarded consumed her thoughts.

A low whinny from the woodlands snapped her attention away. Her pulse quickened. Someone else was here. She wasn't alone. Swallowing her fear, Elsbeth reached for the pistol tucked into the waistband of her trousers. She couldn't be caught. Not like this. The repercussions would be disastrous, and her family's already tarnished reputation would be utterly ruined.

From the shadows emerged a lone figure on horseback. The moonlight glinted off his dark hair, and the sound of his voice sent a chill down her spine. "Don't go," he called out. "I mean you no harm."

Her heart sank.

That voice. She would recognize it anywhere.

Lord Westcott.

For a moment, her instinct screamed for her to flee, to disappear deeper into the woodlands and abandon this foolish confrontation. But her curiosity held her in place. Why was he here? What did he want?

Lowering her voice to disguise it, she asked, "What do you want?"

"I just want to talk," he replied.

She adjusted her mask, her fingers trembling slightly as she tried to maintain her composure. "Talk? At this hour? Out here? Forgive me if I find that hard to believe."

"I want to understand why you are doing this," Lord Westcott replied.

"I do not owe you an explanation."

Lord Westcott urged his horse forward but stopped a short distance away. "No," he admitted, "but you seem driven, purposeful. What compels you to take such a risk?"

He wouldn't understand her reasonings so there was no point in telling him the truth. "It is just something I have to do."

"Are you in need of money?"

Elsbeth frowned. "I am not doing this for the money."

"Then why are you doing this?" Lord Westcott pressed. "After all, you are risking your life by robbing coaches."

"It is a risk worth taking."

Lord Westcott tilted his head, studying her carefully. "Perhaps I could help."

She almost laughed at the absurdity of his offer. "And what, pray tell, could you do, my lord?"

"You remember me, then?"

Elsbeth tightened the hold on her reins, silently chiding herself on the slip of her tongue. "I do," she replied. "You are rather hard to forget."

"I am at a loss since I do not know your name."

The sound of a twig snapping in the distance caused her

head to turn towards the direction of the noise. "Did you come alone?"

"I did."

Perhaps it was just an animal that had made that noise. But a feeling of uneasiness came over her. Why was she chatting with Lord Westcott in the woodlands? She had a mission that she had to accomplish but she couldn't do so with him here.

Lord Westcott's voice drew back her attention. "You can trust me."

"Trust you?" she asked. "Why would I do something so foolish?"

"I can help you."

In a strained voice, she replied, "No one can help me. I must do this on my own."

"That is a sad way to live."

"And what do you know about that?" Elsbeth challenged. What would an earl know about struggles?

The moon shifted and it illuminated his face. It showed a pain that she didn't think he was capable of. "I know what it is like feeling alone," he admitted.

"But you aren't alone."

"Just because someone is surrounded by people, it doesn't mean they can't feel alone," he replied.

"I agree with that sentiment," Elsbeth said, knowing that feeling well. She lived in a home that was filled with servants, but she had never felt more alone. Isolated. Even her own mother didn't quite know what to do with her.

Lord Westcott's voice held compassion. "I am in a position that I can help you."

She decided to ask the most glaring question. "Why do you care?"

"I don't know why, but I recognize a kindred soul when I see one," Lord Westcott replied.

Elsbeth's stomach tightened at his words. "We are not

kindred souls, my lord." They were far from it. He wouldn't be saying such things if he knew her true identity.

Lord Westcott shrugged. "I wouldn't be so quick to dismiss it."

"You are a powerful lord, and I am..." Her words trailed off as she tried to find the right word. "Helpless."

"No one is helpless."

"How naive of you," Elsbeth stated, her words curt. "You are an earl and have the world at your disposal. I am just a woman."

Lord Westcott considered her for a long moment. "You seem like a remarkable woman. One who has a story to tell."

"Everyone has a story to tell."

"Yes, but some are more interesting than others," Lord Westcott contended. "Not many ladies turn to being high-waywomen."

Elsbeth hesitated, his words striking a chord deep within her. For the briefest of moments, she felt an urge to open up, to share her burden. To not feel so alone. But that was foolish. He wouldn't understand. How could he?

Surprising even herself, she revealed, "If you must know, I am searching for something specific."

"Is it a pocket watch?" he asked, a teasing lilt in his voice. "Because I do believe that is still in your possession."

"I still have it. However, I did not want your pocket watch. You left me little choice in the matter," Elsbeth said. "I shall see it is returned to you."

He nodded. "I would gratefully appreciate that. It was my father's pocket watch."

"If that was the case, why did you give it to me?"

"You were robbing me... at gunpoint," he reminded her.

She offered him a weak smile. "I am sorry for that. It was never my intention to steal from you."

"Then why did you?"

"As I told you, I am looking for something specific."

"Which is?" he pressed.

Elsbeth shook her head. "That is not something I can tell you."

The crack of a pistol shot rang out, slicing through the night. Pain erupted in her left arm, hot and sharp, and she barely registered her gasp of shock before instinct took over. Kicking her horse into a gallop, she bolted into the trees, her surroundings blurring as branches whipped past her.

The searing pain in her arm was almost unbearable, and she clenched her teeth to stifle the cry building in her throat. She couldn't stop. Not now. Not when someone had just shot her.

Lord Westcott had tricked her. Anger and betrayal coursed through her as she pushed her horse harder, darting through the woodlands. She glanced over her shoulder repeatedly, her eyes scanning for any sign of pursuit, but the woods seemed empty behind her.

Finally, the familiar outline of her stepfather's manor appeared in the distance and Elsbeth let out a shaky breath of relief. The throbbing in her arm was relentless, and every jolt from the horse's hooves sent waves of pain coursing through her. She reined in her horse. She had made it back home, but not without consequences.

The sound of hurried footsteps greeted her as the white-haired groom, Morton, stepped out from the stables' lantern-lit entrance. She felt a wave of relief wash over her. Morton had been with her family since she was young, and he would not betray her confidence.

"I have been shot," Elsbeth blurted out. Finally allowing herself to cry, she felt tears roll down her cheeks.

Morton's expression hardened, but his tone was steady. "Where?"

"My left arm."

"Do you need help off your horse?"

"No," she replied, sliding down from the saddle. She stumbled slightly, her legs weak, but Morton was quick to steady her.

He took the reins, guiding the horse into the stables. "Come inside," he said. "I will take a look at it."

She followed him into the warm, hay-scented stables. The soft nickering of horses filled the quiet space, but Elsbeth could hardly hear it over the pounding in her ears.

"Sit," Morton ordered, gesturing to a nearby stool. He had never been so direct with her before, but she wasn't about to say anything about it.

Obediently, she sank onto the stool, and removed her wool cloak. Glancing down, she winced at the sight of her sleeve. It was soaked with blood. A wave of dizziness washed over her, and she gripped the edges of the stool to keep from fainting.

Morton pulled another stool beside her and sat down, his frown deepening as he inspected the wound. "You should see a doctor," he muttered, his face grim. "This isn't something I should be handling."

"No, I can't go to a doctor," Elsbeth said. "How would I explain getting shot?"

Morton muttered a curse under his breath as she rolled up her sleeve. She bit back a cry of pain as the fabric peeled away, sticking to the wound.

"The bullet grazed you," he said after a long moment. "Right below the shoulder. You will need stitches, but it could have been much worse."

"Will it hurt?" she asked, though she already knew the answer.

"Yes," he replied bluntly.

Elsbeth squared her shoulders. "All right. Do what you need to do."

Morton rose from his stool. "It has been some time since I

have sewn stitches on a person, not since my days in the Royal Army," he said before he went to retrieve a weathered leather pouch. "It will no doubt leave a scar."

"The scar is the least of my concerns," Elsbeth replied.

Morton returned to his stool and gave her a hard look. "You need to stop this madness, my lady. Nothing is worth risking your life."

"But my stepfather—" she began.

He cut her off. "Who cares if he has secrets? Don't we all?" he asked. "I have been complicit in all of this since I have looked the other way. But enough is enough. You can't go around playing a highwaywoman."

For a moment, Elsbeth considered his words. Maybe he was right. Perhaps she was pushing things too far, taking too many risks. But then she thought of Alfred's locked drawers, the whispered conversations, and the lies. She couldn't let it go. "I need to know what he is hiding," she said quietly.

Morton threaded a needle with practiced hands. "This is the last time I will patch you up," he stated, meeting her gaze. "You need to find another way, my lady."

Elsbeth nodded, though she wasn't sure if she truly meant it. "You are right," she responded. "I wasn't a very good highwaywoman anyways."

Morton's eyes softened with relief. "That is the most sense I have heard you speak in weeks."

As he brought the needle to her arm, she braced herself for the inevitable pain. "This will hurt a little," Morton warned.

The needle pierced her skin, and Elsbeth gasped, her nails digging into the edge of the stool. Hurting a little was an understatement. She bit her lip to keep from crying out, her breaths shallow and quick.

"Lord Westcott," she said suddenly, the name escaping her lips before she could stop herself.

Morton's hand stilled. "What about him?"

"He was the reason I was shot," she admitted. "He distracted me while someone else took aim."

Morton's jaw tightened. "That man has no honor."

"Well, neither do I," Elsbeth replied. "I did rob him of his pocket watch. Perhaps it was his way of exacting revenge."

Morton shook his head as he resumed stitching. "It was a cowardly thing to do. A man should fight his own battles, not ambush a lady."

Elsbeth felt tears sting her eyes again, though this time they were born of disappointment rather than pain. Why had she trusted Lord Westcott, even for a moment? Why had she let herself believe he could be different? He had saved her life in the village, only to betray her in the woods.

Despite the anger coursing through her, she had to acknowledge that Lord Westcott didn't know she was the high-waywoman. Or did he? No. That was impossible. She had been so careful—up until now. He had betrayed the highwaywoman, not her. But did that even matter?

She swore to herself that she would never let her guard down around him—or anyone—again.

Niles sat atop his horse, staring into the dense, shadowy woodlands where the highwaywoman had disappeared moments before. The sound of hoofbeats faded, leaving only the rustling of leaves. He clenched his reins tightly, his jaw tensing with frustration. She was gone, and he knew better than to follow. These woods were unfamiliar to him and pursuing her blindly could prove dangerous. Still, he couldn't shake the sound of her cry after the pistol discharged. He suspected that she had been shot.

Before he could linger on the thought, a deep voice interrupted his musings. "Are you all right, my lord?"

Startled, Niles turned to see a tall, heavy-set man astride a horse riding out from the shadows. The man tucked a pistol into the waistband of his trousers, his stern expression softened slightly in concern.

"Who are you?" Niles asked.

The man inclined his head respectfully. "My apologies. I am Constable West. I was informed of a highwaywoman terrorizing these parts and I came to investigate."

Niles frowned, his mind racing. "Who informed you?"

"Your aunt, my lord," Constable West replied. "She was worried for your safety and felt it was necessary to alert me. When I saw you conversing with the highwaywoman, I feared she might harm you."

"She meant me no harm."

The constable's expression hardened. "Desperate people tend to do desperate things. It is best not to take chances."

Niles tightened the hold on his reins, his knuckles whitening. "I do not believe this highwaywoman is desperate. There is something different about her."

Constable West gave him a skeptical look. "Regardless, she needs to be brought to justice. What can you tell me about her?"

Niles hesitated. He had a choice to make. He could cooperate with the constable and likely ensure the woman's capture, or withhold information and protect her. His instincts pulled him towards the latter. For reasons he couldn't fully explain, he felt compelled to shield her.

"I'm afraid I didn't get a good look at her," Niles lied.

Constable West furrowed his brows. "But, my lord, from what I understand, this is the second time you have encountered her. I was informed she robbed your coach and stole your pocket watch."

"She always wears a mask," Niles said. "I couldn't discern her features."

"It almost seems as if you are protecting her," Constable West said, his tone pointed.

"And why would I do that?" Niles countered, meeting the constable's gaze evenly.

Constable West studied him for a long moment before tipping his head. "I don't rightly know. But if you remember something that might aid the investigation, I trust you will contact me."

Niles was done with this conversation. He wanted to return home and retreat to his own thoughts. "If that will be all," he said.

"Goodnight, my lord," Constable West responded, retreating into the shadows.

Niles urged his horse forward, his mind spinning. He hoped fervently that he had been wrong about the gunshot wounding the highwaywoman, but the thought lingered. The idea of her hurt and alone in the forest unsettled him in a way he didn't expect. Why was he so preoccupied with this woman? She was merely a thief who had taken his father's pocket watch. And yet, she was unlike anyone he had ever met, a mystery he couldn't help but want to unravel.

When the familiar silhouette of his aunt's manor came into view, he dismounted and handed his horse to the waiting groom. He entered the house quietly, noticing a soft light spilling out from the parlor. Finding himself curious, he changed course and stepped inside. Eugenie was there, her legs curled beneath her as she sat in a plush chair, engrossed in a book.

"Why are you still awake?" Niles asked.

Eugenie held up a finger, signaling for him to wait as she finished the page. After a long moment, she placed a ribbon between the pages and closed the book. "Sorry," she said lightly. "I just had to read that last part."

"I assume that's why you're still awake?" he teased, moving to sit across from her.

"That," Eugenie replied with a grin, "and I was waiting for you to return from your... excursion."

He arched a brow. "And why is that?"

Her smile dimmed. "Did you find the highwaywoman?"

"I did," he admitted, leaning back in his chair.

Eugenie placed the book down onto the table. "Did you convince her to abandon her wayward ways?"

"I tried, but I was interrupted by the constable."

"That might have been a good thing. You seem rather preoccupied with this highwaywoman."

A wry smile played on his lips. "Why are you nosing into this?"

"Because I care," she replied, her tone laced with genuine concern. "I just wish you had a healthier obsession."

"Like reading?" he asked dryly.

Eugenie laughed. "Yes, like reading. We could read together and discuss books. Think about how much fun we could have."

Niles shook his head. "That is not likely to happen. Besides, I am not obsessed with this highwaywoman. I simply want my pocket watch back."

With a knowing look, Eugenie replied, "You have spent the last two nights chasing after her. If that is not an obsession, what is?"

"Curiosity," he said with a shrug.

"You are odd, Brother," Eugenie said. "But promise me you will be careful."

"I am always careful," Niles replied, rising from his seat.

"Wait, don't go," Eugenie encouraged.

"Does that mean this interrogation is over?"

Eugenie looked up at him. "I am merely trying to understand. What is it about this highwaywoman that intrigues you?"

Niles ran a hand through his dark hair as he tried to think of an answer. "I suppose I see a kindred soul in this highwaywoman."

"She is a thief."

"I don't think she is," Niles said. "She told me that she is looking for something specific and hadn't intended to rob me."

Eugenie gave him an exasperated look. "And you believe her?"

"I do."

"Where did my cynical brother go?"

Niles offered his hand to help his sister up. "I am still here, and I know what I am doing."

Eugenie took it, standing gracefully. "It is madness, you know," she said. "Aunt Margaret is worried about you."

"Is that why she spoke to the constable?"

"It was," Eugenie replied. "How did you know that?"

Niles started walking towards the door. "I met Constable West after he shot at the highwaywoman."

"Oh, no," Eugenie murmured.

"I suspect she was hit because she cried out in pain before retreating into the woodlands."

Eugenie glanced over at him. "I am surprised you didn't follow her."

"I would have, but the woodlands can be treacherous, especially at night," Niles replied. "It would have been foolish to do so."

As they ascended the grand staircase together, Eugenie asked, "Do you think you will see her again?"

Niles thought for a moment, his gaze distant. "I hope so," he murmured.

They came to a stop at his sister's door and she gave him a

faint smile. "Goodnight," she said before slipping into her room and closing the door behind her.

He lingered there for a moment, her words echoing in his mind. Why was he so preoccupied with this highwaywoman? With a heavy sigh, he turned and made his way down the corridor to his own bedchamber.

The warm glow of candlelight greeted him as he stepped inside. His trusted valet was tidying up the room. At the sound of the door, Wiley glanced up, his expression easing with relief.

"You are back," Wiley said. "I expected you much later."

"I found her," Niles muttered, shrugging out of his jacket and tossing it onto a nearby chair.

Wiley straightened, giving Niles his full attention. "And?"

"And nothing," he grumbled as he dropped onto the settee. "We spoke for a few moments before we were interrupted by the constable."

"That might be for the best."

Niles leaned back, his head resting against the upholstered seat as he stared up at the ceiling. "I can't stop thinking about her," he admitted. "I don't know why. I don't even know who she is."

The valet moved closer, his expression thoughtful. "What is it about her, my lord?"

"There is something familiar about her," Niles said after a long pause. "Something I can't explain. It is like—" He stopped himself, shaking his head. The notion was ridiculous, absurd even. "It feels as if our souls are somehow intertwined."

Wiley's brows lifted slightly. "That is quite the sentiment, my lord."

Niles let out a humorless laugh. "Madness, isn't it? She is a highwaywoman. A thief. I should be condemning her actions, not being obsessed with her."

Wiley took a step closer, folding his hands in front of him.

"Perhaps you see something in her that others don't. Or perhaps she is meant to cross your path for a reason."

Niles huffed. "Don't say that you believe in destiny and whatnot."

Wiley chuckled. "I do, in my own way. I met my wife at a country dance I hadn't even planned to attend. If I hadn't gone that night, my whole life would have been different."

The sincerity in Wiley's tone caught Niles off guard. "And are you happy?"

"Wholeheartedly," Wiley replied, a small smile tugging at his lips. "Marriage is not without its challenges, but it is a partnership. A choice made every day."

Niles grew silent, his thoughts shifting. He had always believed marriage was a matter of practicality. Mutual toleration. Shared goals. Love had seemed unnecessary, even frivolous. Yet Wiley's words stirred something within him, a seed of doubt about his own rigid beliefs.

"Perhaps love does make a difference," Niles murmured, almost to himself. The thought felt awkward, unwelcome even.

The image of Lady Elsbeth came into his mind, and he quickly banished it. Where had that thought even come from? He would no more marry Lady Elsbeth than chew glass.

Shaking his head, he rose from the settee with a groan. Between the highwaywoman and Lady Elsbeth, he doubted he would get even a moment of sleep.

Wiley studied him for a moment. "If I may, my lord, sometimes the answers come when you least expect them."

"I am not looking for answers," Niles said, heading towards the bed. "I am looking for peace and quiet."

With an amused look, Wiley replied, "Then you should not get married."

As Niles sank onto the edge of the bed, he couldn't help but agree.

6

Elsbeth woke with a sharp jolt of pain radiating from her left arm. Sunlight streamed in through the tall windows, brightening the room but doing little to lift her mood. Her memories of the night before flooded in. The gunshot. The searing pain. And the betrayal she hadn't seen coming.

Lord Westcott.

How could she have been so foolish? She had almost trusted him. Almost believed he cared. But no. He had kept her distracted, giving someone the perfect opportunity to ambush her. The infuriating lord had tricked her, and she wouldn't make that mistake again.

A soft knock interrupted her musings before Clara entered the room, balancing a bowl of water and bandages. Her usual cheerful demeanor was replaced by quiet efficiency as she set the bowl down on the table beside the bed.

"Good morning, my lady," Clara said. "It is time we clean that wound before it gets infected."

Elsbeth groaned, reluctantly pushing herself up against the wall. "Do you have to sound so happy about it?"

Clara arched an eyebrow as she reached for the clean linen. "It is hard to be cheerful when I am tending to a lady who insists on behaving like a highwayman." She dipped a cloth into the water, wringing it out with practiced hands. "Do I need to remind you that this would not have happened if you had stayed in bed where you belong?"

"Do you truly have to lecture me now?"

Clara smiled as she moved to sit in the chair beside Elsbeth. "Would you prefer I schedule a lecture for a more convenient time? Perhaps before supper?"

"How can you make jokes at a time like this?"

"It is rather easy, considering I wasn't the one who was shot," Clara quipped.

"I should dismiss you."

Clara grinned. "You could, but you would be lost without me."

Despite herself, Elsbeth laughed. "I would," she admitted. "Very well. I won't dismiss you, but can you stop making jokes?"

"I will stop, but that doesn't mean I won't be thinking them."

"You are insufferable," Elsbeth retorted.

Clara held the damp cloth up. "Brace yourself, my lady. This will sting," she warned before pressing the cloth to the wound.

Elsbeth let out a soft cry as the cool water touched her wound. The pain was sharp and relentless. She turned her face away, breathing through it. "Do you have to scrub so vigorously?"

Clara paused for only a moment. "Would you rather it fester and take your arm?" she asked. "That is what happens to unattended wounds."

"You are far too morbid," Elsbeth muttered.

Clara finished cleaning the wound and secured a fresh bandage around her arm. Sitting back with a sigh of relief, she studied her handiwork. "It looks better than I feared, my lady. You will heal. Though you will have a scar."

"A scar is the least of my worries," Elsbeth murmured, her mind drifting back to her stepfather. Alfred was hiding something, but was that something worth risking her life to discover? She wasn't quite sure how she should proceed.

As Clara began gathering up the used cloths, she glanced over at Elsbeth. "I still cannot believe that Lord Westcott tricked you."

"Can we not talk about him?" Elsbeth asked. "I have had quite enough of Lord Westcott and I do not want to think of him a moment longer than I have to."

Clara straightened. "I will change the subject, then. Your cousin, Lord Bedford, and Mr. Strother are waiting for you in the drawing room."

Elsbeth's stomach dropped. "Why are they here? Today, of all days?"

"I did not ask," Clara said with a shrug. "But you might want to hurry before they come searching for you."

Gesturing towards her bandaged arm, Elsbeth asked, "How am I to explain this?"

"I thought of that," Clara replied, crossing the room to the wardrobe. She pulled out a pink gown with oversized puffed sleeves and held it up. "These sleeves will hide the bandages."

Elsbeth frowned. "That gown is hopelessly out of fashion."

"Perhaps, but it is very practical right now," Clara remarked.

"You make an excellent point," Elsbeth said, resigned as she allowed Clara to help her dress.

A short time later, she emerged from her room and descended the grand staircase. The pain in her arm pulsated with every step, but she kept her expression composed. At least the pain reminded her that she was alive.

Elsbeth entered the room and saw her tall, dark-haired cousin, Charles, rising from his seat beside her mother, his arms outstretched in greeting. "Cousin! You look as lovely as ever," he said in an overly cheerful voice.

She accepted his brief embrace before stepping back, fixing him with a wary gaze. "What brings you to our quiet village?"

"Why, I came to see you, of course," Charles replied.

Her mother interjected, her lips pursed in disapproval. "Dear, why are you wearing that gown? It is an interesting choice to meet callers."

She smoothed down the gown. "I was rushing to see Charles and it was the first gown that I came across in the wardrobe."

"Perhaps next time, you might take a little more time to make yourself presentable," her mother remarked.

Charles gestured towards a short, balding man standing next to a chair. "You remember Mr. Strother, do you not?"

Elsbeth tipped her head. "Of course, he was my father's solicitor," she said. "Good morning, Mr. Strother."

"Good morning, Lady Elsbeth," Mr. Strother replied with a stiff bow. He cleared his throat before adding, "I wish to speak with you about your dowry."

Her brow furrowed. "My dowry? Has something happened?"

"Not at all," Mr. Strother said quickly. "It remains untouched at fifteen thousand pounds. However, Lord Bedford has a proposal that he believes will be mutually beneficial."

Charles motioned for her to sit. "Allow me to explain."

She claimed the seat next to her mother, who looked far too calm for her liking. "I am listening."

Charles returned to his seat. "As you know, the estate your father left behind is struggling. I have retained the entailed properties, but I require funds to bring the estate back to profitability."

"And what does that have to do with me?" Elsbeth asked, suspicion prickling at her.

Charles paused. "I need a wife. And you need a husband. It seems practical for us to marry."

Elsbeth stared at him, certain she had misheard. "Marry? *You*? But we are cousins."

"Second cousins, once removed," Charles corrected, as though that small detail absolved the madness of the suggestion. "It is perfectly legal, I assure you."

"But we call each other 'Cousin,'" Elsbeth stated.

Charles nodded. "We would have to change that if we were to wed."

Elsbeth turned to her mother, stunned. "And what do you say about this?"

Her mother reached for a teapot, avoiding her daughter's gaze. "Perhaps we should all have a cup of tea and discuss this rationally."

"Forget the tea, Mother," Elsbeth said. "Charles just asked me to marry him."

Her mother leaned back in her seat, finally looking at her. "It might not be such a terrible idea, Elsbeth. Given the... circumstances."

Elsbeth rose abruptly, and Charles stood with her. "This is madness," she declared. "I cannot marry my cousin. No matter how far removed."

Charles regarded her with a solemn expression. "It is not ideal, but the estate needs you. I need you. And you need someone who can offer you stability."

Turning to Mr. Strother, Elsbeth asked, "What happens if I refuse this outrageous suggestion?"

Mr. Strother adjusted his spectacles as he glanced between Charles and Elsbeth. "Your dowry is to remain untouched until such time as you marry. There is no provision for you to inherit it at a certain age, should you remain unwed." He hesitated for a moment before adding, "Without marriage, I am afraid those funds will remain inaccessible indefinitely."

Elsbeth stiffened. Her father, for all his faults, had still managed to leave her trapped by this one condition.

Charles, however, seized the moment to step closer. "Elsbeth," he began softly, "I would be a good husband to you. You would be treated fairly and with respect as my countess."

The words made her stomach churn. Charles was her cousin. Her childhood companion. They had climbed trees and raced horses together. Now, as he stood before her speaking of marriage, the very idea felt so unnatural that she had to fight the urge to shudder.

"And what of the scandal? You cannot possibly believe there wouldn't be whispers about such a union," Elsbeth countered.

Charles's lips pressed into a thin line, though his gaze remained steady. "I do not think our name could be dragged any further into the mud than where it already resides," he replied. "Do you?"

The words hit her harder than she cared to admit. Despite their weight, she couldn't argue with the truth of them. The scandal following her father's death—the debts, the mistresses, the illegitimate children—had already cast a permanent shadow over their family. Society had all but turned its back on them. She sank back down to the settee.

Even so... marry Charles? The very notion seemed ludicrous. She couldn't imagine calling him her *husband*, much less sharing the intimacies of marriage. The thought alone sent a shiver of revulsion through her.

Before she could reply, her mother stood, smoothing her skirts with forced calm. "This is a great deal for Elsbeth to consider," she said. "Perhaps we should allow her some time to process everything."

Charles turned to her mother and gave a deferential nod. "I wholeheartedly agree. I do not want to force Elsbeth into anything she is not ready to accept. But," he added with a pointed glance at Elsbeth, "Mr. Strother will be returning to

Town at his first opportunity. It would be best to come to a decision sooner rather than later."

Elsbeth shot to her feet, the sudden movement startling the men into silence. "There is nothing to think about," she declared, her voice resolute. "My answer is no."

The room went still. For a moment, Charles simply looked at her, studying her as though she were some particularly stubborn riddle. Then, to her frustration, he smiled faintly as if her refusal were nothing more than inconsequential. "I think," he said evenly, "it would be wise for you to truly consider it."

She opened her mouth to retort, but before she could speak, her mother interjected. "That is most generous of you, Charles," she said with a pointed look at Elsbeth. "Isn't that right, dear?"

Elsbeth turned to her mother, disbelief tightening her chest. "Generous?" she repeated, barely able to keep the anger from her voice. "This entire discussion is absurd. You would have me marry my cousin?"

Her mother met her gaze with a mixture of weariness and impatience. "Elsbeth," she said, "Charles is offering you stability. Do not be so quick to dismiss it."

"Stability?" Elsbeth scoffed, her hands curling into fists at her sides. "At what cost? I would lose every ounce of self-respect I possess. I will *not* marry him."

Charles took a step back. "I am not here to force your hand, Elsbeth," he said. "But I urge you to think about this rationally. Time may not offer you another opportunity."

"I have thought about it," Elsbeth shot back, her voice cracking with emotion. "And my answer remains the same. No."

Her mother sighed heavily, sitting back down as if the weight of the conversation had become too much to bear. "You are being difficult," she murmured, her disappointment palpable.

Charles bowed stiffly. "I will take my leave for now," he said, glancing between Elsbeth and her mother. "But know this, I only wish to help you."

Elsbeth watched as Charles and Mr. Strother departed the room, leaving behind a lingering tension that seemed to settle into every corner of the space. The door closed, and she turned to her mother. "How could you entertain this?"

"Because," her mother started, "you have no other prospects. Charles is offering you a future."

"A future?" Elsbeth whispered, tears burning at the back of her eyes. "Or a prison?"

Her mother looked away, unable—or perhaps unwilling—to answer.

Elsbeth needed a moment alone. She turned on her heel and left the drawing room without saying another word.

———————～———————

Niles entered the dining room and noted the scene before him. His aunt was sipping her tea while Eugenie, as always, was engrossed in a book even as she absentmindedly nibbled on a scone.

"Good morning," he greeted.

Eugenie glanced up, her finger keeping her place in the book. "Good morning, Brother."

Niles pulled out the chair beside her, his lips curling into a teasing smile. "A book at the breakfast table? Really, Eugenie? I can't believe Aunt Margaret allows such scandalous behavior."

Aunt Margaret laughed. "A young lady who carries a book is never bored."

"Well, my mother would be rolling over in her grave to see such a thing," Niles remarked.

"Rules are far more relaxed in the countryside," Aunt

Margaret replied with a knowing look, "and, dare I say, far more sensible."

"Not that relaxed," Niles argued.

Aunt Margaret lifted her brow. "I understand," she began, her tone shifting with interest, "that you had quite the adventure last night."

Niles met his aunt's gaze. "Adventure?"

His sister lowered her book, clearly amused. "Oh, do not act coy. I told Aunt Margaret all about your moonlit meeting with the highwaywoman."

He groaned softly, setting his cup down with a quiet clink. "Eugenie, must you discuss my business over breakfast?"

Eugenie shrugged, not looking the least bit repentant. "It isn't my fault you have an odd fascination with criminals."

"Fascination is a strong word," Niles retorted, though even he couldn't deny his strange preoccupation with the masked woman. "We spoke briefly until the constable showed up and scared her off."

Aunt Margaret looked thoroughly unimpressed. "A conversation with a thief? Truly riveting, I am sure."

Niles picked up his fork and began to prod at the food placed before him. "It is more complicated than that. She told me she was searching for something specific."

"And you believe her?" Aunt Margaret asked.

"Why wouldn't I?" he countered. Why did he feel compelled to defend the highwaywoman?

His aunt leaned forward. "Perhaps because she is a thief who robs coaches at gunpoint? You should be more wary of charming stories spun by desperate people."

Niles held her gaze. "I don't think she is desperate. If anything, she is... determined."

"Well, it is a good thing I spoke to Constable West about this nonsense. If he hadn't intervened last night, I half-expect you would have ended up at Gretna Green with this highway-woman," Aunt Margaret said.

Niles huffed. "I assure you, I have no intention of marrying a highwaywoman."

"That is a relief," Eugenie chimed in. "Though you must admit, it would make quite the story."

"Enough," Niles muttered, rubbing his temple. "Can we discuss something else, please?"

Aunt Margaret appeared ready to press the subject further when the butler entered the room. "Lady Elsbeth has come to call, my lady."

A pleased smile replaced Aunt Margaret's solemn expression. "Ah, that does save us a trip to her manor today. Please inform Lady Elsbeth that we will join her momentarily."

Rising, Eugenie remarked, "I wonder what brings her here so early. Do you suppose something is wrong?"

"No doubt it is merely a social visit," Aunt Margaret assured her. "Lady Elsbeth frequently joins me for walks in the gardens in the morning."

Niles stood as well, his movements slow and deliberate to hide the conflicted emotions swirling within him. He told himself it was mere curiosity that made him eager to see Lady Elsbeth. Nothing more. But the woman occupied his thoughts far too often for his liking.

Eugenie gave him an expectant look as she tucked her book under her arm. "Are you coming?"

Feigning indifference, Niles placed his napkin down. "I suppose I shall. I wasn't particularly hungry anyway."

"That is convenient," Eugenie teased. "I do hope Lady Elsbeth brought along a book to discuss."

"Which book?" he asked, but he already suspected he knew the answer.

"Does it matter?" Eugenie asked with a smile.

Niles chuckled as they followed their aunt down the hall. "You are incorrigible."

Eugenie laughed, just as he had intended. But Niles could no longer focus on her chatter. His thoughts returned to Lady Elsbeth. Last time they spoke, she had a vulnerability about her that captivated him.

As they entered the drawing room, Niles noticed Lady Elsbeth standing by the window, her back to them. The soft light streaming through the glass highlighted the pale pink gown she wore. It was an absurd dress with far too many frills and ridiculous puffy sleeves. Still, it did little to distract from her beauty.

She turned at the sound of their approach, and Niles knew that something was wrong. Her brow was furrowed, and the usual fire in her eyes was replaced with something more fragile —worry, perhaps, or unease.

Before he could stop himself, Niles asked, "What is wrong?"

Lady Elsbeth's lips tightened, and she tilted her chin slightly, her voice clipped. "Why do you suppose something is wrong?"

Niles faltered. "You seem rather..." He searched for the right word, then settled on one. "Preoccupied."

"I assure you, I am perfectly fine," she said firmly, but the slight tremor in her voice betrayed her.

Aunt Margaret gestured towards the settee. "Come, my dear. Sit with us and tell us what troubles you."

Lady Elsbeth hesitated, then moved stiffly towards the settee. Niles noticed the faint grimace that crossed her features as she lowered herself onto the cushion.

Was she in pain?

Once they were all situated, Eugenie reached for the teapot and poured four cups of tea. She extended one to Lady Elsbeth.

"Thank you," Lady Elsbeth murmured.

They all sat in silence, sipping their tea, until Aunt Margaret cleared her throat. "Now, what has you so troubled?"

Lady Elsbeth exhaled softly. "My cousin, Charles, the Earl of Bedford, came to visit."

"Oh, how delightful!" Aunt Margaret exclaimed.

"No, not delightful," Elsbeth countered. "He has a ridiculous notion that we should marry so he can use my dowry to save his estate."

Aunt Margaret blinked in surprise. "But he is your cousin."

"As Charles reminds me, he is my second cousin, once removed," Lady Elsbeth corrected with evident disdain.

Eugenie moved to the edge of her seat. "What did you say?"

"I told him no, but he thinks I will change my mind," Lady Elsbeth replied. "Which I won't. My mother even invited him to stay at our manor."

Niles set his teacup down, hiding the sudden discomfort that rose within him. The thought of Lady Elsbeth marrying anyone—much less her cousin—left an inexplicable weight on his chest.

Lady Elsbeth continued. "What is worse is that my mother isn't opposed to the idea," she shared. "She thinks it might be my only chance to receive an offer of marriage."

"That is awful," Eugenie muttered. "You can't marry your cousin."

"I know," Lady Elsbeth said.

Aunt Margaret turned to Niles, her sharp gaze landing on him. "What do you say about this, Niles?"

He gave her a blank look. "Why should my opinion matter?" he asked. "This is Lady Elsbeth's decision, and hers alone."

Rather than expressing gratitude, Elsbeth shot him a glare, her words dripping with sarcasm. "How generous of you, my lord."

Niles frowned, utterly perplexed by her reaction. What had

he done now? He thought they were past this disdain for one another.

Eugenie reached for the teapot and refilled Lady Elsbeth's teacup. "More tea? Tea makes everything better."

"Tea won't help this," Lady Elsbeth said.

Aunt Margaret leaned forward, reaching out to lightly touch Lady Elsbeth's left sleeve. In response, Lady Elsbeth flinched and let out an audible gasp.

Aunt Margaret withdrew her hand. "Is something the matter?"

Lady Elsbeth quickly straightened in her seat. "It is nothing. I fell off my horse yesterday. My left arm is just a bit tender."

"Oh, my poor girl!" Aunt Margaret exclaimed. "That must have been dreadful. Is that why you are wearing that hideous dress?"

Lady Elsbeth smoothed her hands over the frills. "Yes. Unfortunately, it is the only gown I own with sleeves full enough to hide the bandage."

At the word *bandage*, Niles's attention sharpened. He set his teacup down with deliberate care. "A bandage? For a bruise?" he asked.

Lady Elsbeth turned her gaze towards him, her eyes flashing with barely concealed annoyance. "Not that it is any of your business, my lord, but when I fell, I landed on a jagged rock, causing a scrape."

Niles frowned. Something about her explanation didn't sit right with him. A rock? A scrape? It seemed far too mild for the visible pain she'd displayed when Aunt Margaret had barely touched her arm. He leaned back in his chair, observing her carefully. "Where, exactly, did you fall?"

Before Lady Elsbeth could answer, Aunt Margaret turned a scolding look on him. "Niles, really. Why are you interrogating the poor girl like she's a prisoner at the Tower of London?"

Lady Elsbeth forced a weak smile. "It's all right, Lady

Margaret. I fell along a path in the woodlands. It was near dusk."

"Near dusk?" Niles pressed, a suspicion flickering in his mind. He kept his voice even, but his sharp eyes were locked on her face, searching for any sign of deception. "Why were you out riding so late?"

Lady Elsbeth's hands tightened where they rested in her lap. "It doesn't matter why, my lord," she replied curtly. "The question is irrelevant."

"I disagree," Niles countered. "It's rather odd, wouldn't you say, that you only injured your left arm after a fall? Most riders would have more extensive bruising or at least a few scrapes elsewhere."

Lady Elsbeth's back grew rigid. "I suppose I was spared that fate."

Niles tilted his head slightly, narrowing his eyes as a thought occurred to him. *Could Lady Elsbeth be the highwaywoman?* The idea was absurd, and yet it seemed entirely probable.

He pressed on, his tone deceptively casual. "Tell me, Lady Elsbeth, were you perhaps riding in the woodlands in the dead of night?"

A flicker of something—shock, guilt, fear—passed across her features, so brief that most wouldn't have caught it. But Niles did.

"Why would I ever do such a foolish thing?" she replied.

Eugenie interjected. "I agree with Lady Elsbeth. No sane young woman would venture into the woodlands at night. That would be madness."

Niles ignored his sister. He leaned forward slightly, his tone hardening. "Then let me see your wound."

Aunt Margaret gasped. "Niles! Have you lost your senses? Asking such a thing of a lady is entirely improper!"

Lady Elsbeth's chin lifted. "I agree with Lady Margaret. It

would be highly inappropriate for me to undress my arm for you."

Niles paused, studying her carefully. "Who treated your injury?"

"Morton, our groom," she replied, her voice tight with irritation. "He served in the Royal Army, and he has experience stitching wounds. I'm fortunate to have his skill at hand."

"How very convenient." Niles decided to try a different tactic. "I assume your mother was terribly worried?"

"I didn't inform her. I saw no need to worry her over something so trivial," Lady Elsbeth replied.

"How gracious of you," Niles replied dryly, though his mind whirled with possibilities. Her explanation sounded plausible enough, but something about it rang false.

Aunt Margaret interrupted with an impatient shake of her head. "Dear heavens, Niles! You're being positively unbearable this morning." She turned to Lady Elsbeth. "I do apologize, my dear. I have no idea what's gotten into him."

Niles rose abruptly, pushing back his chair with a scrape against the floor. "Forgive me, but I believe the stuffiness of the drawing room has clouded my judgment. A turn in the gardens might clear my head." He turned his attention to Lady Elsbeth. "Would you care to accompany me, my lady?"

Lady Elsbeth held his gaze, her expression guarded. "It's rather cold outside, my lord."

"I would be happy to lend you my cloak," Niles replied, unable to resist adding, "assuming, of course, that you'll return it."

Her lips pressed together, pulling downward at the corners. "You need not worry for your cloak, my lord. I have no desire to keep it."

Just his pocket watch.

Niles extended his arm towards her. "Shall we?"

For a moment, she stared at his proffered hand. Then with a

sigh, she placed her hand lightly in his. Niles couldn't help but note the tension in her grip, as though she were bracing herself for battle. And perhaps she was.

He led her towards the door, his mind already plotting his next move. If Lady Elsbeth was the highwaywoman, he would find the proof. And if she wasn't?

Well, then he had an entirely different problem.

Because either way, he couldn't seem to stop thinking about her.

7

H *e knew.*
Elsbeth kept her chin high and her composure steady as Lord Westcott guided her down the garden path. How could she talk her way out of this?

"Lord Westcott..." she began.

"Not here," he interrupted curtly, his tone brooking no argument.

The silence between them stretched as they strolled further into the gardens. The crisp air carried the faint scent of roses, a stark contrast to the storm brewing in her thoughts. At last, Lord Westcott stopped and turned to face her.

"Do you want to explain yourself?" he half-asked, half-demanded.

Elsbeth weighed her options. Should she feign ignorance or confess everything? She didn't trust him, especially after what happened last night. He had betrayed her, and she had no guarantee he wouldn't do so again. Deciding to buy time, she tilted her chin with a faint smile.

"I'm afraid I don't know what you are talking about," she

settled on. It was a weak response, but it was the best she could come up with at that moment.

His brow arched, skepticism etched onto his features. "I know you are the highwaywoman."

Her heart skipped a beat, but she didn't flinch. It would do no good to show any sign of emotions. "And why would you think that, my lord?"

"You were shot last night, and now you claim you were injured by falling off a horse. How very convenient," he mocked.

"How do you know I didn't fall off my horse?" she countered.

"Because that seems rather unlikely, don't you think?"

Elsbeth shrugged. "Perhaps I am a poor rider. Have you considered that?"

Lord Westcott ran a hand through his dark hair. "Why don't you trust me?"

She let out a scoff. "Trust you?" she repeated. "You were the reason why I was shot!"

"So you admit it."

"I admit nothing," Elsbeth snapped, silently chiding herself on the slip of her tongue. "But if I were to admit such a thing, you set me up. You feigned concern, pretended to care, all to keep me there so you could ambush me."

Lord Westcott's expression shifted, guilt flickering briefly across his face. "I had no idea the constable was there."

"You didn't go to him?" she asked, her voice sharp with accusation.

"I didn't," he insisted. "My aunt did. She thought she was protecting me. You must believe me. I would never knowingly put you in harm's way."

Elsbeth shook her head, her emotions a whirlwind of anger and confusion. "It doesn't matter anymore. None of this does. Why did I ever think this scheme would work?"

He took a step closer to her, his voice dropping to a softer tone. "Why are you doing this? This clearly isn't about money."

Her defenses faltered at the genuine concern in his voice, but she rallied quickly. "My reasons are my own."

"They are, but I want to help."

Elsbeth let out a humorless laugh. "Help, my lord? Surely you cannot be serious."

"You said last night that you were searching for something specific," Lord Westcott said. "What is it?"

She hesitated. Could she trust him? Every instinct screamed for her to run, to retreat into the safety of her guarded silence. But then there was that small, insistent voice inside her. The one that urged her to try, to take a chance. And heaven help her, she did want to trust Lord Westcott. There was something about him, something familiar, something safe.

"A key," she said at last.

Lord Westcott furrowed his brow. "A key to what?"

Elsbeth took a steadying breath. This was it. She would tell him the truth, and hope that he believed her. "My stepfather isn't who he claims to be. No one believes me, but I know he is hiding something. He keeps his desk locked, and the key is always in his jacket pocket."

There was a moment of silence as her words hung in the air. She searched his face for any sign of disbelief or mockery but found none.

Finally, when he spoke, he asked, "And you thought pretending to be a highwaywoman would get you that key?"

She frowned, heat rising to her cheeks. "I did, but your coach was the only one that I robbed. I mistook yours for his."

"And my pocket watch? Was that part of your grand plan?" His tone carried both amusement and reproach.

Elsbeth winced. "I had to take something to make it seem believable. I didn't realize it was your father's. I will return it, of course. I have no use for it."

A stern look came to Lord Westcott's expression. "Did you even consider the risks of this charade? Riding alone at night, confronting strangers? You could have been killed."

"I did consider that," she admitted. "But what was I supposed to do? Stand by while my stepfather continues to deceive everyone? My mother adores him, but he's a fraud. I need to prove it."

"And you thought risking your life was the solution?"

"It was the only solution I could think of," she said, her tone more defensive now. "But I realize now that it wasn't enough. That's why I need to find another way."

"This is madness," he said, his voice filled with exasperation.

"No," Elsbeth countered. "Madness is doing nothing. Madness is letting him fool everyone while I stand idly by. I won't let history repeat itself."

Lord Westcott met her gaze. "What do you mean by that?"

Her words were heavy with emotion as she revealed, "My father fooled everyone. No one suspected what he truly was until it was too late. The truth only came out after his death, and it destroyed us. We were left to pick up the pieces of a shattered legacy. I won't let that happen again. Not to my mother. Not to me. We deserve better."

A long silence followed her words, and when Lord Westcott finally spoke, there was a quiet determination in his voice. "Then I will assist you. Let me help."

Her eyes widened in surprise. "You will?" she asked. Frankly, it was the last thing she had expected.

"Yes," he said firmly, "but on three conditions."

"I'm listening," she said, lifting her brow.

"First," he began, "no more highwaywoman antics."

"That's fair," she agreed.

"Second, you'll be honest with me from now on. No more secrets."

Her pause was brief. "Very well. And the third?"

A smile curved his lips. "You'll allow me to call you by your given name."

"That is rather presumptuous of you, my lord."

"No bolder than robbing me at gunpoint," he retorted.

Despite herself, a laugh escaped her lips. "You were never in any true danger," she informed him. "The pistol wasn't even loaded."

Lord Westcott chuckled. "You were a terrible high-waywoman."

"And yet, I managed to steal your pocket watch," she quipped.

"Correction," he said with a grin. "I *gave* it to you."

For the first time, Elsbeth felt a flicker of hope. Perhaps, with Lord Westcott's help, she could uncover the truth. And perhaps, just perhaps, she wasn't as alone as she had thought.

"Are we in agreement, Elsbeth?" His deep voice carried a warmth that sent an unexpected flutter through her chest.

She stiffened at the sensation. It was just a name, after all. "Am I to call you by your given name, as well?"

"I would prefer it."

"Then... Niles, we are in agreement," she replied, letting his name roll off her tongue.

He flashed her a flirtatious grin. "I like how you say my name."

"Well, I find the way you say my name to be utterly bother-some," she shot back, though her words lacked sincerity.

"I don't think that is true," Niles replied. "And did we not just agree to be honest with one another?"

Before she could reply, Eugenie's voice rang out from farther up the path. "Aunt Margaret sent me out here to ensure you two didn't kill one another," she teased. "I should note she bet on Lady Elsbeth."

Niles turned towards his sister. "Lady Elsbeth and I have come to an understanding."

Eugenie raised an eyebrow as she approached. "An understanding?"

He raised a hand to clarify. "Not that type of understanding. We have simply agreed to be cordial to one another."

"How fascinating." Eugenie shifted her gaze to Lady Elsbeth. "Are you sure he didn't coerce you into this? If so, blink twice."

Elsbeth laughed. "We came to this agreement together."

Eugenie's eyes flickered between them. "This seems rather... sudden."

"You are reading far too much into this, Sister," Niles said. "I suspect this is due to your reading mania."

That clearly was the right thing to say because Eugenie placed her hands on her hips and retorted, "There is nothing wrong with reading a book or two a day. Books are the key to a fulfilled mind."

"There is when you should be using your time and energy to find a husband," Niles responded.

"A husband is useless to me," Eugenie contended, glancing at the sky. "Perhaps we should go back inside and continue this conversation. It appears as if it is about to rain."

Niles stepped forward and offered his arm. "This is England. It always looks like it is about to rain."

Eugenie accepted his arm and turned her attention to Elsbeth. "Would you like to go pheasant shooting tomorrow?"

Elsbeth glanced at her arm. Though she knew how to shoot, her injury would make it impossible. "I have never gone pheasant shooting before," she said, opting for a half-truth.

Niles extended his other arm to Elsbeth. "My father indulged Eugenie too much in her youth. He often took her shooting, and now she insists on going at every opportunity."

"And why shouldn't I?" Eugenie asked. "Why should only men enjoy pheasant shooting?"

"I never said it was fair, but it is hardly conventional," Niles replied.

Eugenie ignored him with a wave of her hand. "I am going tomorrow, and you are welcome to join us, Elsbeth."

"I don't think I will be much help with my left arm," Elsbeth said.

"You should still come. We will need someone to balance the numbers. Perhaps bring your cousin," Eugenie suggested. "I would like to meet him."

Elsbeth's back went rigid at the mention of Charles. "I am not sure if that is the best idea. I do not want to encourage him, given the circumstances."

"What if I partner with Charles, and you partner with Niles?" Eugenie questioned. "We will turn it into a friendly competition."

Niles offered Elsbeth an apologetic look. "You will have to excuse my sister. She is always looking for an opportunity to challenge me."

"I did bag more pheasants last time we went," Eugenie reminded him.

"That was pure luck," Niles countered.

Eugenie leaned closer to Elsbeth, shielding her mouth with her hand as if sharing a secret. "I should warn you, Niles is a dreadfully sore loser. Truly unbearable."

"Don't listen to her," Niles said, looking heavenward. "She is an insufferable gloater."

Elsbeth found the whole conversation to be rather amusing. And, despite it all, the thought of spending time with Niles while they engaged in pheasant hunting seemed rather enjoyable.

Niles sat in the darkened coach as it rumbled along the short journey to Lady Elsbeth's manor. She had invited them to dinner, hoping to navigate the difficult situation with her cousin. He couldn't blame her. Being offered marriage by one's own cousin was a predicament no one deserved.

The silence inside the coach was broken by Eugenie's soft, worried voice. "I'm concerned about Aunt Margaret. She wasn't feeling well enough to accompany us this evening."

"I wouldn't give it much heed," Niles replied evenly, though he understood his sister's anxiety.

"Perhaps we should fetch the doctor," she suggested, her concern etched across her delicate features.

Niles shook his head. "Let's not overreact, Eugenie."

Her hands fidgeted with the ribbon on her gown. "I can't help it," she admitted. "It started this way with Mother and Father. They were unwell, and it only got worse and worse until..." Her voice faltered, trailing into silence. "Until they died."

His heart clenched at the pain in her words. He reached out, covering her hands with his own. "It's not the same, Eugenie," he said gently. "Aunt Margaret isn't going anywhere. She'll live a long life."

"That's what was supposed to happen with Mother and Father," she whispered, her voice trembling. "What if she doesn't? What will we do then?"

Niles leaned closer. "No matter what happens, you'll always have me."

Her gaze met his, searching for reassurance. "And what happens when you marry?"

He gave her a pointed look. "That's not likely to happen anytime soon."

Eugenie's lips quirked into a faint smile. "I think it'll happen sooner than you think."

Leaning back in his seat, Niles said firmly, "Regardless, you don't need to worry about your future. I'll always take care of you."

"Thank you, Brother."

The coach came to a halt in front of the Stockton estate. Niles stepped out without waiting for the footman, turning to offer his hand to Eugenie. She took it gracefully, stepping onto the gravel path with practiced ease.

As they approached the manor, the heavy door swung open, revealing the butler. The entry hall glowed warmly, and Elsbeth stood waiting just inside. Relief softened her features as her eyes landed on them.

"Thank you for coming," she said, her voice carrying a hint of gratitude.

"There's no place I'd rather be," Niles responded sincerely.

Elsbeth's lips twitched with amusement. "I can think of several places I'd rather be than having dinner with a cousin who's proposed to me."

He chuckled. "Fair point."

Turning to Eugenie, Elsbeth added, "You look lovely this evening."

Eugenie smoothed down her pale blue gown. "Thank you. I see you've changed your gown."

Elsbeth's hand instinctively went to her sleeve, where a bandage peeked out from beneath the fabric. "Yes. I told my mother about my fall from the horse. There was no need to keep it hidden anymore. And, quite frankly, that gown was awful."

"How did she take the news?" Eugenie asked.

Elsbeth sighed, a trace of exasperation in her voice. "She's forbidden me from riding for the foreseeable future. She thinks I take too many risks."

Eugenie nodded sympathetically. "Perhaps that's for the best."

Elsbeth managed a small smile. "Come, let me introduce you to my cousin, Lord Bedford."

As they entered the drawing room, Eugenie came to an abrupt halt. Niles, distracted by her sudden pause, nearly ran into the back of her.

"What is it?" he asked, glancing at her curiously.

Eugenie's gaze was fixed on a tall, dark-haired man standing near the hearth. Her expression was a mixture of surprise and unease.

"Charles," Elsbeth said, motioning towards the man. "Allow me to introduce you to Lady Eugenie and Lord Westcott."

The man's eyes widened as he stared at Eugenie. "You."

Elsbeth looked between them in confusion. "Are you two already acquainted?"

Eugenie's cheeks turned pink as she stammered, "No! Not... not formally."

Charles pressed his lips together. "We may not have been formally introduced, but we've met before."

Eugenie waved her hand dismissively. "It was merely in passing. Hardly worth mentioning."

"I recall it rather differently," Charles said.

"You're mistaken," Eugenie said quickly, her voice rising slightly. "Has the dinner bell rung yet? I'm positively famished."

Niles raised an eyebrow, noting his sister's uncharacteristic fluster. There was clearly more to this story, and he intended to get to the bottom of it later.

Before anyone could speak further, Lady Isabella and Mr. Stockton entered the room. Lady Isabella smiled warmly. "I was just informed that dinner is ready to be served."

"Wonderful!" Eugenie exclaimed, spinning on her heel and walking briskly towards the dining room.

Niles exchanged a glance with Elsbeth, who seemed just as

intrigued by Eugenie's odd behavior. He was about to offer his arm to Elsbeth when Lord Bedford stepped forward.

"Allow me to escort you to the dining room," Lord Bedford said, extending his arm.

She hesitated before placing her hand lightly on his arm. "Thank you, Cousin."

"Charles," he corrected gently.

Elsbeth pressed her lips into a thin line, clearly biting back a response. "Of course," she murmured.

Niles trailed behind them as they made their way to the dining room. He told himself that it didn't matter that Elsbeth wasn't on his arm. But it did. He found the situation irksome, though he couldn't quite say why.

The dining room was bright and warm, the long table set with flickering candles. Niles moved to sit beside Eugenie, directly across from Elsbeth.

Lady Isabella, seated at one end of the table, smiled graciously. "We are so thankful to have everyone with us this evening."

"Quite right," Mr. Stockton agreed from the other side of the table, raising his glass in a toast.

"Thank you for inviting us," Eugenie said politely.

"It is a shame that Margaret was not feeling up to joining us this evening," Lady Isabella remarked.

"Indeed," Eugenie replied. Her gaze darted towards Lord Bedford, but she quickly dropped her eyes to her plate as the footmen began placing bowls of soup in front of the guests.

Niles picked up his spoon, hoping to enjoy the meal in relative silence, but that hope was short-lived.

Lady Isabella turned towards Niles with a bright expression. "I understand that you will be partnering with Elsbeth for pheasant shooting."

He inclined his head. "I do believe that is what we decided."

Eugenie interjected, her tone a little too eager. "It might be best if I partnered with Lady Elsbeth instead."

Niles arched an eyebrow, sensing there was more to her suggestion than she let on. "And why would that be?"

With a tight, guarded smile, Eugenie said, "We could make it a competition. Women versus men. Wouldn't that be grand?"

Lady Isabella didn't quite look convinced. "I do think the men would have an unfair advantage."

Before anyone else could comment, Lord Bedford chimed in. "I say we keep the partnerships as they are. I'm quite looking forward to shooting with Lady Eugenie."

Eugenie opened her mouth, likely to argue, but let out a resigned sigh instead. "I suppose they can remain as they are."

"Wonderful," Lady Isabella stated. "But I do not want my daughter handling a rifle, not with the injury on her arm."

Lord Bedford turned to Elsbeth with a reproachful look. "You should be more careful when riding."

Elsbeth sat straighter in her chair, her tone defensive. "I am quite proficient at riding a horse. It was merely an unfortunate accident."

"Like the time you stood on the back of a horse?" Lord Bedford teased.

Lady Isabella gasped, her hand flying to her chest. "You did what?"

Elsbeth shot her cousin an exasperated look. "It was hardly my fault," she insisted. "Charles bet me a guinea that I couldn't do it."

"You could have broken your neck!" Lady Isabella exclaimed.

"But I didn't," Elsbeth replied, lifting her chin defiantly. "And besides, I was only ten at the time."

Lady Isabella frowned. "That doesn't make it any better."

A rueful grin spread across Lord Bedford's lips. "I tried to warn her, Aunt Isabella, but she wouldn't listen."

"You did no such thing," Elsbeth huffed. "If anything, you were encouraging me the entire time."

Lord Bedford feigned an innocent expression. "I do not recall that."

Elsbeth rolled her eyes. "How convenient."

The playful exchange dissipated into a brief but heavy silence around the table. Niles, sensing an opportunity to shift the focus of the conversation, decided to direct his attention to Mr. Stockton.

Clearing his throat, he met the man's gaze. "I understand you own a fleet of merchant ships, Mr. Stockton."

Mr. Stockton nodded. "That is correct."

"Has the war affected your business dealings?" Niles inquired.

The man's face grew solemn as he considered the question. "I'm afraid the war has forced me to adapt my methods significantly."

"In what way?" Niles pressed.

Mr. Stockton opened his mouth to answer but hesitated, his gaze flicking towards his wife. Lady Isabella gave him a warning glance. He let out a soft sigh. "I suspect my wife would rather we refrain from discussing business tonight. Perhaps we could continue this conversation later, over a glass of port."

"I would appreciate that."

The footmen moved with practiced precision, stepping forward to clear away the soup bowls and replacing them with plates for the next course. As Niles reached for his glass, he noticed Elsbeth watching him from across the table. Their eyes met and he winked at her.

Her eyes widened slightly before she quickly averted her gaze, a faint blush dusting her cheeks. She picked up her fork and focused on the plate before her, refusing to look his way again.

Why had he done such a thing? Flirting with Elsbeth was

entirely inappropriate. And yet, he couldn't seem to help himself. There was something captivating about her, something that drew him in despite his better judgment.

As beautiful and intriguing as she was, there could be no future for them. He was certain of that.

Niles tore his gaze away from Elsbeth and focused on his plate, determined to push his thoughts aside. But the question lingered in the back of his mind: why had he agreed to help her in the first place?

8

As the morning light poured into her bedchamber, Elsbeth sat stiffly on the edge of her bed while Clara secured a fresh bandage around her injured arm. She tried not to let her discomfort show, despite the ache that pulsed with every movement.

"That should do," Clara said, leaning back to assess her work. "But do try to be careful when you go pheasant shooting today."

"You needn't worry," Elsbeth replied with a small smile. "I have no intention of firing a rifle."

"Then why bother going?"

Elsbeth rose from the bed and walked towards the dressing table. "Because I'll be partnering with Lord Westcott. It will give us the perfect opportunity to discuss how to uncover the truth about my stepfather's lies."

Clara let out a sigh of exasperation. "Not this again. Why do you insist on seeing only the worst in Mr. Stockton?"

Elsbeth met Clara's gaze in the mirror. "Because he is hiding something."

"Aren't we all, my lady?"

"Not like him," Elsbeth retorted, sitting down and removing her cap.

Clara retrieved a brush and began working through her mistress's hair. "I think this entire endeavor is reckless. You should be focusing on recovering, not on scheming against your stepfather."

Elsbeth's lips tightened as she stared at her reflection. "Once I get that key to his desk, I'll know what he's hiding."

"And if you find nothing?"

"I'll find something," she said firmly, though doubt briefly flickered in her voice.

Clara twisted Elsbeth's hair into a neat chignon before reaching for a pale green gown. "Let's dress you," she said, holding it up.

Elsbeth sighed as she stood, slipping out of her dressing gown and into the fresh attire. As Clara fastened the buttons down the back of the gown, she spoke softly. "I just worry about you."

"I know what I'm doing," Elsbeth attempted.

"Do you?"

Elsbeth turned to face her. "I'm not wrong."

Clara's expression remained skeptical. "If you insist. But..." She hesitated. "I might have a way to help you secure that key."

Elsbeth's eyes widened. "You do? How?" she asked in an eager tone.

Clara nodded. "I'm on friendly terms with Mr. Stockton's valet. I could ask for his assistance. He's a discreet man."

A spark of hope lit in Elsbeth's chest. "Yes, please. Ask him."

Clara held up a finger. "But if I do this, and you find nothing in the desk, will you agree to drop this madness?"

"I promise."

"Very well," Clara said, straightening. "Now, hurry. You're already late for breakfast."

Elsbeth exited her bedchamber but abruptly stopped when

she found Charles leaning casually against the wall just outside her room.

"What are you doing loitering by my door?" she asked, arching a brow.

Charles straightened, offering his arm. "I came to escort you to the dining room."

Elsbeth forced a polite smile as she accepted his arm. "How thoughtful."

"You're lying," Charles said, a smirk tugging at his lips. "I know you too well."

"Exactly," Elsbeth replied. "Which is why a union between us would never work. No matter how distantly related we are, I consider you family."

Charles sighed heavily. "It would be the perfect solution for both of us. I would have the funds to restore the estate, and you'd be welcomed back into Society as my countess."

"It's not as simple as that."

"Perhaps not," Charles admitted, his tone softening. "But I'm worried about you."

Elsbeth stopped and turned to face him. "Worried? About me? Why?"

"Your mother wrote to me. She said you've been terribly unhappy here."

The realization dawned on Elsbeth. "You offered for me out of pity," she whispered.

"No!" Charles protested. "I don't pity you. I only—"

"Do you even want to marry me?" Elsbeth pressed, her voice rising.

Charles winced. "I do... because it's my responsibility. I take that role seriously."

Elsbeth shook her head, resuming her walk down the hall. "You don't want to marry me, Charles. You're just trying to do the honorable thing."

"Is that so wrong?" he asked, catching up to her. "You could return to your home. Your friends. Your old life. Isn't that what you want?"

"My old life is gone," Elsbeth said, pausing at the top of the staircase. "And it is time I accept that."

"It doesn't have to be."

"It does," she insisted. "My friends abandoned me at the first hint of a scandal, and the only home I knew now belongs to you."

Charles stepped closer. "Marry me, and I will ensure you are happy."

Elsbeth heard the sincerity in his voice, but she knew why he was doing this. He was doing the honorable thing and she wouldn't let him throw his life away for her. "My answer is no."

"But you aren't happy in this life."

"True," she admitted. "But I won't trap you in a marriage you don't want."

Charles opened his mouth to argue, but she raised a hand, silencing him. "Thank you, Cousin, for your kindness. But my decision is final."

He studied her for a moment, then conceded. "Your mother won't be pleased."

"I'm used to disappointing her," Elsbeth said with a faint smile.

Charles gave her a bemused look. "Your mother loves you. You know that, right?"

"I do, but she's so enamored with my stepfather. It is maddening."

"Perhaps the problem isn't her, Elsbeth," Charles said pointedly. "Perhaps it's you."

Elsbeth blinked. "I beg your pardon?"

Charles folded his arms. "Just because you were born a lady doesn't make you better than anyone else, including a merchant."

Her cheeks flushed. "I never said I was."

"No," Charles said, his tone calm but firm. "But you think it. Judge a man by his actions, not his station."

"That is easy for you to say. You are an earl," she shot back. "Besides, you do not know what you speak of."

"Then enlighten me."

Elsbeth was done with this ridiculous conversation. How dare her cousin accuse her of thinking herself better than her stepfather. Her issues with Alfred stemmed from his secrets. Didn't they? But the more she thought about it, the more she had to concede that Charles might have a point. Had she treated Alfred differently because he was only a merchant?

No.

She treated him differently because he was hiding something and not because of his profession. Or at least that is what she wanted to believe.

Charles placed a hand on her shoulder. "Alfred is a good man. You should give him a chance."

"You don't understand—" she began, but her words were cut short by her mother's voice.

"Are you two going to join us for breakfast?" Her mother stood at the bottom of the staircase, her expression one of polite impatience.

Charles withdrew his hand and turned to face her. "Yes, Aunt Isabella. We will be down in a moment."

As they descended the stairs, Charles glanced at her. "You were saying?"

"Not now," she muttered.

Charles tipped his head in understanding. "Very well."

Once they arrived in the dining room, Elsbeth saw Alfred was sitting at the head of the table with newssheets in his hand. He began to rise when she entered, but she waved him back down and took her seat.

"Good morning, Elsbeth," her stepfather greeted. "I trust you slept well?"

"As well as I could with my injury," she replied.

Alfred set the newssheets aside, his gaze briefly resting on her arm. "I do hope you will be careful today."

"I will be," she assured him. But why did he care? Was it genuine concern or something else entirely?

Her mother's voice cut through her thoughts. "Did you two come to an understanding yet?" she asked, her gaze shifting between Elsbeth and Charles.

Elsbeth placed a napkin onto her lap before saying, "We have decided it would be best if we did *not* marry."

"I do not think that is wise," her mother said.

"I know, but I refuse to let Charles throw away his life for me," Elsbeth remarked. "He deserves to find love."

Charles nearly choked on his tea, setting the cup down with an awkward cough. "Love?" he repeated. "I'm afraid love isn't a luxury I can afford. I must marry an heiress to restore my estate."

"Surely you can achieve both," Elsbeth pressed.

"I doubt it," Charles said. "My estate and my responsibilities come first. I know my duty and I'll do what is expected of me."

Elsbeth felt a pang of sadness at her cousin's words. She wanted him to be happy, but she knew all too well the duty and expectations of being born into this life. She had always dreamed of a love match, but was it just as unattainable for her as it was for Charles?

A footman placed a plate of food in front of her and she reached for her fork. As she took her first bite, her mother said, "I think we should host a soiree."

"A soiree?" Elsbeth repeated, her tone tinged with skepticism.

"Yes," her mother said with a smile. "It's been far too long since we've entertained. It would be a kind gesture for the villagers."

Elsbeth wiped her mouth with her napkin. "That's a terrible idea."

Her mother's smile didn't falter. "Well, I'm sorry you feel that way since I've already sent out the invitations."

"What?" Elsbeth's brows shot up. "Who did you invite?"

"Just a few of Alfred's friends and some of our neighbors," her mother replied.

Elsbeth resisted the urge to groan. The last thing she wanted was to host a soiree filled with strangers, forced politeness, and shallow conversations. The thought alone was exhausting.

Her mother turned towards Charles. "Please say that you will stay until our soiree. It would mean so much to us."

"I would be delighted," he replied.

Elsbeth felt her stomach twist. She returned her gaze to her plate and poked at her food with her fork, her appetite gone.

Surely today could not get any worse.

———————— ⌒ ————————

Niles sat in the coach as it jostled along the winding road to Lady Elsbeth's estate. His gaze drifted to his sister Eugenie, who stared out the window with a contemplative expression. This was the perfect opportunity to address the matter that had been gnawing at him since last night. How exactly was she acquainted with Lord Bedford?

Clearing his throat, he broke the silence. "How exactly did you say you knew Lord Bedford?"

Eugenie turned towards him, offering a weak smile. "We met in passing. Hardly worth mentioning."

"That is precisely what you said last night," he remarked, narrowing his eyes.

"Well," she replied, "it makes it no less true."

He shifted tactics, probing further. "Where did you meet him?"

"At Lady Britton's ball," she said casually, brushing an invisible speck off her gown.

"Did you dance with him?"

She waved her hand dismissively. "Heavens, no. We met in the library. It was all entirely innocent, I assure you."

"I recall you mentioning going to the library at that ball," Niles said slowly, "but you never mentioned you weren't alone."

Eugenie's lips pressed into a thin line. "I was reading when a man entered the room. We spoke briefly, and then he went on his way."

"You spoke to a man you weren't acquainted with?" Niles asked in disbelief.

"Yes," she replied with a slight edge in her voice. "The situation didn't allow for an introduction. Besides, no one saw us."

"You were most fortunate," he said, his tone growing stern. "If anyone had seen you alone with him, your reputation could have been ruined."

Eugenie shrugged lightly. "No one did, not even when we kissed."

The air in the coach seemed to freeze. Niles shot upright in his seat. "*What*?! You kissed?"

Eugenie met his gaze with a composed expression. "We were debating a book, and somehow... we ended up kissing. It was rather confusing, and I'm not quite sure how it happened."

"You cannot go around kissing strangers, Eugenie!" His voice rose slightly, his frustration evident.

"I am well aware," she said, nodding with mock seriousness. "And it won't happen again."

"It shouldn't have happened at all!" he exclaimed.

"Regardless," Eugenie continued, "after the kiss, Lord Bedford slipped out of the library, and I haven't seen him since."

Niles rubbed his temples, trying to rein in his growing irritation. "Do you realize what could have happened if anyone had caught you kissing?"

"It's a good thing no one did, then," Eugenie said matter-of-factly.

"Eugenie..." he began.

She cut him off with a knowing smile. "You can save the lecture, Brother. I know precisely what you're going to say."

"I doubt that," he countered.

In a deep voice, mimicking him, Eugenie said, "You must protect your reputation at all costs."

Dropping his hands to his sides, Niles scowled. "It makes it no less true. You don't want to be forced into an unwanted marriage with a stranger."

"You're right," she conceded.

"I know I'm right," he replied firmly.

Eugenie leaned back against the seat, lifting a brow. "Can this lecture be over now? I promise I won't ever kiss Lord Bedford—or any other stranger—again."

The coach came to a halt in front of the manor, and Niles sighed. "Fine. But I'll be partnering with Lord Bedford for the pheasant hunt."

"You will do no such thing," she said sharply. "If we switch partners, he'll know I told you about the kiss."

"So you want me to pretend I don't know?"

"Yes."

He stared at his sister, incredulous. "And why would I do that?"

"Because, Brother," she said, her tone imploring, "I don't want him to think I dwell on that kiss."

"Do you?" he asked, arching a brow.

She let out a huff, but it lacked conviction. "Heavens, no! I hardly think about it."

Niles wanted to press her further, but the coach door

opened, and a footman extended his hand to assist them. Stepping out first, Niles reached back for Eugenie, helping her onto the gravel drive.

As they approached the manor, the main door opened, and Elsbeth stepped out with Lord Bedford by her side, a hunting rifle resting casually on his shoulder.

Elsbeth's smile lit up her features, and Niles felt a strange lightness in his chest. "Lord Westcott. Lady Eugenie," she greeted.

"Lady Eugenie," Lord Bedford said with a bow.

Niles glanced at his sister, noting the slight flush on her cheeks. Interesting. Despite her protests, it was clear she wasn't entirely immune to Lord Bedford's charms.

"It was most generous of your stepfather to allow us to pheasant shoot on his property," Niles said, turning his attention to Elsbeth.

Her smile grew tight. "It was, wasn't it?"

"Shall we walk to the pond?" Niles suggested, eager to shift the mood.

Once they retrieved their rifles, the group set off down a narrow path leading to the woodlands. Silence settled over them until Eugenie, clearly uncomfortable, turned to Lord Bedford and asked, "Do you like the weather?"

Lord Bedford looked at her, perplexed. "I... suppose so."

Eugenie glanced up at the sky, her voice overly bright. "It's quite an unremarkable day, isn't it?"

"It is," Lord Bedford replied.

Niles observed that Elsbeth brought a hand to her lips to hide a smile, though the amusement in her eyes was unmistakable. He could understand the humor in the situation, but he felt a pang of sympathy for his sister. Eugenie was trying so hard to engage Lord Bedford in conversation and it clearly wasn't working.

A short time later, they reached the pond, surrounded by a

blend of tall trees and dense holly undergrowth. Eugenie surveyed the area and gave a satisfied nod. "This is a good spot to flush out pheasants."

"I concur," Lord Bedford remarked.

Pointing towards a clearing in the distance, Eugenie said, "That would be the perfect place to shoot."

Lord Bedford adjusted his grip on his rifle, his expression focused. "Shall we?"

As Eugenie and Lord Bedford walked towards their designated shooting spot, Niles stole a glance over at Elsbeth. "I don't trust Lord Bedford," he confessed.

Elsbeth's brow furrowed as she looked at him. "Whyever not?"

Niles began methodically loading his rifle, using the moment to think carefully about his response. He couldn't betray Eugenie's confidence, but he needed to voice his concerns. "He just strikes me as... well, a rake."

Elsbeth threw her head back with a laugh that echoed lightly through the woods. "Pardon me, my lord, but my cousin is no rake."

Her laughter softened the tension in Niles, though only slightly. Still, it was good to see her in such high spirits, even if just for a moment.

Elsbeth's smile dimmed into something more thoughtful. "Charles and I both agreed a union between us would be madness," she shared, her tone shifting. "Apparently, he only offered for me because he pitied me. My mother wrote to him and told him how terribly unhappy I was here."

Niles lowered his rifle, suddenly more interested in her words than the hunt. "Why are you unhappy here?"

Elsbeth sighed, her gaze wandering to the horizon. "How could I not be? I once had the world at my feet in Town—balls, opera houses, intelligent conversation—and now I'm tucked away in this far-off coastal village with little company beyond Lady Margaret."

"There are worse companions," Niles teased, hoping to coax a smile from her again.

To his relief, she grinned. "True. I am grateful for your aunt's friendship, but it is still terribly lonely."

"Have you told your mother this?"

She shook her head. "No. She's far too consumed with Alfred. He's bewitched her. She has no idea who he truly is."

"And you do?" Niles pressed.

"Not yet," she admitted. "But I will gather the proof I need."

Their conversation was interrupted by the approach of a short man with a bushy beard, his leather boots crunching on the gravel. He raised a hand in greeting. "My lord, my lady."

Elsbeth turned to him with a warm smile. "Good morning, Mr. White." She glanced at Niles. "Mr. White is my stepfather's gamekeeper."

Mr. White gestured towards a group of beaters standing in formation nearby, some holding leashes of eager hunting dogs. "The beaters are ready, my lord. On my command, they'll start driving the pheasants out."

"Excellent," Niles replied, his gaze flicking briefly to where Eugenie and Lord Bedford were stationed a short distance away. "I believe we're ready."

At Mr. White's command, the beaters surged forward into the undergrowth, their sticks thrashing through the dense vegetation. Moments later, a flurry of wings erupted as several pheasants broke cover, soaring skyward. Niles raised his rifle with practiced ease and fired. One of the birds plummeted to the ground, and a hunting dog darted forward to retrieve it.

"Well done," Elsbeth said with genuine admiration.

Niles shrugged, lowering his gun. "It was just one bird. If I don't put on a good show today, Eugenie will never let me hear the end of it."

Elsbeth studied him for a moment before saying, "You and your sister seem quite close."

"We are," Niles replied, beginning to reload his rifle. "We had to be after our parents died so suddenly. We learned to rely on each other."

"I always wished I had a sibling," Elsbeth admitted wistfully.

Niles glanced at her. "It's not as enticing as you might imagine. A sibling can be your greatest ally or the bane of your existence."

"You make it sound so appealing," she joked, her smile returning.

He grew solemn, his curiosity piqued by her vulnerability. "May I ask how your father died?"

Elsbeth's smile faded, replaced by a shadow of sadness. "He was trampled by horses," she revealed. "He was drunk, as usual, and stumbled in front of a coach outside a gambling hall. The coroner believed he didn't even look before crossing."

"I'm so sorry," Niles said, his voice tinged with genuine regret. He wished he could offer more comfort, but he was at a loss as to what to say.

Her jaw tightened. "It was his fault. He loved his vices more than he loved us."

"You can't know that for certain," Niles attempted.

"I can," she asserted. "He seemed to only care for himself."

Before Niles could respond, Mr. White stepped forward, his voice brisk. "The beaters are in position again, my lord."

Niles nodded, adjusting his grip on his rifle. "Give the command."

As the beaters resumed their task, the woods filled with the rustle of undergrowth and the rhythmic drumming of sticks. Niles raised his rifle, his focus trained on the sky. Just as he took aim, the sharp crack of a gunshot pierced the air, followed by the splintering of wood in a tree mere inches from Elsbeth's head.

9

Someone had shot at her.

Elsbeth's heart raced as she turned her wide eyes towards the tree where the bullet had struck, leaving a fresh gouge in its bark. The realization settled in—she could have died. The thought sent a chill coursing through her, and she felt the blood drain from her face.

Niles lowered his rifle and stepped closer, his gaze scanning her for injury. "Elsbeth, are you all right?" His voice was laced with worry.

She opened her mouth to answer but no sound came out. Instead, she found herself staring at him, unsure how to articulate the storm of emotions brewing within her. That bullet had missed her by mere inches.

Niles placed a steadying hand on her shoulder. "Elsbeth, talk to me," he urged, his voice gentler now but no less urgent.

Finally, she managed to say, "That bullet... it was so close." Her voice trembled, the words barely above a whisper.

Niles's eyes darted to the tree. "I know," he responded, his tone grim.

"Elsbeth!" Charles's voice rang out, cutting through the

moment. She turned to see her cousin hurrying towards her, his face etched with panic.

Niles dropped his hand from her shoulder but remained close. For reasons she couldn't quite explain, his nearness made her feel steadier, safer.

Charles reached them, breathless. "Elsbeth, I'm so sorry," he said, his words tumbling out in a rush. "I was focused on the pheasant... I didn't see—please, say you're all right."

Niles's sharp voice cut through Charles's apology like a blade. "You almost shot her," he growled. "Where did you even learn how to hunt?"

Charles winced, his remorse evident. "I know, and I'm terribly sorry. It was an accident, I swear. I didn't think I was that close to Elsbeth, but I heard the sound of splintering wood."

"Terribly sorry?" Niles repeated, his voice rising. "Do you think that makes it better? She could have been killed!"

Eugenie appeared beside Charles. "Perhaps we should all take a moment to breathe," she suggested. "It was an unfortunate accident—"

Niles whirled on his sister. "An accident?" he exclaimed. "Lady Elsbeth *almost died*! I don't want to take a breath."

Elsbeth finally found her voice. "It's all right," she said, though her hands still trembled. "I'm fine. Truly."

Mr. White stepped forward and addressed Elsbeth. "Are you all right, my lady?"

"I am," Elsbeth replied. "Thank you for your concern, but I do think I've had enough of pheasant shooting for one day."

Niles's jaw clenched, his frustration evident, but he nodded. "I'll walk you back to the manor."

"Cousin..." Charles began again, his face a portrait of guilt. "I am so, so sorry."

Elsbeth gave him a faint smile, trying to ease his obvious distress. "I know you are, Charles," she said. Without waiting for a reply, she turned towards the path leading back to her stepfather's estate.

Niles fell into step beside her, his watchful gaze flicking towards her every few moments.

"You don't need to keep looking at me like that," she said. "I'm fine."

Niles leaned in slightly, lowering his voice. "I don't trust your cousin."

Elsbeth halted abruptly, spinning to face him. "Not this again. Why?"

"What if that shot wasn't an accident?"

Her breath caught. "Why would you even suggest such a thing?"

He stepped closer, his piercing gaze holding hers. "It seems... convenient," he said carefully. "If something were to happen to you, your dowry would revert to the estate. To Charles."

Her mouth fell open in shock. "You can't honestly believe Charles would intentionally try to harm me!"

"I'm saying it's not out of the realm of possibility," Niles replied, his voice unwavering.

She scoffed, turning away from him. "That's absurd," she muttered, quickening her pace.

Niles caught up easily, falling into stride beside her. "Just think on it," he pressed.

"I don't need to think on it," she retorted, her voice rising with frustration. "Charles would never hurt me. He's my family."

"And didn't you say he's desperate to save his estate?" Niles countered.

"Yes, I did. But what you're suggesting is... it's ludicrous!"

Niles didn't reply immediately, but the weight of his silence said everything.

They continued towards the manor in silence, and with

every step Elsbeth took, she grew more outraged by Niles's suggestion. Charles would never try to kill her. She was sure of that. It had just been an accident.

So why did she feel a little uneasy?

When she arrived at the manor, Niles rushed ahead to open the door and followed her into the entry hall. He turned towards the butler and ordered, "Lady Elsbeth would care for a cup of tea."

Elsbeth bristled, shooting him a glare. "You do not get to give orders in my home, my lord."

"I merely thought a cup of tea might help calm your nerves."

She opened her mouth to retort but stopped herself as she caught the genuine concern in his expression. Despite her irritation, she couldn't deny that tea sounded like a good idea.

As if sensing her inner turmoil, Niles stepped closer. "I'm glad you're all right."

She softened at his words, murmuring, "Thank you."

"But I do think you should take a moment to yourself and rest," he encouraged. "What happened today... what almost happened to *you*..." His words trailed off, his voice tight with emotion.

For reasons she couldn't quite explain, Elsbeth reached out, resting a hand on his sleeve. "I do appreciate your concern."

He paused, glancing down at her hand on his arm. "We are friends, aren't we?"

She tilted her head. "Are we?"

"You are maddening and stubborn," he admitted. "But yes, I do consider you a friend."

Elsbeth allowed herself to smile. "I feel the same."

"Good," he said with a small nod. "Then as your friend, I insist that you rest."

Before she could respond, the front door swung open, and Eugenie and Charles entered, their voices carrying through the hall. Elsbeth immediately withdrew her hand, stepping back, but not before noticing the curious glance Eugenie shot her.

Eugenie smiled, breaking the tension. "We should head back, Niles. If we leave now, I'll have time for a quick nap before supper."

Niles chuckled. "My sister does love her naps."

Not quite ready to part ways, Elsbeth spoke up. "Would you care to join us for dinner this evening?"

Niles's answer came quickly. "Yes."

Eugenie laughed. "Well, I suppose we'll be seeing you later tonight."

"Please bring Lady Margaret, assuming she's feeling up to it," Elsbeth added.

Niles offered her a parting glance before escorting Eugenie to their awaiting carriage. Once the door closed, Charles approached Elsbeth, his expression filled with remorse.

"Again, Cousin, I'm so sorry," he said earnestly.

"It's forgotten," Elsbeth replied, though her tone was clipped.

Charles hesitated, as if wanting to say more, but eventually nodded. "Very well. Excuse me."

Elsbeth watched him walk away, doubt creeping into her thoughts. He seemed sincere, but could it all be an act? No. Charles loved her. He was willing to marry her to secure her future. Why would he now try to harm her?

Shaking off the unsettling thoughts, Elsbeth made her way upstairs to her bedchamber. Opening the door, she found Clara tidying up. The lady's maid looked up with a smile. "Good, you're back."

Clara approached her, holding up a small brass key. "I was able to get the key to your stepfather's desk."

Elsbeth's eyes widened. "How did you manage that?"

A faint blush crept up Clara's cheeks. "I spoke to Thomas,

the valet. When I explained your concerns, he assured me Mr. Stockton is hiding nothing. He gave me the key to prove it."

Elsbeth accepted the key and gripped it tightly. "Thank you, Clara. This means everything to me."

"But it won't be as easy as you think," Clara warned. "You'll need to sneak into the study without anyone seeing."

Elsbeth nodded determinedly. "I'll think of something."

Clara grinned. "Since I managed to retrieve the key, could I possibly take tomorrow afternoon off?"

"That's fair," Elsbeth agreed.

Before Elsbeth could utter another word, the door swung open, and her mother entered, her face etched with concern. "Oh, Elsbeth, are you all right?" she exclaimed, her voice trembling. "Charles told me what happened."

Elsbeth straightened, discreetly tucking the small key into the folds of her gown. "I'm fine, Mother," she assured her.

Her mother crossed the room in swift strides and enveloped her in a tight embrace. "My poor child," she murmured. "I don't know what I'd do if something happened to you."

Elsbeth felt the warmth of her mother's arms and returned the embrace. "I'm perfectly well," she said softly, hoping to alleviate her mother's fears.

After a lingering moment, her mother pulled back, carefully studying Elsbeth. "No more pheasant hunting," she declared.

Elsbeth managed a weak smile. "I'm not going to argue with that."

Her mother's expression softened as she changed the subject. "I understand we're to have guests this evening for dinner?"

"I do hope that's all right."

Her mother's smile grew. "Of course. I simply adore Lady Eugenie and Lord Westcott. I'll inform the cook while you rest. You've had a most taxing morning."

"I agree," Elsbeth said, nodding as she made her way towards the bed. "I think a nap would do me some good."

Her mother reached out and brushed a loose strand of hair from Elsbeth's face. "Rest well, my dear. I'll leave you to it."

As her mother exited the room, Clara, who had been quietly observing from the corner, stepped forward. "Dare I ask what happened this morning?"

Elsbeth sighed, waving her hand dismissively. "My cousin was aiming at a pheasant and almost hit me instead."

"How terrifying," Clara remarked.

"It was merely an accident," Elsbeth said firmly. "Charles would never intentionally hurt me."

"I never said that he would."

"Good," Elsbeth muttered, the faintest trace of relief in her tone. At least someone saw reason.

Clara moved towards the door, her hand resting on the handle. "Would you care for a bath after your nap?"

"That would be lovely," Elsbeth replied.

"I'll see to the arrangements," Clara said with a nod before slipping out of the room.

Alone, Elsbeth lay back on her bed, staring up at the ceiling as the events of the morning replayed in her mind. She longed for rest, but her thoughts refused to quiet. She loved her cousin; she knew he loved her in return. So why was she questioning whether he'd ever hurt her?

Drat.

Niles had gotten into her head, planting seeds of doubt.

Niles sat in the darkened coach, the gentle sway of the conveyance doing little to settle his restless thoughts. Across from him, his sister Eugenie stared out the window, her face a mixture of curiosity and contemplation, while Aunt Margaret remained silent beside her. He was grateful for the quiet, though he doubted it would last.

Sure enough, Aunt Margaret soon broke the stillness. "I am so pleased that you two are friends with Elsbeth. She's such a delightful young woman."

Niles bristled slightly, careful to keep his expression neutral. "We tolerate one another."

Eugenie smirked, turning away from the window to fix him with a knowing look. "You two do more than tolerate each other."

"Fine," he admitted reluctantly. "We are... friends. But if there are stages of friendship, we're at stage one. It's barely worth mentioning."

"I'd say Elsbeth and I are at stage five. I find her to be utterly charming," Eugenie said.

Niles pressed his lips together, unwilling to prolong the conversation. He didn't want to talk about Elsbeth—not when thoughts of her already consumed him more than he cared to admit. Thankfully, the coach slowed and stopped in front of the manor. He exited first, stepping onto the gravel drive, and turned to help Eugenie and Aunt Margaret down.

As they approached the entrance, the main door opened, and they were ushered inside by the butler. The drawing room was warm and inviting, with a fire crackling in the hearth. Elsbeth sat on the settee, her hands clasped tightly in her lap. When she turned and saw him, her eyes seemed to light up. Or perhaps it was his imagination.

"Lord Westcott," she greeted with a small smile.

"Lady Elsbeth," he replied, inclining his head.

She rose and closed the distance between them. "I have the key," she whispered.

Niles's brows lifted in surprise. "How?"

"My lady's maid retrieved it for me," she said, a glint of

excitement in her eyes. "My stepfather is out. Shall we open his desk?"

"Now?"

"Do you have a better suggestion?" Elsbeth asked with an arched brow.

Niles glanced back at his aunt and sister, who were deep in conversation and paying them no mind. "Very well. How do you propose we sneak away?"

Elsbeth's lips curved into a mischievous smile. "I have an idea."

"Is it a good idea?"

"I believe so."

"Then I'll trust you," he said, though he couldn't help teasing.

Her smile widened. "That's rather bold of you. But sometimes the simplest plans are the most effective."

There was something about her smile, so unguarded and genuine, that made it hard for him to look away. It drew him in, stirring something he wasn't entirely ready to name.

Raising her voice, Elsbeth asked, "Lord Westcott, would you care to accompany me to the study to select a book?"

"It would be my pleasure," Niles replied, hoping not to sound too eager.

"Wonderful," Elsbeth acknowledged.

As they left the drawing room, Niles followed her down the corridor. "What's the plan once we're there?" he asked.

"I'll search the desk," Elsbeth said. "You keep watch."

"I can manage that." His gaze drifted to her bandaged arm. "How is your injury?"

"It aches now and then, especially at night," she admitted. "I do not recommend getting shot."

"Duly noted."

They reached the study, and Elsbeth paused at the door. "Stay here and alert me if anyone approaches."

"Understood."

Taking a deep breath, she added, almost to herself, "This is it. Let's hope I was right, or this will be a colossal waste of time."

Niles placed a reassuring hand on her sleeve. "No matter what you find, you're following your convictions. That's what matters."

"But I don't want to be wrong."

"No one does," he replied. "But sometimes, being wrong leads to answers we didn't know we needed. Now go, before we're caught."

Elsbeth didn't hesitate. She slipped inside the study and crouched behind the desk, pulling open the drawers. Niles kept watch, his ears straining for any approaching footsteps. A gasp from inside the study made him turn.

"What is it?" he asked, stepping into the room.

Elsbeth held up a file, her expression a mix of confusion and disbelief. "It's a collection of clippings from the newssheets. They are all about my father's death."

"All of them?" Niles asked, moving to her side.

She flipped through the articles. "It seems so. Why would Alfred keep these?"

Niles took the file, scanning its contents. "Did your stepfather know your father?"

"I don't think so," Elsbeth said, her voice uncertain. "I'll have to ask my mother."

Placing the clippings back into the file, Niles asked, "Did you find anything else?"

Elsbeth shook her head, her shoulders sagging. "No. Just this. It doesn't make sense."

"Keep looking," he urged. "I'll return to stand watch."

Elsbeth nodded, determination flickering in her eyes. "There has to be something else here. There has to be."

Niles returned to his post outside the study. As he scanned the corridor, the steady sound of approaching footsteps drew his attention. He straightened as Mr. Stockton appeared, his face betraying a hint of curiosity.

Clearing his throat loudly, Niles greeted him. "Good evening, Mr. Stockton."

Mr. Stockton stopped in front of him. "Good evening, Lord Westcott. Dare I ask why you are loitering outside my study?"

Niles offered a casual smile, though his heart beat a little faster. He hoped Elsbeth had managed to restore everything to its rightful place. "Lady Elsbeth is collecting a book from your study. I thought it prudent to remain in the corridor, for propriety's sake."

"Ah," Mr. Stockton replied.

Before either could say more, Elsbeth emerged from the study, holding a book in her hand. Her expression was serene, but Niles caught the subtle tension in her posture.

"I found the book I was searching for," she announced, holding it up.

Mr. Stockton glanced at the book in her hand, his expression shifting to one of mild amusement. "Farming machinery? I didn't realize that topic was of interest to you."

Elsbeth didn't appear fazed. "Yes, I find it utterly captivating," she said with a practiced smile.

Mr. Stockton chuckled. "I must admit, I found that particular book rather dull, but to each their own."

The distant chime of the dinner bell echoed through the manor, breaking the moment. Mr. Stockton glanced over his shoulder at the study door before pulling it shut. "It seems I won't have time to work before supper," he remarked, gesturing down the hall. "Shall we?"

They began walking towards the drawing room, the corridor quiet except for the sound of their footsteps. The silence stretched until Elsbeth broke it.

"It's a fine evening, isn't it?" she asked.

Niles bit back a groan. The weather? Of all topics? Still, he decided to play along. "Yes, it is a fine evening indeed."

Mr. Stockton shifted his attention to Niles. "How long do you plan to stay in our village, Lord Westcott?"

"My sister was hoping for a fortnight," Niles replied. "But, of course, it depends on whether my aunt grows tired of us."

Mr. Stockton chuckled lightly. "I'm sure she's enjoying the company. It's not every day she has visitors from London."

Niles nodded. "It has been a welcome reprieve, though my responsibilities at my estate call for my return soon."

"I can only imagine the weight of those responsibilities, being a lord and all," Mr. Stockton said with a hint of admiration.

They arrived in the entry hall, where the rest of the household was assembled. Lady Isabella watched their approach with a warm smile. "Dinner is ready to be served," she announced.

Elsbeth held up the book. "If you'll excuse me, I'll just place this in the drawing room." Without waiting for a reply, she disappeared into the adjacent room.

When she returned, Niles offered his arm, and together they followed the others towards the dining room. As they walked, he leaned closer, lowering his voice. "Did you find anything else?"

Elsbeth let out a quiet puff of frustration. "No."

"What were you hoping to find?" he pressed.

Her gaze flickered away. "I'm not sure," she admitted. "But I was hoping for something that would prove my stepfather is not who he claims to be."

"Perhaps he isn't hiding anything," Niles suggested.

Elsbeth's lips tightened. "Everyone is hiding something."

Niles came to a stop, turning to face her. "Is it so hard to believe that your stepfather might not be hiding anything? That this suspicion might be misplaced?"

Her eyes burned with defiance. "Then why would he have all those clippings about my father's death?"

"I can't answer that," Niles replied. "But there might be a simple explanation. Perhaps one you haven't considered yet."

Elsbeth's expression was a mix of frustration and doubt. "No, I am right about my stepfather. I have to be."

Her voice held an edge of desperation, and Niles studied her for a moment, noticing the tension in her shoulders and the fire in her eyes. She wasn't just trying to convince him, but rather she was trying to convince herself.

"Elsbeth..." he began, choosing his words carefully, "I understand why you feel this way. But sometimes, our emotions can cloud our judgment."

Her eyes snapped to his. "This isn't just a feeling. He's hiding something, I know it."

Niles sighed. "And if you're wrong?"

She flinched at his words, her gaze dropping to the floor for a moment before rising again. "I can't afford to be wrong," she whispered. "If I am, then everything I've done... everything I've risked... would have been for nothing."

Her vulnerability struck a chord within him. Niles couldn't help but feel a pang of sympathy, but alongside it was a growing unease. Was this pursuit of the truth truly worth the potential cost?

"You're certain about this, then?" he asked.

She lifted her chin with stubborn resolve. "I am."

Niles hesitated, glancing down the corridor towards the dining room where the rest of the party waited. He had promised to help her, and he was a man of his word. But doubt gnawed at the edges of his conviction.

Was this truly the right course of action? Or were they barreling towards a truth that might shatter more than it would heal?

"Very well," he finally said. "I gave you my word, and I intend to keep it. But promise me one thing, Elsbeth."

Her brow furrowed. "What is that?"

"If it turns out you're wrong—if your stepfather's secrets aren't what you think they are—promise me you'll let this go. Promise me you'll allow yourself to move on."

Her lips parted as if to argue, but she stopped herself. After a long, tense moment, she nodded. "Fine," she said. "But I won't be wrong."

Niles didn't reply, but as they resumed walking, a shadow of doubt lingered in his mind. Was he helping her uncover the truth or merely enabling a dangerous obsession?

10

The early sunlight spilled gently into her bedchamber as Elsbeth sat beside Clara, who was carefully dabbing honey onto her wound. The faint stickiness of the salve was the least of her concerns. Her thoughts were tangled with fragments of the conversation she'd had with Niles the night before.

What if I'm wrong about Alfred?

What if I've been the problem all along?

She quickly dismissed the idea as absurd, but the doubt lingered. Alfred's collection of newssheet clippings about her father's death had rattled her. Why keep them locked away? Why not discard them altogether? It was suspicious, wasn't it?

Clara's voice broke through her spiraling thoughts. "The honey should prevent infection," she said, securing the bandage. "Did I hurt you?"

"No," Elsbeth replied absently, her gaze fixed on the corner of the room.

"You seem rather distracted, my lady," Clara observed.

"I am," she admitted. "I used the key you gave me to unlock

my stepfather's desk and all I found was newssheet clippings about my father's death."

"That is strange."

"Exactly," Elsbeth said. "It is not the proof I was looking for, but it is something. Isn't it?" Clara leaned back in her seat. "Perhaps it's just what it appears to be. Mere curiosity about your father's passing. It doesn't mean he's hiding anything."

"Then why lock them away?" Elsbeth countered. "There's nothing illegal about owning newssheet clippings."

"It's still... odd," Elsbeth insisted, pulling down the sleeve of her pale green gown. Her movements were sharp, betraying her frustration.

Clara gave her a knowing look. "There's no shame in admitting you're wrong, my lady."

"But I'm not wrong," Elsbeth snapped. "I just need more time."

"I fear time won't change anything."

Rising abruptly, Elsbeth crossed the room to her dressing table, picked up the small key, and handed it to Clara. "Please return this to Alfred's valet."

Clara accepted the key with a faint sigh. "I will, but I wish you would let this go."

"I can't. Not now," Elsbeth murmured.

The feeling of disappointment was palpable in the room. She understood why Clara felt the way she did, but Elsbeth knew in her heart that her stepfather was not the man he was pretending to be. Why could no one see it but her?

"Will there be anything else, my lady?"

Elsbeth shook her head. "No, thank you."

Once her lady's maid departed from the room, she walked over to the window. Niles was helping her fight this battle... for now. She suspected he would stop when she couldn't find further proof about her stepfather.

Her stomach grumbled and she decided it would be best to

go down for breakfast. She dreaded nearly every interaction with her stepfather. He would smile, act cordial, but she knew it was just an act.

She departed from her bedchamber and the sight of Charles in the corridor brought a smile to her lips. "Good morning, Cousin."

Charles returned the smile, though it lacked its usual warmth. "Good morning," he said. "I trust that you slept well?"

"I did," Elsbeth lied as she noticed the deep-set shadows beneath his eyes. "Although, I suspect you cannot say the same."

Charles exhaled heavily, raking a hand through his already disheveled hair. "I did not. I couldn't stop thinking about how I almost shot you. It kept replaying over and over in my mind." His voice wavered slightly before he steadied it. "I want you to know how terribly sorry I am, Elsbeth."

She placed a reassuring hand on his arm. "It is all right, Cousin. Consider it forgotten."

Charles's lips pressed into a thin line. "You are most gracious," he murmured, though there was a stiffness to his tone, as if he struggled to believe she could forgive him so easily.

Together, they made their way down the grand staircase, the rich mahogany railing cool beneath her fingertips. Charles glanced at her arm as they reached the last step. "How's the wound?"

"Sticky," she said with a wry smile. "Clara applied honey to it this morning."

Charles nodded approvingly. "An old remedy, but an effective one." He sneezed abruptly, pulling a handkerchief from his pocket.

"Are you catching cold?" Elsbeth asked.

"Hardly. I slept with my window open," Charles admitted, dabbing his nose. "The fresh air is worth a sneeze or two."

"My mother would scold you for such recklessness," Elsbeth teased.

Charles chuckled and reached into his pocket, pulling out a small tin. "I've been taking these lozenges. They work wonders. Care to try one?"

She hesitated before accepting a lozenge and placing it in her mouth. The faint taste of rosewater was surprisingly pleasant. "They're quite good," she admitted.

"They are, indeed," Charles replied with a grin. "My cook prepared a fresh batch for me before I left."

Entering the dining room, Elsbeth found Alfred seated at the head of the table. He rose politely as they approached.

"Elsbeth," he said. "Lord Bedford."

"Please, call me Charles," he corrected. "Family does not make use of titles."

Alfred seemed pleased by Charles's remark as he returned to his seat. "I'm afraid Isabella was not feeling well this morning and she requested a tray be sent to her room."

"That is unfortunate," Elsbeth said as she sat down.

Breakfast was served swiftly, but Elsbeth barely touched her plate. Her thoughts raced as she decided whether to broach the subject of the clippings. Finally, setting her fork down, she turned to Alfred.

"Did you know my father?" she asked.

Alfred looked momentarily surprised before answering. "I knew *of* him but never had the privilege of an introduction. Our paths rarely crossed in Society."

"His death must have been a shock to you," she pressed.

"As much as it was to anyone," Alfred replied.

"Some people have a morbid fascination with death," Elsbeth said lightly, watching him closely.

Alfred frowned. "I suppose some do, but I've never understood it. It seems a waste of one's time."

"Have you ever visited the site of a death?" she asked pointedly. "It's quite the trend in London."

Alfred's frown deepened. "I find such things distasteful. If you'll excuse me, I have work to attend to."

Pushing back his chair, Alfred left the room, leaving Elsbeth to wonder if his measured answers were as innocent as they seemed or carefully constructed lies.

"Do you want to explain what that was about?" Charles asked, his tone more accusatory than curious.

"Nothing," Elsbeth said quickly, hoping to dismiss the subject before her cousin asked more questions.

Charles arched a skeptical brow. "Try again, Cousin."

Elsbeth sighed, lowering her voice. "Did you know that my mother and Alfred grew up in the same village?"

"I did not," Charles admitted, leaning back slightly, "but why does that matter?"

"Doesn't it seem... unusual to you?" she pressed, watching his reaction carefully.

Charles chuckled. "Not at all. If anything, it explains why they married so quickly after your mother came out of mourning."

"Does it?" she asked, her tone laced with doubt. "I found clippings from the newssheets about my father's death in Alfred's desk."

"Why were you searching his desk?"

"That is not the point—"

He cut her off. "Then what is the point?"

With a glance over her shoulder, she lowered her voice. "My stepfather is keeping secrets and I intend to discover what they are."

The humor drained from Charles's face, replaced with a serious expression. "Why can't you just be happy for your mother?"

The question landed heavily, stirring guilt deep in Elsbeth's chest. "It's not that—"

"Then what is it?" he interrupted.

She reached for her cup of chocolate. "I would do anything for my mother," she murmured. "Even if it means I go about it alone."

Charles's brows furrowed in concern. "Elsbeth..."

She cut him off, turning the conversation back on him. "What about you, Charles? Would you do anything to keep your estate afloat?"

His lips pressed into a thin line, his hesitation speaking volumes. "There are some things I wouldn't do," he said firmly.

Returning her cup to the saucer, she leaned forward. "Didn't you say you'd marry for convenience rather than love? You'd sacrifice your happiness for the survival of your estate?"

"That's different."

"Is it?" she challenged.

Charles abruptly stood, his chair scraping against the floor. "I'm going riding," he announced, his tone clipped. "Perhaps when I return, we can have a frank conversation about how not to be troublesome."

"I'm not trying to be difficult," Elsbeth countered. "I'm merely trying to make a point."

He stepped closer and placed a hand gently on her shoulder. "If you continue down this path, you're going to push everyone away."

She looked up at him, her heart heavy with the truth in his words. "I've become well acquainted with loneliness," she admitted, her voice barely above a whisper.

"That's by choice, Cousin," he said, letting his hand drop before walking out of the room.

As the door closed behind him, Elsbeth groaned softly, leaning back in her chair. She hated that Charles might be right, and that thought gnawed at her more than she cared to admit.

Her stomach churned unexpectedly, and a wave of nausea washed over her. She pushed her chair back, intending to leave, but as she stood, dizziness overtook her, and she clutched the back of the chair for support.

A nearby footman rushed to her side, his face etched with concern. "Are you all right, my lady?"

"I... I think so," she said faintly, sinking back into her seat. "I just need a moment."

The room seemed to spin, and the thought of climbing the stairs to her bedchamber felt impossible. Instead, she rested her head on the table, hoping the feeling would pass.

The footman's voice was urgent. "I'm going to send for the doctor."

"Thank you," she murmured, though the words barely left her lips. Her focus was consumed by the effort to keep her stomach from rebelling.

***

The rain lashed against the windows in relentless sheets, obscuring the gardens from view as Niles stood by the window. He was restless. And that was so unlike him. He had a myriad of things to do but he couldn't quite bring himself to do anything. It had been two days since Lady Isabella's note arrived, informing them that Elsbeth had fallen ill.

He told himself he should focus on his ledgers or correspondence, anything to keep his mind occupied. But every time he tried, his thoughts strayed back to Elsbeth. Why did her illness trouble him so much? He had no reason to be so preoccupied. Yet he was, and that truth unsettled him.

Niles turned to see Eugenie sitting comfortably on the

settee, a book balanced in her lap. Her serene demeanor only magnified his inner turmoil. As if sensing his gaze, she looked up and gave him a pointed look.

"Do sit down, Brother. You are making me anxious by just looking at you."

He sighed and crossed the room, settling into a chair across from her. "What are you reading?"

Eugenie perked up. "Do you truly wish to know, or are you merely bored out of your wits?"

"Perhaps a little of both," he admitted. "There's little else to occupy me at the moment."

Her lips twitched with amusement. "Your enthusiasm is truly inspiring. Tell me, why are you moping about? It can't simply be the rain."

"I am not moping," he retorted, though even he heard the defensive edge in his tone.

"You most certainly are," she countered. "And it began right after we received word that Lady Elsbeth was unwell. Quite the coincidence, wouldn't you agree?"

Niles leaned back in his chair, folding his arms. "You've been reading too many novels."

"This has nothing to do with my love of books," Eugenie said, leaning forward with a mischievous glint in her eyes. "It just begs the question, have you developed affection for Elsbeth?"

His huff of indignation was immediate. "Good heavens! How can you even suggest such a thing?"

"Because it's glaringly obvious," she said with a knowing smile.

He straightened in his seat, determined to put an end to her teasing. "For the record, I would not marry Lady Elsbeth if she were the last woman on earth. I am simply concerned for her wellbeing, nothing more."

Eugenie raised an eyebrow. "So your interest is purely

innocent?"

"Precisely," he replied curtly. "Though I do find it odd that she fell ill so suddenly. She appeared perfectly well the last time I saw her."

Eugenie placed her book aside, her eyes dancing with mock drama. "Do you suspect foul play, Brother? Was she poisoned?"

His expression grew somber. "That would explain it."

Eugenie blinked, startled by his seriousness. "And who, pray tell, do you think poisoned her?"

"Lord Bedford," he said without hesitation.

Her mouth fell open. "You cannot be serious! Why on earth would Lord Bedford poison his cousin?"

"It makes sense," Niles insisted.

"No, it does not," Eugenie argued. "Lord Bedford did not poison his cousin."

Niles wasn't quite convinced. "He did take a shot at her."

"I'm not entirely sure that was Lord Bedford," Eugenie argued. "He wasn't aiming at Elsbeth."

He arched his eyebrow. "Are you saying there was another shooter there, and he was aiming for Lady Elsbeth?"

Eugenie winced slightly. "I know that sounds ludicrous."

"It does," Niles replied.

"It is more plausible than Lord Bedford trying to kill Elsbeth," Eugenie remarked.

Before they could debate further, Aunt Margaret entered the drawing room, a letter in her hand. "I've just received word from Lady Isabella. Elsbeth is feeling much improved. The doctor believes it was merely a bout of food poisoning."

Niles frowned. Food poisoning? That didn't sit well with him. Many poisons mimicked those symptoms, and the timing seemed too convenient. He stood abruptly, straightening his waistcoat. "We should call on Lady Elsbeth."

Aunt Margaret studied him for a moment, then nodded. "I

agree. I'll join you." She turned to Eugenie. "Would you like to come as well?"

Eugenie hesitated before rising to her feet. "I suppose I should."

Aunt Margaret smiled knowingly. "It's a good thing I had the coach brought around. I suspected we'd all want to visit Elsbeth at once."

As they prepared to leave, Niles couldn't shake the sense of urgency gnawing at him. Something about Elsbeth's sudden illness didn't sit right. There were too many unanswered questions, and he was determined to find clarity.

Eugenie stepped beside him. "People fall ill all the time, Brother. I wouldn't be so quick to assume the worst."

He didn't respond. Instead, he climbed into the awaiting coach, settling into the seat opposite his sister and Aunt Margaret. The coach jolted forward, and Niles turned his attention to the rain-streaked window. He had no interest in idle chatter, but Aunt Margaret didn't share his sentiment.

"I received an invitation to Lady Isabella's soiree," she announced brightly. "I thought it would be nice for us to attend."

"That sounds delightful," Eugenie said, smoothing her pale pink gown.

Niles shifted uncomfortably in his seat. "I'll pass," he muttered. The idea of mingling at a soiree held little appeal.

Aunt Margaret adopted a feigned look of innocence. "Oh, dear. I'm afraid it's too late for that. I've already confirmed our attendance. I didn't think you'd object."

He narrowed his eyes. "How convenient."

Eugenie grinned. "Don't sulk, Brother. You've been in a foul mood ever since Elsbeth's illness was announced. Perhaps seeing her will lift your spirits."

"I'm not sulking," he snapped. "And my concern for Elsbeth is purely platonic."

"Yes, of course," Eugenie said, her tone dripping with mock sincerity. "We all believe you."

Niles looked heavenward, since he was done with the conversation. His sister was seeing connections where there were none, or so he tried to convince himself. He couldn't have feelings for Elsbeth. He wouldn't.

But, blast it all, he did.

The coach came to a stop in front of Elsbeth's manor, pulling him from his thoughts. He stepped out onto the gravel path, helping his aunt and sister descend, and led the way to the door. It swung open before they reached it, and the butler greeted them with a bow.

"Lady Elsbeth is resting in the drawing room and is expecting you," the butler informed them. "Please, follow me, and I shall announce you."

Niles nodded but felt Eugenie's hand on his arm as they walked. "A word of caution," she murmured. "Don't go making Elsbeth paranoid about Lord Bedford. You've no proof of your suspicions."

Just his gut, but he knew his sister would not appreciate that remark. "I understand," he decided to reply.

Eugenie looked pleased with his response and strode confidently into the drawing room. Niles followed, his gaze immediately finding Elsbeth. She was seated on the settee, a blanket draped over her lap. Her cheeks had a healthy flush, and though she looked tired, she didn't appear gravely ill. Relief coursed through him.

Aunt Margaret wasted no time in taking the seat beside Elsbeth, clasping her hand warmly. "My dear, we've been so worried about you."

Elsbeth smiled faintly. "The doctor believes it was just a bout of food poisoning."

Niles stepped closer, his brow furrowed. "And what do you believe?"

Elsbeth offered him a bemused look. "I see no reason to doubt the doctor's conclusion. It explains my symptoms."

"Did you experience nausea, vomiting, and diarrhea?" Niles asked bluntly.

A deep blush spread across her cheeks. "I'd rather not discuss that, my lord."

Aunt Margaret gasped. "For heaven's sake, Niles! One does not ask a lady about such things!"

"My apologies," he said quickly, though his curiosity remained unabated. He needed to speak with Elsbeth privately, but how?

Eugenie chimed in, her tone light. "I had food poisoning once, and I haven't been able to stomach baked apples since. Just the smell makes me queasy."

"That sounds dreadful," Elsbeth acknowledged.

Niles watched her carefully. She was putting on a brave face, but something about her demeanor left him unsettled. He resolved to find a moment alone with her to press further. Whatever was going on, he wasn't about to let it go unanswered.

11

E lsbeth could tell that something was troubling Niles. The tightening of his jaw was a subtle but telltale sign. It was one of the many small habits she had begun to notice about him. And therein lay the problem. She shouldn't be noticing anything about him. They were merely friends. Nothing more.

Yet, the gnawing need to address his unease refused to leave her alone. She needed to speak with him privately, but what excuse could she possibly offer that wouldn't raise suspicion?

Eugenie's animated discussion about a book she was reading provided an unexpected spark of inspiration. It wasn't the most brilliant idea, but it would suffice.

Elsbeth tossed the blanket from her lap and rose. "Eugenie, I have a book that you might enjoy."

Her friend's eyes lit up with interest. "Which book?"

Drat. She hadn't thought this through. She had no specific book in mind. But Eugenie was waiting expectantly, so she managed a weak smile. "It's a surprise."

Eugenie frowned. "I do not like surprises."

Niles chuckled from his seat nearby. "That much is true," he said. "She's managed to ruin every present I've given her over the past few years."

"This is a good surprise," Elsbeth said with more confidence than she felt. Was it? Would she even find a book in the library that Eugenie might enjoy?

Eugenie relented with a sigh. "Very well. I suppose I can wait."

Elsbeth turned to Niles. "Would you care to accompany me?"

He sprang to his feet, looking uncharacteristically eager. "I'd be happy to." His enthusiasm was almost suspicious. "Shall we?" he asked, offering his arm.

She accepted, and together they left the drawing room. Once in the quiet corridor, she leaned closer to him. "What is troubling you?"

"Why do you suppose something is troubling me?"

"You were clenching your jaw," she said plainly.

He arched a brow. "Pardon?"

"You clench your jaw when you're upset. So tightly, in fact, that a vein pulsates just above it," she explained.

"You noticed that?"

Heat rose to her cheeks. She struggled to sound indifferent. "It's fairly obvious. Anyone with eyes could see it."

Niles smirked. "I'll take that as a compliment."

"You may take it however you like," she said, waving her hand dismissively. "Now, tell me, what has you so troubled?"

His expression turned serious. "Do you know what caused your food poisoning?"

"No, but it could have been anything."

He paused. "What if you were poisoned?"

Elsbeth stopped abruptly and turned to face him. "I beg your pardon?"

He raised a hand to placate her. "Hear me out before you

dismiss the idea. I believe your cousin might have poisoned you."

Her brow furrowed. "Why would you think such a thing?"

"Did he give you anything to eat or drink? Was he ever alone with your food?"

"No, he wasn't alone with my food, but he did give me a lozenge. That hardly means he poisoned me."

"Did you get sick after eating it?"

"Yes, but—"

"Did he eat one as well?" Niles interrupted, stepping closer.

"No, but—"

"Then surely you see the problem," he pressed.

She threw up her hands. "Why do you insist on believing Charles means me harm?"

"Did you eat anything else that could have caused your illness?"

"I had my usual breakfast—one egg, one piece of toast, and ham," she replied impatiently. "I admit it doesn't look good for Charles, but that doesn't mean he poisoned me."

Niles gave her a pointed look. "He shot at you."

"That was an accident."

"Was it?"

Before she could retort, muffled shouting reached them from the direction of her stepfather's study. She raised a finger to her lips, signaling Niles to follow her.

They approached the study quietly. The door was ajar, allowing her to peer inside. Alfred sat at his desk, his face set in a scowl. A man she had seen only once before stood before him, speaking in hushed but heated tones.

"Why is Lord Bedford poking around in matters that do not concern him?" Alfred demanded.

The man shrugged. "Do you want me to take care of it?"

"Yes," Alfred said sharply. "But make sure it can't be traced back to me."

"I can be discreet."

Alfred's expression darkened further. "If Lord Bedford keeps asking questions, it'll be his funeral."

Elsbeth's breath caught in her throat. Her stepfather's words echoed ominously in her mind.

"I won't disagree with you there, Sir. I'll handle it," the man responded before he turned to leave.

Elsbeth's pulse quickened at the sight. They needed to hide, and quickly. Without hesitation, she reached for Niles's hand and pulled him into the nearest room, a parlor just off the corridor. The soft click of the door closing behind them felt deafening in the tense silence. She leaned against it, taking a steadying breath to calm her racing heart.

Niles remained close. "What do you make of that conversation?" he asked in a low voice.

"I'm not sure," she replied. "But it doesn't bode well for Charles. What could he be poking around in that has my stepfather so agitated?"

"Do you know who that man was with your stepfather?"

"I've seen him once before, the last time I overheard my stepfather in conversation. He's not someone I recognize from our social circles."

As the words left her mouth, she became acutely aware of the warmth of Niles's hand in hers. She froze, the realization sending a wave of mortification through her. What must he think of her, dragging him around like this? Quickly, she released his hand and took a step back, putting a bit of space between them.

"Now do you believe me?" she asked, hoping to distract Niles from her embarrassment. "My stepfather is not who he pretends to be."

Niles's gaze lingered on her, thoughtful. "I'll admit, that conversation was... troubling."

"Troubling?" she echoed, her voice full of incredulity.

"What is he involved in? And why would he want to harm my cousin?"

"I know that look. You're about to go off half-cocked, aren't you?"

She straightened her posture, indignant. "No, I'm merely considering my options. For instance, I think it's time I follow my stepfather and see where he's been going. He travels to the next village over far too often for it to be a coincidence. What business could he possibly have there?"

"It might be perfectly innocent," Niles suggested, though his skeptical tone betrayed his true thoughts.

"Or it might be illicit," she countered.

He crossed his arms over his chest, his expression stern. "Elsbeth, you promised me you wouldn't play highwaywoman ever again."

"I did," she agreed with a sigh. "But following someone discreetly is hardly the same thing."

"And if you're caught?"

She shrugged. "Who says I'll be caught?"

Niles stared at her, his exasperation palpable. After a long pause, he relented. "Fine. But I'm coming with you."

Elsbeth blinked, surprised by his quick concession. "I never asked you to."

"True," he said, a wry smile tugging at the corner of his lips. "But I think we both know it's for the best. Someone needs to ensure you don't get yourself into more trouble. And, more importantly, that you stay safe."

His earnestness gave her pause. For a moment, she could only look at him, uncertain of how to respond. Finally, she nodded, her voice softer than before. "Thank you, Niles."

"Just don't make me regret it."

She found herself staring into his eyes—deeper than she ought to—and noticed, for the first time, the faint brown flecks scattered within the green. It was a detail so minute, so personal, that it made her pulse quicken. She shouldn't be this close to him. But she was. And to her dismay, she rather liked the nearness of him.

The sound of her own breath brought her back to reality. They were alone in the parlor, a situation that could lead to talk if anyone happened upon them. It may be the countryside where propriety was a touch more forgiving, but not so much as to excuse a moment like this.

"Shall we return to your sister and aunt?" she asked, her voice more steady than she felt.

For a fleeting moment, she thought she caught a flash of disappointment in his eyes. Or had she imagined it? "Of course. But shouldn't we fetch the book you promised Eugenie first?"

Elsbeth winced. "I'll admit, there is no book. I only said that to have an excuse to speak with you privately."

The corners of his mouth lifted slightly. "Ah, I see. Well then, perhaps we can make good on that promise. Let's find a book together that might pique my sister's interest."

"A reasonable suggestion." She crossed to the door and opened it just enough to peek into the corridor, ensuring it was empty before stepping through.

Niles followed, his footsteps light on the carpet as they made their way towards the library.

"What kind of books does your sister enjoy?" Elsbeth asked, breaking the silence.

He chuckled. "I'm not sure there's a book my sister doesn't enjoy. Her tastes are varied, to say the least."

"Noted. So, we're looking for anything and everything?"

"Precisely."

As they approached the library doors, Elsbeth couldn't help but glance sideways at him. He seemed so at ease, so comfortable in her presence, and she realized with some surprise that she felt the same. She wasn't quite sure what to make of that, but she knew it was a thought that was best left for another time.

She approached one of the towering bookshelves that lined the back wall of the library. Her eyes roamed over the spines, her fingers trailing along the textured leather bindings as she searched for a title. At last, she paused and tilted her head. "What about *Nathan der Weise*?"

Niles stepped closer, far closer than she had expected. "I think it's a perfect choice."

"Good."

Without thinking, they both reached for the book at the same time. Their fingers brushed—a fleeting, accidental touch, but it sent an unwelcome jolt up her arm.

Niles quickly withdrew his hand. "My apologies," he murmured.

"No harm done." She turned her attention to the book, attempting to ignore the way her skin still tingled where their hands had met. She grasped the book, pulling it carefully from its spot on the shelf.

Niles cleared his throat. "Allow me to escort you back to the drawing room?"

She glanced at his proffered arm and hesitated. Did she trust herself? Each time they touched, it felt as though something unspoken passed between them, something she couldn't afford to examine too closely. And yet, propriety dictated her response.

She placed her hand lightly on his sleeve, determined to remain composed, and forced a polite smile to her lips. "Thank you," she said.

As they walked back towards the drawing room, Niles asked, "Would you care to join me on a picnic this afternoon?"

"That sounds wonderful."

He smiled. "I shall see to the arrangements then."

Niles tugged on the reins, bringing the carriage to a halt in front of Elsbeth's manor. The soft crunch of gravel beneath the wheels filled the otherwise quiet afternoon. He leaned back for a moment, his grip tightening on the reins as he took in the grand façade of the manor. Why had he suggested a picnic? The answer was both obvious and unsettling. He wanted to spend more time with Elsbeth. Alone.

What was wrong with him?

Why did he care so much about her plight? He had offered to help her uncover the truth about her stepfather, but somewhere along the way, his role as a mere ally had begun to blur into something more personal.

With a frustrated sigh, Niles secured the reins and stepped down onto the gravel path. Before he could make his way to the door, it opened, and Lord Bedford strode out with a purposeful look on his face. His usual easy demeanor was replaced by something sharper, more serious.

"A word, Westcott," Bedford said, closing the distance between them.

Niles raised an eyebrow, unsure of the cause for this sudden confrontation. "Bedford," he replied, his tone cautious.

Bedford stopped just short of him. "What are your intentions towards my cousin?"

"My intentions?" Niles repeated, incredulous. "I have none beyond taking Lady Elsbeth on a carriage ride and sharing a picnic. Surely, even you can find no fault in that."

"I expect you to behave honorably."

Niles couldn't suppress a scoff. "Why do you care so much about propriety when you were the one who nearly shot her?"

Bedford stiffened, his jaw tightening. "That was an accident."

Niles allowed himself a pointed smile, the words coming out more biting than he intended. "And I daresay Lady Elsbeth will be safer in my company than she ever was in yours."

Bedford's eyes narrowed. "I beg your pardon?"

Before Niles could retort, the door opened again, and Elsbeth stepped outside. She looked beautiful, her jonquil gown accentuating her graceful figure, and her hair arranged in a delicate chignon. But it was her smile that captivated him the most.

"Lady Elsbeth," Niles said, brushing past Bedford to offer his arm. "You look lovely."

"Thank you," she murmured, her cheeks coloring slightly as she accepted his arm.

He assisted her into the carriage, his focus entirely on her. From behind them, Bedford's clipped voice called out, "Enjoy your picnic."

Elsbeth glanced back, watching her cousin retreat into the manor. She turned to Niles with a curious look. "Dare I ask what Charles spoke to you about?"

Niles climbed into the carriage and sat beside her, reaching for the reins. "He wanted to ensure that I intended to behave honorably during our outing."

"That was kind of him."

Niles lifted an eyebrow, the reins taut in his hands. "Kind, yes. Much like the kindness he showed when he nearly shot you or when he poisoned you."

Elsbeth sighed. "You have no proof that he did such things."

"Perhaps not," Niles admitted, urging the horses forward. "But his behavior is suspect."

"My cousin is a good man," Elsbeth insisted. "He would never intentionally hurt me. I'm certain of that."

Niles refrained from arguing further, focusing on the road ahead. But the tension in his jaw betrayed his thoughts. "And what of your stepfather? Would he try to hurt you?"

Elsbeth clasped her hands tightly in her lap. "I don't know what he is capable of," she confessed. "And that frightens me the most. He presents himself as kind and warm, but I believe it's all an act."

"Then you need to be cautious around him," Niles advised.

She nodded but then added, "I overheard him telling my mother that he intends to travel to the village tomorrow."

Niles glanced at her, catching the glint of determination in her eyes. "And I suppose you want to follow him?"

A mischievous smirk curved her lips. "You're starting to know me too well."

That was the truth. Niles turned his attention back to the road, trying to suppress the flicker of admiration her boldness inspired in him. It wasn't just her quest for answers or her resilience that drew him in. No. It was Elsbeth herself. And that was both thrilling and terrifying.

Niles realized he had no interest in discussing Bedford or Mr. Stockton anymore. What he truly wanted was to learn more about Elsbeth. He turned to her. "Will you tell me about yourself?"

A playful glint sparkled in her eyes. "That's rather vague. What exactly do you wish to know?"

That was an excellent question. What did he want to know about her? He decided to start small. "Besides dressing up as a highwaywoman, what else occupies your time?"

"The usual pursuits for a young lady, I suppose. My mother was determined that I excel at needlework and the pianoforte."

"That sounds... thrilling."

Her smile faltered slightly. "My life has grown rather dull since we moved to this godforsaken village," she admitted, her voice carrying a tinge of bitterness.

"I find the village quaint."

"Perhaps to visit," Elsbeth countered, "but living here is an entirely different matter. There's precious little to do, and most of the villagers don't know quite what to make of me. Apart from your aunt, I have no other friends here."

Her words carried a sadness that tugged at him, and Niles felt an inexplicable urge to remedy it. "I'm sorry your friends abandoned you."

She gave him a rueful look. "Thank you, but I can't say it surprises me. That's what happens when scandal strikes."

"That doesn't make it right."

"No," she agreed, "but if I'm being honest, I probably would have done the same. A lady's reputation is everything. When someone jeopardizes their own, it's easier to walk away than risk being tainted by association."

Niles studied her, the vulnerability behind her words surprising him. "I worry about Eugenie," he admitted after a moment. "She can't seem to pull her nose out of a book long enough to think about finding a husband."

Elsbeth's expression softened. "Your sister is resilient. When the right suitor comes along, I have no doubt she'll put her book down."

"I hope you're right," he remarked. "I swore to my father that I'd always look after her, that I'd make sure she's taken care of."

"You're a good man," Elsbeth said simply.

He winced at her words. "I don't feel like one. I'll never be the man my father was. He had this presence about him. He could command a room with just a glance. I doubt I'll ever be like him."

She gave him a thoughtful look. "And you don't think you have that same ability?"

"Hardly," Niles replied with a huff of frustration. "In Parliament, the other lords barely notice me. I have to fight to make myself heard, and even then, they dismiss my views as unimportant."

"Then speak louder."

Niles let out a humorless laugh. "I doubt the volume of my voice will make a difference."

"I envy you," Elsbeth said. "You're in a position to enact real change. You can do things most people can only dream of."

"I'm failing at it," he admitted.

She reached out and placed her hand gently on his sleeve. "You're not failing. You're finding your way, and when the time comes, you'll make them listen. I have no doubt."

Her faith in him, so freely given, settled something inside him. For the first time in a long while, Niles felt that maybe, just maybe, she was right.

Elsbeth withdrew her hand, and Niles found himself missing the warmth of her touch. Clearing his throat, he ventured cautiously, "Were you close with your father?"

"Hardly," she replied, her voice steady but tinged with a trace of sadness. "He was rather indifferent to me."

"I'm sorry to hear that," Niles said, unsure what else to offer.

A weak smile curved her lips. "He wasn't cruel, not intentionally. But as I grew older, it became painfully clear just how different we were. My father couldn't understand why I would spend my time making clothing for the orphans at the workhouse. He believed poor people deserved their circumstances."

Niles glanced at her. "But you don't believe that."

"Heavens, no," she said emphatically. "It's hardly a child's fault they were born into poverty. They're denied opportunities from the start. How could they possibly be expected to rise above it without help?"

"I feel the same," Niles said, his voice filled with conviction.

She nodded. "It's refreshing to meet someone who shares that perspective. Most of the people I know are content to ignore such realities."

"What first brought the workhouse to your attention?"

She shifted slightly on the bench to face him, her posture more animated. "I read an article in the newssheets. It painted such a grim picture that I didn't want to believe it was true. But when I visited one myself, I realized the reality was even worse than I had imagined."

"I've toured a few workhouses myself," Niles said grimly. "The conditions are appalling. They are cramped, unsanitary, and dehumanizing. People barely survive. That's when I knew I had to act."

Elsbeth glanced down at her hands, her expression troubled. "I once asked my father to help, to use his influence to make a difference. He dismissed me outright and told me to stop being nonsensical. He believed if the poor truly wanted to improve their lives, they would work harder."

"Unfortunately, that is a general consensus amongst the members of Parliament," Niles replied, his tone laced with frustration.

Elsbeth sighed deeply. "Perhaps we should change the subject. The weather, perhaps?"

Niles chuckled at her attempt to lighten the mood. "I have no interest in discussing the weather."

Feigning offense, she teased, "Do you not like weather, my lord?"

A genuine laugh escaped him. "I think we've progressed past the point in our friendship where small talk about the weather is necessary."

Her face softened. "I'm glad we're friends."

"As am I, Elsbeth." And he meant it. Despite the complexities surrounding them, he had come to genuinely value her company. "What was your childhood like?"

The question brought a wistful smile to her lips. "It was idyllic, in its way. I grew up at our country estate, surrounded by gardens and rolling hills. My mother doted on me something fierce."

"But not your father?" Niles probed.

She shook her head. "He was always busy in meetings,

social engagements, and whatnot. I can count on one hand the number of times I truly spent time with him as a child."

"That must have been hard for you."

"It was familiar," she corrected. "Not that he was absent from my life entirely. He made decisions, like hiring a governess for me. We became quite close until my mother abruptly dismissed her."

"Dare I ask why?"

Elsbeth grew visibly tense. "Apparently, my father and the governess had grown... too close. When she began increasing, my mother refused to allow the scandal to tarnish our household."

Niles tightened his grip on the reins. "Pardon me for saying so, but your father sounds like a cad."

"You wouldn't be wrong," Elsbeth admitted. "He had many flaws, but at the end of the day, he was still my father. That's all I know."

"Are you close to your mother?"

Elsbeth pressed her lips together. "We used to be close, before she married Alfred. Things were different then. Simpler. But now... now she's constantly frustrated with me. She can't understand why I'm so insistent that Alfred isn't the man she believes him to be. She dismisses my concerns, utterly convinced that I'm wrong."

Niles leaned forward. "Has Alfred ever been unkind to you?"

"No," Elsbeth replied. "And that's part of the problem. He's been nothing but kind to me, almost overly so, as if he's trying to replace my father."

"Has he ever said that?"

"Well, no," she responded. "But why else would he act so... accommodating? It's almost unnerving."

Niles hesitated, carefully weighing his next words. "Have you tried being kind to him in return?"

Her head snapped towards him, her eyes narrowing slightly. "I don't throw rocks at him, if that's what you're asking."

A grin tugged at his lips. "That's a start. But what I mean is, have you tried treating him as someone who might genuinely care for you, instead of assuming his motives are purely self-serving?"

Elsbeth fidgeted with her hands in her lap. "Your suggestion implies that I've been the one making things difficult."

"I'm not saying Alfred doesn't have his secrets," Niles clarified. "He very well might. But what if his kindness isn't a calculated move? What if it is genuine? Would it hurt to show him the same courtesy?"

Elsbeth's expression grew guarded, but her eyes revealed a flicker of something. Was it regret? Annoyance? Uncertainty? He couldn't quite place it.

"You're asking me to do something I'm not sure I'm capable of," she said at last.

"I'm asking you to consider the possibility," Niles replied. "That's all."

For a moment, neither spoke. The only sound was the rhythmic clatter of the carriage wheels against the road. Elsbeth finally let out a soft sigh, her shoulders relaxing just slightly.

"I'll think about it," she murmured.

It wasn't much, but it was a start.

12

Elsbeth sat at the dining table, absently pushing her food around on her plate with her fork. The clinking of cutlery and low murmur of conversation surrounded her, but she felt detached from it all.

Her thoughts lingered on her earlier conversation with Niles. His words had struck deeper than she cared to admit. He wasn't the first to suggest she should be kinder to Alfred, but somehow, coming from him, it carried more weight. It gnawed at her. Could she truly soften towards the man who had so thoroughly disrupted her life?

She sighed quietly, longing for a simpler time when her father was alive, her family unbroken, and her world unmarred by scandal and suspicion. But the past was an unreachable dream, and the present demanded her attention.

Her mother's voice broke through her reverie. "Dear, are you not hungry?"

Elsbeth set down her fork and knife, carefully masking her inner turmoil. "I do apologize. I was woolgathering."

Charles, seated across the table, raised an eyebrow. "Were you thinking of Lord Westcott?"

"Heavens, no," she replied a little too quickly. "I try not to think of him at all."

Charles grew solemn. "Good, because I'm not entirely sure I trust him."

Elsbeth had to fight the urge to laugh. If Charles only knew what Niles thought of him. Instead, she maintained her composure. "Lord Westcott is a good, honorable man. I trust him."

"You're far too trusting, Cousin," Charles responded.

This time, she nearly did laugh. If only Charles knew how deeply she questioned nearly everyone in her life.

Alfred, seated at the head of the table, interjected. "Did you have an enjoyable time on your picnic with Lord Westcott?"

"Yes, I did," Elsbeth replied.

Alfred nodded in approval. "It was a fine day for a picnic."

The old Elsbeth would have retorted with a sharp comment, but she was trying to heed Niles's advice and be kinder. It was an uphill battle.

Charles leaned forward slightly and asked, "What do you actually know about Lord Westcott?"

"I know that he has been kind to me," she responded. She kept her expression guarded, unwilling to betray that she and Niles were working together to uncover Alfred's secrets.

The footmen moved in to clear their plates, providing a temporary reprieve. But Charles wasn't ready to let it go.

"I think you should stay away from Lord Westcott," he said bluntly.

"And why is that?" Elsbeth asked, her voice laced with challenge.

Charles gave her a pointed look. "Your reputation is already in tatters. Any lord with sense would steer clear of you. So it begs the question: what does Lord Westcott truly want?"

Her breath caught at his words. As much as she hated to admit it, Charles had a point. Why had Niles agreed to help her? What was his true motive?

"Well, I, for one, think it's wonderful that Elsbeth is spending time with Lord Westcott," her mother chimed in.

"I concur with my lovely wife," Alfred said.

Elsbeth bit back the urge to roll her eyes. Alfred's constant agreement with her mother was maddening, though she couldn't quite place why it irked her so much.

A footman placed pudding in front of her mother, who looked up with a bright smile. "I've invited Lord Westcott, Lady Eugenie, and Lady Margaret to join us for a game of Snapdragon this evening. They should be here shortly."

"Wonderful," Alfred said with a grin. "I haven't played Snapdragon in ages."

Charles groaned dramatically. "That's not the word I would use."

The butler entered, his voice cutting through the chatter. "My lady, your guests have arrived."

"Thank you," her mother replied, pushing back her chair. "Shall we all adjourn to the drawing room?"

Elsbeth's heart began to race at the prospect of seeing Niles again. Why did he have this effect on her? She longed to feel indifferent towards him. But she couldn't. His presence stirred something in her she couldn't quite name.

After they rose from their seats, Charles came to her side and whispered, "Promise me you'll be careful with Lord Westcott."

"I will," she said, matching his tone.

"Good," he replied. "Because he'll be leaving soon enough, and I don't want to see you get hurt."

The thought of Niles leaving made her chest tighten. Of course, he would leave. He had a home, a life outside this village. And she? She would remain here, in the tangled mess of her family's secrets and her own unspoken fears.

That was the way it should be.

At least, that's what she told herself.

As they walked towards the drawing room, Elsbeth's eyes sought out Niles almost instinctively. He stood by the window, the light of the flickering fire casting shadows across his features, looking deucedly handsome.

When he caught her gaze, he smiled. It was a smile that disarmed her entirely. Against her better judgment, she returned the smile. But she didn't approach him. Not yet. Instead, she turned her attention to Eugenie and Lady Margaret, who were standing in the center of the room.

"Good evening," Elsbeth greeted as she came to a stop beside them.

Lady Margaret enveloped her in a warm embrace. "You are looking well, my dear. Much better than when I last saw you."

"Thank you," Elsbeth replied graciously.

Before she could think of something else to say, Niles's voice came from behind her, close enough that it sent a shiver down her spine. "It must have been all those biscuits she consumed during our picnic."

She turned towards him. How had she not noticed him approach? "I do have a fondness for sweets, my lord."

Niles grinned, his eyes twinkling mischievously. "I think that was evident by the way you devoured those biscuits. Impressive, truly."

Feigning indignation, she placed a hand over her heart. "A gentleman would never speak of such things!"

"My apologies, Lady Elsbeth," he said. "I would hate to wound your delicate sensibilities."

Her mother's voice broke through their playful exchange. "Gather around the bowl, everyone!" she called brightly. "It's time to play Snapdragon."

The group moved towards the center of the room, where a large, shallow bowl of raisins soaked in brandy sat atop a low table. A footman stepped forward, lighting the brandy, and blue flames flickered to life, casting ghostly shadows across the room as the candles were snuffed out.

"Who will go first?" her mother asked.

"I will." Niles stepped forward, his movements confident, and deftly plucked a raisin from the flames before popping it into his mouth. "Delicious," he declared with a triumphant smile.

Not one to be outdone, Elsbeth reached into the fiery bowl and retrieved two raisins in one quick motion. "I do believe I'm winning," she said with a playful tilt of her head.

Niles chuckled. "Slow down, my lady. The game has only just begun."

Eugenie removed her gloves and approached the flames, her expression one of determination. "I beat my brother the last time we played Snapdragon," she informed them.

Niles smirked. "You won by a single raisin, Eugenie, and only because the bowl was empty."

"Excuses, as always," Eugenie retorted, rolling her eyes.

Lady Margaret took a cautious step back from the fiery bowl. "This is very much a young person's game," she remarked. "I think I'll observe from a safe distance."

"You're unlikely to catch fire, Lady Margaret," Elsbeth said, trying to reassure her.

"But not entirely impossible," the older woman replied with amusement in her eyes.

Charles joined Eugenie at the table, his expression contemplative. "It's said that whoever retrieves the most snapdragons will meet their true love within the year."

"That's an old wives' tale," Eugenie dismissed, though her cheeks colored slightly.

As the game continued, laughter filled the room, mingling with the scent of brandy and the crackling of flames. For the first time in what felt like ages, Elsbeth felt truly at ease. She couldn't recall the last time she had laughed so freely or felt so unburdened. Surrounded by friends and family, she allowed herself to savor the moment.

When Niles plucked the final raisin from the bowl, he held it up. "And with this raisin, I declare myself the victor!" he announced with mock grandeur.

"Barely," Eugenie muttered.

Elsbeth turned to him. "Well done, my lord. It appears you excel at this game."

Niles's grin widened. "I excel at all games I play, my lady."

Eugenie groaned. "Now you're just being insufferable, Brother."

"You are only upset because you lost," Niles said.

A footman extinguished the flames and carried the bowl away, while the candles were relit, restoring the room to its warm glow.

"Would anyone care for tea?" Elsbeth's mother offered as she gestured to the tea cart.

Niles placed a hand on his stomach, feigning a grimace. "I fear I've eaten far too many snapdragons."

"Serves you right," Eugenie quipped.

Her mother turned towards her. "Would you care to pour the tea, Elsbeth?"

Elsbeth nodded and rose, making her way to the tea tray. The fine porcelain gleamed in the soft candlelight as she lifted the pot and began pouring. One by one, she handed out the cups as everyone settled into their seats around the room.

"What a delightful game that was," her mother declared.

Elsbeth arched an eyebrow. "I couldn't help but notice that you didn't play, Mother."

Her mother waved a hand dismissively. "Oh, I thought it best to step back with Margaret and let you young people enjoy yourselves."

As Elsbeth's gaze swept the room, her brow furrowed

slightly. "Where is Alfred?" she asked, the question slipping out before she could think better of it.

Her mother seemed unconcerned. "He had a meeting in the village."

"At this hour?" Elsbeth pressed, her eyes darting to the darkened windows. The moon hung low in the sky, casting a silvery glow over the gardens. It was late for business, even for a merchant.

Eugenie interjected. "Did you know this village is notorious for smuggling?" She paused, catching the startled looks her comment garnered. "Not that I am accusing Mr. Stockton of any such thing," she added hastily. "It's just an interesting fact."

Her mother's lips pursed as she straightened in her seat. "My husband is not a smuggler, Eugenie," she said firmly, though her voice remained polite. "Sometimes his ships dock later than expected, and he is obliged to meet with associates at odd hours. It's the nature of his business."

Elsbeth tightened her grip on her teacup, the warmth seeping into her palms as her thoughts churned. Her mother's words were plausible enough, yet they settled uneasily in her mind.

Leaning back in her seat, Elsbeth tried to appear composed, though her resolve was hardening. She would see for herself what her stepfather was up to during these mysterious meetings. Answers didn't come from sitting idly by.

The moon was high in the sky as Niles approached the stables on Elsbeth's property. He had seen the determined look on her face earlier and he had a feeling that she was going to do something intolerably stupid.

The faint flicker of a lantern spilled from the stables. He

pushed open the heavy wooden door, its hinges creaking softly in protest.

Inside, the scent of hay and leather was heavy in the air. A white-haired groom sat on a worn chair, his fingers curling around the handle of a pitchfork resting nearby. The man's eyes narrowed as he straightened his posture.

"What do you want?" the groom demanded, his voice sharp and wary.

Niles raised his hands, palms out in a gesture of peace. "I mean no harm."

The groom's grip on the pitchfork tightened. "I'll be the judge of that."

Niles took a measured step forward, the crunch of hay beneath his boots filling the silence. "I'm here to ensure Lady Elsbeth doesn't do something she'll regret."

The man's expression softened slightly, though his grip on the pitchfork didn't waver. "Who are you?"

"I am Lord Westcott," Niles introduced himself with a disarming smile.

The groom's eyes darkened, and he rose from his chair with surprising speed for his age. "You're the reason Lady Elsbeth was shot."

Niles flinched but held his ground. "That was a misunderstanding," he rushed to explain.

"A misunderstanding that nearly cost her life," the groom snapped, his voice laced with accusation.

"I had no knowledge of the constable's presence," Niles said. "I was only there to speak with her."

The groom scrutinized him for a long moment, the weight of his judgment palpable. "Well, as you can see, Lady Elsbeth isn't here—"

The door swung open before he could finish, and Elsbeth slipped inside. She froze the moment her gaze landed on Niles.

"Lord Westcott?" she asked, her voice a mix of surprise and suspicion. "What are you doing here?"

Niles crossed his arms, his expression as stern as he could muster. "I might ask you the same question."

Elsbeth shifted uncomfortably under his gaze. "I came to visit my horse," she offered weakly.

His brow arched in disbelief. "The truth, if you please."

She hesitated, then sighed. "I'm going to the village to see who my stepfather is meeting with."

"And you thought it wise to go alone?" Niles pressed, his voice rising slightly. "Do you truly think it is safe for a young woman to wander the village in the dark?"

"I am perfectly capable," she retorted, though her tone lacked conviction.

"I don't doubt that," he countered. "But I thought we agreed we would work together."

Elsbeth winced, guilt flickering across her features. "We did. I'm sorry."

Niles uncrossed his arms. "Then let's do this together. Shall we?"

Her lips curved into a small smile. "I'd like that."

A short time later, they were galloping down the road towards the village, the sound of hooves echoing into the night. As the dim lights of the village came into view, Niles slowed his horse and cast a questioning glance at Elsbeth.

"Do you have a plan?" he asked.

Elsbeth shook her head. "I don't."

"That's a fine way to get caught."

"It's not as though my reputation could get any worse," she muttered.

Niles pulled his horse to a halt and turned to face her. "You are more than your reputation, Elsbeth."

She let out a soft, bitter laugh. "Easy for you to say. You're a wealthy lord with an impeccable reputation. I'm destined to be a spinster."

Niles leaned forward slightly, his gaze intent. "No," he said, his voice softer now. "You're a beautiful, intelligent young woman who has a great deal to offer the right man."

Her eyes searched his, vulnerability shining through. "You think I'm beautiful?"

"I do," he replied simply, his tone leaving no room for doubt.

She lowered her gaze, her voice tinged with sadness. "It has been a long time since a gentleman has told me that I am beautiful."

"It makes it no less true."

Elsbeth lifted her eyes to meet his. "I thought my life would be much different than this," she confessed.

"What is so wrong with your life?"

She let out a small huff, her frustration spilling into her words. "I'm riding through the night, alone with you, chasing after my stepfather to uncover his secrets. I'm risking my future, my reputation—what little remains of it—all for what?"

Niles tightened his grip on the reins. "You can't alter the past or foresee the future, but you can ruin the present by worrying about both."

A faint smile tugged at her lips, but it was fleeting. "I should have gotten married when I had the chance," she said. "The Earl of Pembroke offered for me."

"Why did you refuse him?"

Her smile turned sheepish. "You'll think me silly, but I wanted a love match. Not a marriage of convenience to a man old enough to be my father."

"For what it's worth, I think you made the right choice."

"Did I?" she countered, her tone skeptical. "If I'd married him, I wouldn't have ended up in this godforsaken village, living under my stepfather's roof."

Niles glanced at her. "You need to change your perspective. You have more than most people could dream of."

"You're right," she admitted, groaning softly. "I hate saying that out loud."

"That I'm right?" he teased.

"Yes, because it means I'm wrong," she said, her voice filled with mock indignation.

He grinned. "I'm glad to be in a position to keep you humble."

She considered him for a moment before asking, "What about you? Do you want a love match?"

"Love matches are rare. I'm too much of a pragmatist to believe I'll find one. But I know they're possible since my parents were desperately in love."

"I thought my parents loved each other, too," Elsbeth said, her voice wistful. "But now... I'm not so sure."

A small, bittersweet smile curved Niles's lips. "It was hard when my parents passed so close to one another, but it wasn't surprising. They did everything together."

"How I envy you."

He raised a brow. "At least your mother is still alive. I'd give anything to say the same."

Her shoulders slumped slightly as she nodded. "Life is strange, isn't it? We long for what we don't have and fail to truly appreciate what we do."

Niles turned his gaze to the road ahead, his voice tinged with an unspoken weight. "I just hope, wherever he is, my father is proud of the man I've become."

"I think he would be," she said.

Niles's heart tightened at the sincerity in her voice, and for a moment, he simply nodded, words failing him. Her belief in him meant more than he cared to admit.

Elsbeth turned her attention to the flickering lights of the village ahead, her expression hardening. "My stepfather is somewhere in that village, doing who knows what."

"What if your mother is right? What if he's simply meeting an associate about one of his ships or business dealings?"

Her lips pressed into a thin line. "Perhaps," she admitted. "But I intend to find out for myself." With that, she urged her horse forward, the determination in her posture leaving no room for argument.

Niles followed her lead, wondering what it would take to get through to her. The sound of their horses' hooves echoed against the cobblestone streets, the village eerily quiet at this late hour. Lanterns glowed dimly in windows, their light spilling onto the damp stones below. The scent of rain lingered in the air, though the skies had long since cleared.

They came to a stop in front of a coaching inn, a modest structure with peeling paint and sagging shutters. Securing their horses to a nearby post, Elsbeth wasted no time, slipping around to the alleyway that ran alongside the building.

"We should check the coaching inn first," she whispered, her voice barely carrying above the soft rustle of the night breeze. Without waiting for his reply, she crept forward, her movements purposeful.

Niles followed behind until they reached one of the dirt-streaked windows. Elsbeth pressed her hands lightly against the glass, peering inside. Her sharp intake of breath made him step closer.

"What do you see?" he asked in a low voice.

She gestured for him to join her. "It's him," she murmured. "My stepfather. He's speaking with someone."

Niles leaned in, squinting through the window. Inside, the flickering light of a lantern illuminated two men. Mr. Stockton stood with a composed but grave expression, speaking intently to a balding man that he did not recognize.

"Who is the other man?" he asked.

Elsbeth turned her gaze towards him. "That's Mr. Strother," she explained, her voice tight. "He was my father's solicitor. But Charles said he was returning to Town. So why is he still here, meeting with my stepfather?"

"That is an excellent question," Niles muttered as he studied the men through the window.

Elsbeth pulled back from the window, her brows furrowed in thought. "None of this makes sense," she murmured, more to herself than to Niles.

"It doesn't," he agreed. "But whatever they're discussing, it's important. Important enough for both men to take risks."

Her gaze flickered to his, her resolve evident. "We need to find out what they are discussing."

"Agreed. But not here, not now. We need to be careful, Elsbeth. If they suspect you're on to them..."

"I know," she said, swallowing slowly. "But I can't walk away from this."

"You're not alone in this," he reminded her. "We'll figure this out. Together."

"Thank you, Niles."

He offered her a reassuring smile. "Let's head back. We'll need a proper plan before we do anything else."

Elsbeth bobbed her head as she followed him out of the shadowed alley, their steps quiet against the cobblestone streets. As they traveled back to her estate, Niles couldn't help but wonder what business Mr. Stockton could have with Elsbeth's father's solicitor, especially so late at night. And why meet at the coaching inn in secret? Why not have the meeting at his estate? None of this made any sense. Not yet. But Niles was determined to find out why.

13

The moonlight seeped through the curtains as Elsbeth entered the back door of her manor, her footsteps muffled against the stone floor. Her mind raced as she ascended the servants' stairs, eager to reach her bedchamber without anyone noticing her late return. However, the moment she opened the door, she froze.

Charles.

He was sitting on her bed, his expression thunderous. His penetrating gaze bore into her, and his voice was sharp. "Where have you been?"

Elsbeth closed the door behind her, her hand lingering on the handle as she prepared herself. "I can explain."

"Can you?" he asked, his tone dry. "I'm all ears."

She clasped her hands tightly in front of her, trying to maintain composure. "I went to the village to see who Alfred was meeting with—"

Charles threw his hands up. "Not this again! This obsession of yours is becoming more than troublesome." His voice rose with each word. "You can't just go to the village alone at night..." He paused, narrowing his eyes. "You *were* alone, weren't you?"

Elsbeth hesitated, knowing her answer would only fuel his anger. "I was with Lord Westcott."

Charles's jaw dropped in disbelief. "Are you mad?" he barked. "Traipsing around in the dead of night with Lord Westcott? Have you lost all sense of propriety? You must think of your reputation!"

"My reputation is already in tatters," she replied, her voice tinged with defiance. "Why should it matter?"

His gaze softened momentarily, but his tone remained firm. "You don't truly believe that, do you?" He stood, pacing the room. "You still have a dowry of fifteen thousand pounds—"

She cut him off. "And who would want me? A fortune hunter?"

Charles stopped pacing and turned to face her. "You don't know what the future holds," he said. "But you must stop actively ruining your prospects."

"I am doing no such thing," she argued. "My stepfather is not who he claims to be. He was meeting with Mr. Strother at the coaching inn."

Charles's brows knitted together. "That's impossible. Mr. Strother returned to Town a few days ago."

"I know what I saw," Elsbeth said. "Why would Alfred meet with Mr. Strother in secrecy?"

Charles crossed his arms. "It was hardly secret if they were meeting at the coaching inn in plain view of anyone who cared to look."

"Yes, but—"

"This has to stop!" Charles shouted, his voice echoing in the quiet room. "I think it's best if I take you away from here for a while. We'll leave for my country estate tomorrow."

Her eyes widened in alarm. "No, I can't go. Not now."

"And why is that?" he demanded. "And don't say it's because of Alfred."

The thought of leaving Niles tightened her chest, but she

couldn't admit that. Instead, she scrambled for another excuse. "What about my mother's soiree? We can't leave before then."

Charles sighed heavily, clearly displeased. "Fine. But we'll depart at first light the next morning." He strode to the door. "This is for your own good."

Elsbeth's temper flared. "My own good?" she repeated. "You claim to be protecting my reputation, yet here you stand—in my bedchamber. Alone."

He barely spared her a glance as he reached for the doorknob. "We are cousins."

She scoffed, folding her arms. "Did you not propose marriage to me only a few days ago?" Her sharp tone halted him mid-motion. "Furthermore, what will the *ton* think when I take up residence with you in Town? Do you honestly believe they will accept such an arrangement without question?"

"My mother resides with me. That should be enough to appease the gossips."

Elsbeth frowned, her mind racing. He was being infuriatingly pragmatic, as always. But she wasn't done yet. "Don't you want to know what secrets my stepfather is keeping?" she asked, her voice laced with challenge.

Charles turned, his expression both weary and exasperated. "Alfred is a good man, and you'd see that if you took two seconds to get to know him."

"I know he's hiding things—"

"Enough!" Charles's shout silenced her. "You're hellbent on proving Alfred is a terrible person. For what purpose? Your mother is happy for once. Let her have that."

"My mother was happy with my father," she said, her voice trembling slightly. She needed to believe that was true.

Charles huffed. "There's so much you don't know."

"Then tell me."

"No," he replied. "I'm trying to protect you. I don't want to ruin the memories you have of your father."

Elsbeth straightened her shoulders. "I'm not a child. I can handle the truth."

"Can you?" Charles asked, stepping closer to her, his expression grave. "Well, here's some truth for you: Alfred is twice the man your father ever was."

"That is not true!" she shot back, her voice breaking.

Charles's gaze didn't waver. "I'm sorry, but it is. In time, you'll see that."

Elsbeth shook her head, her voice trembling with conviction. "Alfred has secrets, and I will uncover them. You'll see he's deceived you all."

Charles sighed deeply, placing a hand on her sleeve, his touch unexpectedly gentle. "This is my fault. I was so consumed with running the estate that I failed you. You deserved so much more."

Her back grew rigid. "I'm not wrong. Niles believes me."

"Niles?" Charles's brow furrowed in displeasure. "You are calling him by his given name?"

She realized her mistake too late. "He gave me leave to. We are friends."

His jaw clenched. "You need to stay away from Lord Westcott."

"Why would I do that?" she countered. "He's the only one who believes me, the only one who's stood by me."

"I don't want to see you get hurt," Charles said.

"Niles won't hurt me."

Charles's eyes narrowed, his voice hard and cutting. "Instead of talking you off a cliff, he's encouraging you to jump. That's no friend."

Elsbeth's lips pressed into a firm line. "You're wrong."

"There can be no future between you and Lord Westcott. You do realize that, don't you?" he asked, his gaze unyielding.

She stiffened at his words. "I never said anything about having a future with Niles."

"No, you haven't," Charles replied. "But your actions suggest otherwise. Lord Westcott will eventually leave, Elsbeth. He'll return to his estate and his life, leaving you behind."

She turned her face away, unwilling to let him see the flicker of pain in her eyes. "I am well aware of that fact."

"Good," Charles said firmly. "Because Lord Westcott is not the man I envisioned for you."

She was done with this conversation. It was going nowhere, and she wanted to be alone. "Goodnight, Charles," she said curtly.

He hesitated, as if he had more to say, but eventually stepped back. "In time, you'll see that leaving with me is the right thing to do."

"I doubt that," she murmured under her breath.

Shaking his head, Charles exited her bedchamber, finally leaving her in peace. Elsbeth waited until the sound of his footsteps faded before walking over to her dressing table. She opened the top drawer and retrieved Niles's pocket watch. Running her fingers over the smooth surface, she let out a sigh.

She needed to return it to him. But a small, selfish part of her wanted to keep it. To have something of his, a tangible reminder of the time they had shared. She cared for Niles far more than she was willing to admit, even to herself. But Charles was right about one thing: Niles would leave. He would return to his world, and she couldn't allow herself to pine after him.

Resolving herself, she decided she would return the pocket watch tomorrow.

A soft knock interrupted her thoughts, and her brow furrowed. Had Charles come back to argue further? Before she could answer, the door opened, and Clara slipped inside.

"I'm sorry, my lady," her lady's maid began, her words tumbling out in a rush. "Lord Bedford was insistent that I tell him where you'd gone."

Elsbeth placed the pocket watch back in the drawer and gave Clara a reassuring look. "It wasn't your fault."

Clara winced, wringing her hands. "I may have been eavesdropping outside your door. I've never seen Lord Bedford so furious."

"He wants me to leave with him for his estate after my mother's soiree."

"That is a good thing, isn't it?" Clara asked, stepping closer. "You'll be leaving this place, going back to your home."

Elsbeth shook her head, a tinge of sadness in her voice. "It's not my home anymore, Clara. Not really."

Clara's brows knitted together in concern. "What do you want to do?"

Sinking into the chair at her dressing table, Elsbeth replied, "I want to uncover my stepfather's secrets, but I fear I've run out of time."

"Maybe that's for the best," Clara suggested cautiously as she picked up a hairbrush, moving to stand by her.

Elsbeth's shoulders slumped. "My poor mother. She'll continue to be deceived by a man she claims to love."

Clara carefully removed the pins from Elsbeth's chignon and began brushing her hair with gentle strokes. "By all accounts, your mother seems happy with him. Perhaps there's no deception at all."

"Appearances can be deceiving," Elsbeth countered.

A comfortable silence stretched between them until Clara broke it hesitantly. "Do you not want to leave because of Lord Westcott?"

"Lord Westcott has nothing to do with this," Elsbeth lied, but the faint warmth that spread across her cheeks betrayed her.

Clara set the brush down and reached for a delicate lace cap. "You have been spending a lot of time with him lately."

"We are merely friends."

"Pardon me for saying so, but you two appear much closer than just friends."

Elsbeth remained silent as Clara carefully placed the cap on her head, adjusting it to sit just right. "Niles is helping me uncover my stepfather's secrets. That is all."

Clara tilted her head slightly, her expression thoughtful. "But why did he agree to help you in the first place?" she asked. "This was never his fight, yet he's been by your side since he arrived."

The question hung in the air like a challenge, and for a moment, Elsbeth found herself unable to respond. Why had Niles agreed to help her? He had no obligation, no reason to involve himself in her troubles. And yet, he had.

Her mind flitted to the moments they had shared. The teasing banter. The genuine concern in his eyes. The quiet support he offered when she felt like the world was against her. A flicker of doubt surfaced. Could his motives be more than just a sense of duty? Or worse, was she allowing herself to see more than what was truly there?

Clara interrupted her thoughts. "Forgive me, my lady. I didn't mean to overstep."

Elsbeth forced a small smile, her heart a confusing tangle of emotions. "You didn't overstep," she assured her. "I suppose I haven't given it much thought."

Clara's eyes filled with a quiet understanding. "Perhaps it's worth thinking about, my lady."

Yes.

It was most definitely worth thinking about.

With golden streams of the morning sunlight flooding the

manor, Niles descended the stairs. He barely reached the entry hall when a sharp knock echoed through the manor. The butler moved to answer, revealing Elsbeth on the threshold.

She stepped inside, looking radiant in a pale pink gown that complemented her olive complexion, her hair arranged in an intricate chignon that framed her face perfectly. The early hour didn't diminish her beauty but only seemed to enhance it.

Niles inclined his head in greeting. "Elsbeth."

She dropped into a graceful curtsy. "Niles," she replied, her tone more formal than usual.

"What brings you here so early?"

Her expression grew serious as she approached, her reticule dangling lightly from her wrist. "I came to visit Lady Margaret," she said. "But I was hoping to speak to you as well." Reaching into the small bag, she retrieved his pocket watch. "This is yours. I am sorry it has taken me so long to return it."

Niles took the pocket watch, its familiar weight settling in his palm. He stared at it for a moment, then back at her. Without thinking, he said, "Keep it." The words tumbled out before he could reconsider.

Elsbeth blinked, clearly startled. "Pardon?"

"I want you to have it," he said, surprising even himself.

Her brows knitted in confusion. "But this watch... it means so much to you."

"It does," Niles admitted. His voice lowered as he added, "But so do you."

Her eyes widened. "What are you saying?"

He hesitated, the vulnerability of his own words catching him off guard. "I'm saying I want you to have something to remember me by," he said, extending the watch towards her. "Please, take it."

She looked down at the watch, uncertainty flickering across her face. "Are you certain?"

"I am."

Elsbeth tentatively reached out and accepted the watch, clutching it close to her chest. "I promise I will treasure this always."

He smiled. "I'm glad. I've enjoyed our time together, more than I can say."

A shadow passed over her features. "Charles wants me to leave with him to his estate after my mother's soiree."

Niles stiffened. "Absolutely not," he said, his voice rising. "That man tried to shoot you and may have poisoned you."

Elsbeth shook her head, a hint of exasperation in her voice. "The shooting was an accident, and I don't believe he poisoned me. Charles is not a threat."

"I disagree," Niles said, his frustration bubbling to the surface. He raked a hand through his hair. "I can't let you go with him. What if something happens to you?"

"What do you propose I do?"

Without thinking, his next words slipped out. "Come with me to my estate."

She frowned. "What are you saying?"

"You'd be safe there," he insisted, stepping closer. "I can take you far away from your stepfather, from this village."

"And what of my mother?" she countered, crossing her arms.

"She could visit whenever she wishes," Niles replied, though he could sense her hesitation. "It's the best solution."

Elsbeth's frown deepened. "Do you not realize how improper that would be? My reputation is already in ruins. I cannot travel with you without scandal."

"That's why I would hire you as Eugenie's companion," he blurted.

Her face fell, and the hurt in her eyes was immediate. "You want to hire me?" she repeated, her voice soft and pained. "Do you think so little of me?"

Niles reached out instinctively, but she stepped out of his reach. "Elsbeth, I didn't mean it like that—"

"But that's what you said," she interrupted, her voice trembling. "I have a dowry of fifteen thousand pounds. I am not destitute."

He felt his heart drop. "I know that. I just want to keep you safe."

Elsbeth's lips tightened as she stepped closer, pressing the pocket watch back into his hand. "You may keep this, my lord. I don't want it. Not anymore."

"Elsbeth—"

She silenced him with a raised hand, her tone firm. "I thought we were friends, but I see now I was wrong. You're no different than my so-called friends who abandoned me when scandal touched my name."

Before he could say anything more, she turned on her heel and strode out of the manor, her footsteps echoing in the quiet hall.

Niles stood there, stunned and furious with himself. He wanted to run after her, to explain, to beg for forgiveness, but something stopped him. He needed to give her space, even if every instinct screamed for him to follow.

"Was that Elsbeth?" Eugenie's voice cut through the heavy silence behind him.

Niles barely turned his head. "It was."

"Then where is she now?"

"She left," he answered, his tone short and clipped. He hoped his sister would take the hint and let the matter drop. But Eugenie was never one to back down.

Her voice shifted to an accusatory tone. "What did you say to her?"

He sighed. "Why do you automatically assume I said something?"

Eugenie stepped around him, her piercing gaze locking on to his. "Because Elsbeth didn't stay long enough to exchange pleasantries, which means you likely gave her a reason to leave."

"I didn't—" Niles began, but Eugenie's sharp glance cut him off.

Her eyes darted to his hand, and her brow furrowed. "Where did you find your pocket watch?"

He held up the object in question. "Elsbeth found it and returned it to me."

"That was kind of her," Eugenie acknowledged with a nod. "And you thanked her by insulting her, didn't you?"

Niles groaned in frustration. "Must we do this now? I haven't even had breakfast."

Eugenie planted her hands on her hips, her expression unrelenting. "Yes, now. Because I'll keep pestering you until you tell me what happened." Her tone carried the kind of determination he knew all too well.

Realizing there was no escaping her interrogation, he decided to relent. "Fine. I may have suggested that Elsbeth accompany us to our estate... as your companion."

Eugenie swatted his arm. "Are you mad?" she demanded. "Elsbeth is the daughter of an earl, Niles! She does not need an income."

"It was a practical suggestion," he defended weakly, though even to his ears, it sounded absurd.

"Practical?" Eugenie repeated. "Practical for whom? You might as well have told her she was unworthy of her station!"

"That wasn't my intention," Niles protested, though his guilt was growing heavier by the second.

"Intentions mean nothing when your words do the damage," Eugenie retorted. "Do you even understand how insulting that must have sounded to her?"

He rubbed the back of his neck. "I was trying to help her. To keep her safe."

Eugenie shook her head in disbelief. "Safe? Niles, you've likely hurt her more with your thoughtless offer than any danger she's facing at her stepfather's manor."

"I just wanted—" he started, but Eugenie cut him off again.

"I know what you wanted," she said. "But you went about it in the worst way imaginable."

He met his sister's gaze, frustration and regret warring within him. "So what do you suggest I do?"

Eugenie tilted her head. "Fix it, of course. Apologize. Explain yourself. And maybe this time, use that charm everyone seems to think you have."

"All right. I'll make it right."

Eugenie's lips curved into a small smile. "Good. Because Elsbeth deserves better than your clumsy attempts at kindness."

As she turned to leave, he called after her. "And how exactly do I fix this?"

Eugenie glanced over her shoulder. "You're a clever man, Brother. Figure it out."

Left alone in the entry hall, Niles stared down at the pocket watch in his hand. He had made a mess of things, but one thing was certain—he wasn't going to let it end this way. Not with Elsbeth.

Clenching his jaw, he made a decision. Turning towards the butler, who stood quietly near the wall, Niles commanded, "Bring the coach around. Immediately."

"Yes, my lord," the butler replied with a quick bow before hurrying off.

Niles barely had time to turn towards the stairs when a voice from the doorway of the drawing room stopped him in his tracks. "You're doing the right thing."

He turned sharply, startled to see his aunt standing there, a knowing expression on her face.

"How long have you been there?" he asked.

His aunt's smile was faintly apologetic but didn't waver. "Long enough to overhear a few things I probably shouldn't have." She took a step forward. "Do you truly believe Lord Bedford intends Elsbeth harm?"

"I do."

Her smile faded entirely, replaced by a look of quiet resolve. "Then you must do whatever it takes to keep her safe."

"My thoughts exactly," Niles responded.

His aunt's eyes dropped to the pocket watch in his hand, and she tilted her head in mild curiosity. "How exactly did Elsbeth come to find your pocket watch?"

The lie was on his lips before he could think better of it. "She didn't say."

The corners of her mouth twitched with amusement, making it clear she didn't believe him for a second. "Well," she said lightly, "it was very thoughtful of her to return it to you."

"It was," he replied.

His aunt stepped closer, studying him carefully. "You care for her, don't you?"

"I don't want to see her hurt. That's all," he said, the words feeling too shallow, too inadequate. Elsbeth meant something to him, but he didn't quite know what that was at the moment.

His aunt gave him a look that seemed to see right through him. "Be honest with yourself, Niles. Before it's too late."

The weight of her words struck him harder than he cared to admit. Honesty—with himself, with Elsbeth—was a luxury he wasn't sure he could afford. There were so many reasons to keep his distance, so many reasons to guard his heart. But none of them mattered when he thought of her walking away, hurt and vulnerable.

Before he could muster a reply, the butler returned. "The coach is out front, my lord."

Niles didn't need to be told twice. "I need to go."

"Go, then," his aunt encouraged. "And make things right."

With quick strides, he made his way to the door, determination sharpening his every step. He walked outside and the crisp morning air bit at his skin. It was time to act. He would do whatever it took to keep Elsbeth safe.

14

E lsbeth sat in the coach as she wiped away the tear slipping down her cheek. Her chest felt tight with humiliation and frustration, the sting of Niles's offer echoing in her mind. Employment. He had offered her employment. Did he truly think so little of her? Did he believe she had fallen so far? The mortification of it all weighed heavily on her heart.

She clutched her hands in her lap, the reality cutting deeper than she cared to admit. She had allowed herself to care for Niles, and that had been her mistake. Foolish, really, to think he might see her as more than just a friend. But now, for the first time in a long while, Elsbeth realized she deserved more.

The coach came to a stop, and Elsbeth took a deep breath, bracing herself. Exiting onto the gravel path, she straightened her back and walked briskly towards the manor. The butler opened the door promptly, offering a polite bow, and she forced a brief smile in response before stepping inside.

Her resolve wavered as she went to ascend the staircase

towards her bedchamber, but her mother's voice stopped her mid-step.

"Elsbeth," her mother called from the drawing room.

Pausing, Elsbeth turned reluctantly towards the open doorway. "Yes, Mother?"

Her mother's brow creased. "You've been crying," she observed. "What is wrong?"

"It's nothing," she murmured, desperately wanting to be alone.

Her mother crossed the room swiftly and wrapped her arms around her in a comforting embrace. The unexpected warmth undid her. Elsbeth clung to her mother, the tears flowing freely now as the emotion she had tried to contain spilled over.

After a long moment, her mother pulled back, though she kept a gentle hand on Elsbeth's arm. "Come, let's sit down and have some tea. You can tell me what's troubling you."

Elsbeth allowed herself to be led into the drawing room. Her mother poured a cup of tea and handed it to her before sitting across from her. Elsbeth took a sip of the warm liquid, feeling its soothing effect but knowing it could not erase the turmoil inside her.

"Now, tell me," her mother prompted. "Why are you so upset?"

Elsbeth debated her next words. She could choose to deflect, to guard her pain as she so often did, or she could confide in her mother as she used to. Inhaling deeply, she chose trust.

"I went to visit Lady Margaret this morning, and I saw Lord Westcott," she began, her voice trembling slightly. "He... he offered to hire me as Eugenie's companion."

Her mother's sharp intake of breath betrayed her shock. "How insulting," she said, her tone carrying equal parts disbelief and outrage.

Elsbeth nodded, her grip tightening on the delicate teacup.

"It was mortifying. Does he truly think so little of me? I thought we were friends, but..."

Leaning forward, her mother placed a comforting hand over Elsbeth's. "You are an heiress and the daughter of an earl. You can still make a fine match."

Elsbeth averted her gaze. "I don't think so, Mother. Who would want me now?"

Her mother's expression softened with understanding. "My father had a reputation not unlike your father's, and yet I married the second son of an earl. You mustn't lose hope."

"But you became a countess when Uncle Jack passed," Elsbeth pointed out.

Her mother's smile was bittersweet. "There is more to life than titles, my dear."

The candidness of her mother's tone emboldened Elsbeth to ask a question that had lingered in her heart. "Were you happy with Father?"

Her mother hesitated, her gaze distant as if searching the past. "We had our challenges, as all couples do," she said carefully. "But your father... he was a difficult man to love."

"But you did love him?" Elsbeth pressed.

Her mother sighed. "In my own way, yes. But I can't say your father felt the same. He married me for my dowry."

The revelation stunned Elsbeth. "Father was a fortune hunter?"

"I wouldn't call him that, but he was... calculating," her mother admitted. "He had ambitions, and my dowry supported those ambitions."

The room fell silent as Elsbeth absorbed this, her perception of her father shifting slightly. After a moment, she changed the subject. "Charles wants me to return to his estate with him."

Her mother didn't look the least bit surprised by her revelation. "He's spoken to me about it."

"What do you think I should do?"

"I think you should go," her mother said firmly.

"Is this because of Alfred?" Elsbeth asked, her tone edged with suspicion.

Her mother sighed again, her frustration clear. "You have despised Alfred from the moment I married him. He's a decent man and he saved us from financial ruin. Yet you refuse to see his goodness."

"He has secrets, Mother."

"So do we all," her mother countered. "But you've never tried to understand him. You've let your disdain blind you."

Elsbeth's lips pressed into a thin line. "But what if he's like Father? What if he's deceiving us all?"

"Alfred is nothing like your father. Trust me when I say this."

Before Elsbeth could respond, the butler stepped into the room, his demeanor composed. "Lord Westcott has come to call on Lady Elsbeth."

Elsbeth froze, her heart lurching. "Send him away," she instructed.

Her mother raised a hand to halt the butler. "Wait," she said, her gaze on her daughter. "Are you certain you want to do this?"

Elsbeth looked down at her lap, her emotions in turmoil. "I don't want to speak to him."

"I understand that you're hurt," her mother said. "But I would be blind not to notice the growing connection between you two."

Elsbeth's voice was barely a whisper. "He offered me employment, Mother."

"Perhaps it was a misunderstanding."

"You don't accidentally offer to hire someone," Elsbeth muttered.

As Elsbeth turned to instruct the butler to send Lord West-cott away, the infuriating man strode into the room uninvited, his expression a mixture of determination and something softer—something almost pleading.

"I know you don't want to see me, and I don't blame you," Niles began, his voice rushed. "But please, you must hear me out."

Elsbeth's lips pressed into a thin line. "Very well," she said. "Say what you wish to say and then leave."

Niles's gaze met hers and she caught a flicker of vulnerability in his eyes. A stark contrast to his usual air of confidence. Something about him felt... different. "May we take a turn around your gardens?"

"I don't think that is a good idea..." she began, but he interrupted.

"Please, Elsbeth."

His sincerity gave her pause, and though her mind urged her to refuse, her heart betrayed her. "All right," she said, rising from her seat. "But it is cold outside, so I do not wish to lollygag."

Without waiting for his response, she brushed past him, her skirts whispering against the polished floor as she made her way to the entry hall. The butler stood ready with her cloak, which she draped over her shoulders before stepping outside. The brisk morning air greeted her with an icy sting, biting at her cheeks and nose.

Niles followed close behind, his boots crunching softly against the gravel path as they walked towards the gardens. They moved in silence for a time, and the only sound was the occasional rustle of bare branches in the breeze. Finally, Niles clasped his hands behind his back and broke the stillness.

"I wanted to apologize for what I said earlier," he said. "It was wrong of me."

Elsbeth stopped abruptly, turning to face him. "Then why did you say it?"

He exhaled slowly, his breath visible in the chilly air. "I was trying to find a way to help you," he admitted. "In my overzeal-ousness, I failed to think through the repercussions of what I was asking."

Her brow furrowed as she crossed her arms over her chest. "You offered me employment," she said, her tone curt. "Did you not realize how insulting that was?"

Niles had the decency to look ashamed. "I never meant to insult you."

"But you did," she retorted. "You made me feel as though that was all I was worth."

"Heavens, no," he said, his voice rising with urgency. "I wasn't thinking that at all. I only wanted to keep you safe, Elsbeth. That's all. You must believe me."

Her gaze fell to the gravel path. "It doesn't matter, does it?" she murmured. "You're going to leave here one day, and we won't see each other again."

Niles stepped closer, closing the space between them. "I don't accept that."

She lifted her gaze to meet his. "It doesn't matter what you accept. It's the truth. You have a life beyond this village. You're destined for great things, and I... I'll remain here. Perhaps it would be best to accompany Charles to his country estate."

"I don't trust your cousin."

"I know," Elsbeth replied. "And he doesn't trust you either. It seems no one trusts anyone around here."

"Do you trust me?"

A weak smile came to her lips. "I do. You're the only one who believes in me. Everyone else thinks I'm mad for my obses-sion with my stepfather and his secrets."

Niles stepped closer still, forcing her to tilt her head to look up at him. His presence was overwhelming, his nearness igniting a warmth in the frigid air. "I don't think you're mad," he said softly. "I think you're determined. Stubborn. But more importantly, I see you. The real you. The one you keep hidden from the world."

"Niles..."

He spoke over her. "Please forgive me for my thoughtlessness. I don't want to lose you over this."

She studied his face, the rawness in his eyes speaking volumes. He was in earnest, and she couldn't deny the sincerity of his words. "You won't lose me."

"Good," he replied, his voice heavy with emotion. "Because I wasn't ready for you, Elsbeth. But here you are, and somewhere, at some moment, you became my favorite coincidence."

"What are you saying, Niles?"

"I don't rightly know, but I—"

Niles was abruptly cut off by the sound of Charles's booming, irate voice. "I thought I told you to stay away from Lord Westcott!"

Elsbeth spun around to face her cousin, who was storming towards them with a thunderous expression. His fists were clenched at his sides, and his jaw was set as though he were barely containing his anger.

"We were just taking a turn around the gardens," she said.

"Is that what you were doing?" Charles's tone dripped with disbelief. "Because from where I stood, you two looked entirely too familiar with one another."

Elsbeth tilted her chin. "Well, you would be wrong."

Charles came to an abrupt stop directly in front of Niles, his glare unwavering. He pointed a finger at him, his voice sharp. "You will stay away from Elsbeth."

Niles stood his ground. "No," he replied simply. "Lady Elsbeth and I are friends, and that is her decision to make, not yours."

Friends.

The word echoed in Elsbeth's mind. Friends. Why did that

word sting so deeply? Why had she dared to hope that he might see her as more?

Charles stepped closer to Niles. "I should challenge you to a duel."

Niles raised a brow, his voice steady and without a hint of hesitation. "Name the time and place."

"Enough!" Elsbeth snapped. Both men turned to look at her, startled by her outburst.

"There will be no duel," she continued, glaring at both of them. "You're behaving like insolent children, and I refuse to be a part of this. Good day to both of you."

Without waiting for a response, she turned on her heel and marched back towards the manor. She kept her head high, refusing to let either of them see the turmoil churning inside her.

Why had she hoped for something more? Why had she allowed herself to believe, even for a moment, that Niles might care for her as anything beyond a friend? She clenched her fists at her sides, willing herself not to cry.

As she neared the manor, Niles's words lingered in her mind, replaying over and over like a cruel taunt.

Friends. Always just friends.

Niles watched Elsbeth retreat, her figure rigid as she strode away, but not before he had caught the flicker of hurt in her eyes. The sight unsettled him deeply. What had he said to provoke such a reaction? Was it his reference to their relationship as mere friendship? It was, after all, the partial truth. He cared for her—more than he was willing to admit—but he also knew the reality of their situation. Her tarnished reputation would make any future together impossible. And beyond his own feelings, he had to consider Eugenie and the future she deserved.

Lord Bedford's sharp voice sliced through his thoughts. "I told you to stay away from my cousin."

Niles turned, meeting Bedford's piercing gaze. "Is that what *she* wants?"

"No," Bedford admitted, though reluctantly. "But it's what she deserves. You're going to leave eventually, Westcott. Why not do it now?"

"I will leave," Niles replied, his words deliberate. "But not until I know Elsbeth is safe."

"Safe?" Bedford scoffed, his arms folding across his chest. "Safe from what? Or should I say safe from *whom*? Me?"

Before Niles could respond, a loud, sharp crash echoed through the gardens. Both men spun towards the source of the noise, their gazes landing on Elsbeth, sprawled on the ground beside the shattered remains of a large stone planter.

Without hesitation, Niles sprinted towards her, his heart pounding in his chest. He crouched beside her, his eyes frantically scanning her for injuries. "Elsbeth!" he said, his voice edged with panic. "Are you hurt? What happened?"

Her face was pale, her breaths shallow as she pointed upward towards the balcony above them. "I heard a noise... I looked up and saw the planter falling. I couldn't move in time."

Niles's gaze snapped to the remnants of the planter, its jagged edges scattered across the path. A chill swept over him. If it had hit her, she would have been dead.

Bedford arrived a moment later, his expression grim. "This wasn't an accident," he said, his voice tight. "That planter was far too heavy to have simply fallen on its own."

Niles shot him an annoyed glance. "What an astute observation, Bedford. Truly, your talents are wasted."

Elsbeth drew in a shaky breath. "Who would want to kill me?"

"That's what we need to find out," Niles said, his gaze flickering to Bedford. The man appeared genuinely concerned, but was it an act? Niles wasn't prepared to rule anything out.

Bedford extended a hand to Elsbeth. "Let's get you inside."

After a moment's hesitation, she accepted his help, though as soon as she was on her feet, she subtly shifted closer to Niles. Her movement was slight, but it spoke volumes. She was beginning to suspect the same thing he did.

As they entered the manor, the tension was palpable. Niles could feel Elsbeth's fear radiating from her, and it unsettled him in a way he couldn't quite articulate. He needed to protect her, to ensure that whoever was behind this would not succeed in harming her.

Bedford turned to a footman, his voice commanding. "Clean up the mess in the gardens and send for the constable. Immediately."

The footman scurried away, and Niles guided Elsbeth towards the drawing room. Once inside, he helped her to the settee and sat beside her, his protective instinct taking over. "Would you like some tea?" he offered.

"I would," she replied as she moved her trembling hand towards the teapot.

He brushed her hand away. "Allow me."

"Dear heavens, I have never had a gentleman serve me tea before," Elsbeth said lightly, but there was a terseness to her words.

"There is a first time for everything," Niles responded as he poured a cup of tea. He extended her the cup and saucer.

Elsbeth took a sip before saying, "Someone tried to kill me."

"I know," Niles said, his jaw tightening.

She glanced towards the doorway, her voice barely above a whisper. "Do you think it was Charles?"

Niles shook his head. "He and I were arguing when it

happened. His concern seemed genuine. But that doesn't mean he's not involved."

She placed the teacup back on the tray with a trembling hand. "The tea isn't helping."

"It's all right to be upset," he assured her.

Her eyes met his. "Good, because I am *very* upset," she said with an edge of defiance. Then, softer, she added, "I'm glad you're here, Niles."

A faint smile tugged at his lips as he leaned slightly closer. "We'll figure this out," he promised. "Together."

Bedford stepped into the drawing room and cleared his throat. Loudly. "I think you've tended to Lady Elsbeth long enough, Lord Westcott."

If Bedford thought he could intimidate Niles into leaving, he was gravely mistaken. Niles had no intention of leaving Elsbeth's side until he was absolutely certain she was safe.

Before he could respond, Lady Isabella swept into the room. She rushed to Elsbeth's side and knelt beside her on the settee. "Elsbeth!" she exclaimed. "I just heard about the terrible accident."

Niles raised an eyebrow, his sharp gaze flicking to Bedford.

Accident?

Bedford caught his questioning look and gave a subtle shake of his head, silently urging Niles to hold his tongue. The implication was clear: he didn't want Lady Isabella to know that someone had deliberately tried to harm Elsbeth.

Lady Isabella gently wiped the dust from her daughter's cheek. "You poor thing. You should take a warm bath and rest immediately."

"That would be nice," Elsbeth murmured.

Now confident that Elsbeth was in capable hands, Niles rose to his feet and strode over to Bedford. He leaned closer, keeping his voice low. "Accident?"

Bedford shrugged. "I didn't think we should alarm my aunt unnecessarily."

"And what happens when the constable arrives?"

"We'll cross that bridge when we come to it," Bedford replied. "For now, we need to keep a close eye on Elsbeth."

"*We?*"

Bedford gestured towards the entry hall. "Let's talk privately."

Niles reluctantly followed him, spinning on his heel once they were alone. He folded his arms and fixed Bedford with an expectant look. "Well?"

Bedford's expression turned solemn. "I think I know who tried to kill Elsbeth." He paused. "Alfred."

Niles furrowed his brow. "Why do you suspect him?"

"I didn't want to take Elsbeth to my estate just because of her obsession with Alfred's secrets," Bedford admitted. "I wanted to keep her away from him."

"And why would Alfred want her dead?" Niles pressed.

"Because she's asking too many questions," Bedford replied. "Alfred has been investigating my uncle's death."

Niles's gaze sharpened. "You mean the late Lord Bedford?"

Bedford nodded grimly. "Yes. I suspect my uncle was murdered."

Niles exhaled slowly, the weight of the revelation settling over him. "Murdered by Alfred?"

"I don't know," Bedford admitted. "But I do know Alfred paid for the coroner's silence. Why else would he do that?"

"None of this explains why I should trust you," Niles said.

"Whether you trust me or not, we have the same goal—protecting Elsbeth."

Before Niles could respond, Lady Isabella appeared in the doorway. "Lord Westcott, Elsbeth has asked to see you."

Niles nodded and took a step towards the drawing room, only for Bedford to place a hand on his sleeve, halting him.

"Think about what I said," Bedford urged.

"I will," Niles replied before heading into the drawing room. As he entered, his eyes immediately sought out Elsbeth. She was still seated on the settee, but her color had returned, easing some of his worry. He approached her, his voice gentle. "How are you faring?"

Rather than answer his question, she asked one of her own. "What is wrong?"

"Not now."

Her eyes searched his for a moment longer before she gave a reluctant nod. "Very well. But you will tell me?"

"I will," he promised as he moved to sit down next to her on the settee.

Elsbeth lowered her gaze to her lap. "My mother insists I should rest."

"That's a good idea. But have a maid or someone you trust stay with you."

"Do you truly think that's necessary?" she asked, bringing her gaze back up to meet his.

His attempt at a reassuring smile fell short, even to him. "Better safe than sorry. Until we know more."

Lady Isabella approached and extended her hand to her daughter. "Come, my dear. Let's get you comfortable."

Elsbeth rose and Niles stood as well. "I'll call on you later, assuming you have no objections," he said.

"I'd like that," Elsbeth replied.

As they exited the drawing room, Niles walked behind the two women, his focus fixed on Elsbeth's every step. When they reached the base of the stairs, she paused and turned back to face him.

"Thank you, Lord Westcott," she said. "For everything."

He bowed. "Enjoy your rest, my lady."

She gave him a weak smile, but the sadness in her eyes struck him like a blow. What he wouldn't give to remain by her side, ensuring her safety, offering her the comfort she so clearly needed.

The soft shuffle of boots drew his attention, and he turned to find Bedford stepping closer. "I'll send word when the constable arrives."

"Thank you," Niles replied.

He started to leave, but Bedford's voice stopped him midstep. "Alfred was supposedly in his study when the planter fell."

Niles turned back, his expression hardening. "Supposedly?"

Bedford's gaze flicked towards the direction of Alfred's study. "That's what he claims. He said he was reviewing shipping manifests."

"That is rather convenient," Niles remarked. "Was anyone with him to corroborate his story?"

"No," Bedford admitted. "And that's what troubles me."

Niles was still unsure. "But why would he try to harm Elsbeth? What could he possibly gain?"

"I told you, Alfred's been digging into my uncle's death. If he thinks Elsbeth knows something or might uncover the truth, it could be reason enough."

Niles clenched his jaw. The idea of someone so close to Elsbeth harboring such dark intentions was intolerable. "We need proof."

"Agreed," Bedford said. "But for now, we need to keep Elsbeth out of harm's way."

"That is something we both can agree on."

The two men stood in tense silence for a moment, their shared goal uniting them despite the animosity that still simmered beneath the surface. There was much to unravel, and time was not on their side.

Could he even trust Bedford?

15

E lsbeth sat quietly, her arm resting on the edge of her chair, as Clara deftly removed the stitches from her wound. Her thoughts, however, were far from the present moment. Someone had deliberately tried to kill her that morning. There was no denying it now. The planter had not simply fallen by accident. It had been purposefully dropped, with the clear intent to harm her.

She struggled to process the realization. Could Charles truly be behind such a heinous act? She wanted to trust him, wanted to believe he wasn't capable of such treachery. His reaction after the incident had seemed genuine enough, but was it all an act? The cold, hard truth lingered in her mind: if she died, her substantial dowry would revert to the estate, providing Charles with the funds he desperately needed.

The weight of suspicion pressed down on her chest. The only person she could trust completely was Niles, but even that trust brought its own complications. How could he possibly keep her safe when he wasn't residing in the manor?

Clara's voice pulled her from her spiraling thoughts. "That should do it," the lady's maid said with a satisfied nod as she finished. "Now, do try to avoid getting shot again, if you please."

Elsbeth let out a soft, humorless laugh. "I will do my best."

Clara immediately looked contrite. "I shouldn't joke about such things. Not with everything that's happened."

"There's no need to apologize," Elsbeth assured her. "If anything, I welcome the distraction from my thoughts."

Clara studied her with concern. "How are you faring? Truly?"

Elsbeth hesitated before replying, "I am... managing. To be honest, I don't know what to feel or who to trust in this household."

"Well," Clara said with a small smile, "you can trust me."

"And for that, I am eternally grateful," Elsbeth replied sincerely.

Clara's gaze swept over her. "Now, we need to fix your hair. Your mother would be rather upset if you came down to dinner looking less than perfect."

Recognizing the truth in her maid's words, Elsbeth moved to sit before the dressing table. Clara began removing the pins from her hair, brushing it through before gathering it up into an elegant style. She left two soft curls to frame Elsbeth's face, giving her a look of composed grace.

Just as Clara was finishing, a knock came at the door. Clara crossed the room to open it, revealing Charles standing in the corridor.

"Cousin," Elsbeth greeted, forcing a polite smile as she rose from her seat.

Charles stepped into the doorway but did not enter the room. "I came to escort you down to dinner."

"How thoughtful," Elsbeth murmured, her voice tight.

As they walked down the corridor together, Elsbeth clasped her hands in front of her to steady herself. She hated the unease she felt around her cousin, hated how suspicion had crept into her mind and taken root. But how could she ignore her fears? He had taken a shot at her—accidental, he claimed —and possibly poisoned her. Or was she overthinking everything?

Charles broke the silence. "I know you don't entirely trust me, but I promise you, Elsbeth, I would never hurt you."

She kept her gaze forward, saying nothing. She didn't know what to believe anymore.

He continued. "While you were resting, I spoke with the constable. He's been made aware of the circumstances."

"You didn't think to wake me?" she asked, irritation creeping into her voice.

"There was no need," Charles replied evenly. "I was there, and I provided him with all the necessary information. Besides, I didn't want to alarm the household, especially your mother."

She bit back her retort, knowing he had a point. There was no sense in upsetting her mother unnecessarily, not without more concrete information. Still, the fact that Charles had made the decision without consulting her bothered her greatly. "I would have preferred to speak with the constable myself," she said.

"I didn't mean to offend you," Charles responded. "Of course you're more than capable of speaking on your own behalf."

"Indeed, I am," she replied, tilting her chin slightly.

They continued down the corridor in silence. Elsbeth saw no reason to fill the space with meaningless words. Her thoughts were already too loud, and the questions swirling in her mind refused to be silenced.

As they reached the entry hall, Charles paused and turned, his expression solemn. "Let's forget about the soiree. We can leave tomorrow morning for my estate."

She took a deliberate step back, creating space between them. "No. My mother would be furious if I left so abruptly."

"I know," Charles admitted. "But I'd feel much better if you were far away from this place, this village... from Alfred."

Her brows furrowed as she studied his face, searching for the meaning behind his words. "Why Alfred?"

His gaze locked on to hers, the urgency in his eyes unmistakable. "I used to think highly of Alfred. I truly did. But recent events have made me question if I ever knew him at all." He stepped closer, his voice dropping to a whisper. "He's been looking into the death of your father."

"I suspected as much from the newssheet clippings that I found in Alfred's desk."

Charles frowned. "That was reckless, Elsbeth. Foolish, even. What if you had been caught?"

Her back went rigid. "Are you truly lecturing me right now?"

Charles glanced over his shoulder, ensuring the corridor was still empty, then turned back to her. "I'm not lecturing you. I'm worried about you."

His words sounded so sincere, so genuine, but the shadow of fear kept her from fully trusting him. Before she could respond, Alfred's voice echoed from down the corridor, his words light.

"Why the long faces?" he asked with a polite smile as he approached.

Charles quickly stepped closer to Elsbeth, as though shielding her. "Good evening, Alfred."

The butler appeared and handed Alfred his top hat and cane. Alfred placed the hat on his head with practiced ease. "You'll have to excuse me," he said. "There's some business I must attend to in the village."

"Mother will not be pleased that you're missing dinner," Elsbeth remarked.

Alfred chuckled lightly. "That she won't. But business is business."

The moment the door closed, Elsbeth turned to Charles, her voice a low murmur. "We should follow him. See who he's meeting with this time."

"No," Charles responded. "It would raise too much suspicion if we were caught."

"Then we won't get caught," Elsbeth countered.

Charles crossed his arms, his expression resolute. "I have a better idea. While he's gone, I'll search his study."

She shook her head. "That's a waste of time. I've searched his study more times than I care to admit, and the only thing I found were those newssheet clippings."

"Then why do you think Alfred is looking into your father's death?" Charles pressed.

"I don't know," she admitted. "But if he's hiding something, it must be important."

Charles's eyes grew distant, as though he were replaying old memories. "I've always thought the circumstances surrounding your father's death were rather suspicious."

"But the coroner ruled it an accident," Elsbeth pointed out, though the doubt in her voice was evident.

Charles's jaw tightened. "It just seemed too convenient," he said slowly. "That your father would meet his end by being run down by a coach. It never sat right with me."

A heavy silence followed his words. Elsbeth's mind raced, her suspicions growing sharper. She finally broke the silence. "Do you think Alfred had something to do with my father's death?"

Charles sighed deeply, his expression heavy with reluctance. "I don't know for certain, but I do know he paid the coroner to keep quiet. Why would he go to such lengths if he had nothing to hide?"

The weight of his words pressed down on her, but before she could respond, the ringing of the dinner bell echoed through the manor.

As they turned towards the source of the sound, Elsbeth's mother appeared at the top of the grand staircase. Her elegant figure was poised as always, but Elsbeth noticed something different. Her mother's eyes seemed tired, their usual sparkle dimmed, and her steps, though graceful, lacked their usual energy.

Descending the stairs, her mother spoke. "I've just been informed that Alfred will not be joining us for dinner. Shall we adjourn to the dining room?"

Charles stepped forward immediately, offering his arm with a respectful bow. "Allow me to escort you, Aunt Isabella."

"Thank you, Charles," her mother said with a faint smile, accepting his arm.

Together, they walked towards the dining room in a silence that felt heavier than usual. Elsbeth followed behind, her thoughts still swirling with doubt and unease.

When they reached the dining room, the footmen stood ready to serve. Everyone took their seats as the footmen placed bowls of rich soup in front of them.

Elsbeth picked up her spoon and took a sip. The warmth of the soup did little to ease the chill settling in her chest.

Her mother broke the silence, her voice bright but carrying an edge of forced cheer. "The soiree is just two days away," she said, looking across the table at Elsbeth. "I was hoping you might play a piece on the pianoforte for our guests."

Elsbeth glanced up from her bowl. "Of course, Mother. I'd be happy to."

Her mother looked pleased by her response. "Thank you, Dear. I know everyone will enjoy it."

Charles remained silent, his expression unreadable as he spooned his soup. Elsbeth tried to focus on the simple act of eating, but her mind drifted back to her father, to Alfred, to the questions that seemed to grow louder with every passing moment.

Across the table, Charles placed his spoon down and wiped his mouth with a white linen napkin. "Would you care to go riding tomorrow, Elsbeth?"

Before she could respond, her mother interjected. "I do not think that is a wise decision, considering Elsbeth is still recovering from her last fall."

"I think I would be fine," Elsbeth countered. "I've missed my morning rides, and the fresh air would do me good."

Her mother's skeptical gaze lingered on her, the lines of worry deepening around her eyes. "And what if you fall again?" she asked pointedly.

"I won't," Elsbeth said quickly. "I'll be cautious, I promise."

Her mother's expression softened slightly. "You always promise to be cautious, and yet trouble seems to follow you."

Charles chuckled softly, but his humor didn't reach his eyes. "I'll ensure she doesn't get into any trouble," he offered.

"I appreciate that, Charles," her mother said. "Just don't stay out too long. We have much to do to prepare for the soiree."

"Of course," Charles replied, his polite smile unchanging.

Elsbeth looked between the two of them, her frustration bubbling just below the surface. She felt like a child being managed rather than a woman capable of making her own decisions. "Thank you for your concern, Mother, but I will be fine. I do not need a nursemaid following me about."

Her mother gave a reluctant nod. "Point taken, but please, do be careful."

"I will," Elsbeth promised.

Charles met her gaze briefly, and she wondered what his true intentions were. Was he offering to ride with her as an act of protection or something more? Regardless, she would need to remain vigilant.

The rest of the meal passed in polite conversation, but Elsbeth's thoughts remained distant. Tomorrow would bring answers—or so she hoped.

With shafts of the morning sunlight filtering through the curtains, Niles paced the length of the drawing room, his boots tapping against the polished floor. His thoughts were a whirlwind, all circling the same point: Elsbeth. He was worried, deeply so, and the hours seemed to drag unbearably as he waited for a respectable time to call upon her. The gnawing need to see her, to confirm she was safe, consumed him entirely, leaving no room for rational thought.

Eugenie's voice broke through his turbulent musings. "Will you kindly stop pacing?" she asked, her tone carrying a playful edge. "You're making me anxious just watching you."

Niles halted abruptly and turned to face his sister, who sat perched on the settee, a book resting in her lap. "I'm sorry. I was just—"

"I know what you're doing," Eugenie interrupted, a knowing smile curving her lips. "You're waiting for the appropriate hour to call upon Elsbeth. But at this rate, you'll wear a path into the carpet."

His brows knitted in surprise. "And how could you possibly know that?"

Her smug expression deepened. "Brother, you're many things, but subtle is not one of them. It's written all over your face. You care for Elsbeth."

For a moment, he considered denying it, brushing her observation aside. But what purpose would that serve? He had spent too long denying his feelings already. "I do care for her," he admitted, sinking into the chair opposite her. "But there can be no future for us."

Eugenie arched an eyebrow. "And why, pray tell, is that?"

He sighed, leaning forward to rest his elbows on his knees. "It revolves around the scandal surrounding her family. It could jeopardize your chances of making an advantageous match. I have a duty to protect your prospects, and I cannot risk tainting our name."

"So you would sacrifice your own happiness for me?"

"It's not about me," Niles said. "It's about what Father would have wanted. He entrusted me with your future, and I won't fail him."

Eugenie huffed in exasperation, placing her book beside her. "Father would have told you to follow your heart. To marry for love, just as he did with Mother."

Niles straightened, growing defensive. "I said nothing about love."

Her smirk returned, maddeningly knowing. "You didn't have to."

His pulse quickened. "I do not love Elsbeth," he insisted, though his voice lacked conviction. He couldn't. Not now. They hadn't known each other long enough, and yet... in his heart, he knew he was more than halfway there. And that was the problem.

Eugenie leaned back in her seat. "What if I choose not to marry at all? Wouldn't that make your sacrifice entirely pointless?"

"Regardless of what you choose, I cannot risk bringing scandal to our name by marrying Elsbeth."

Eugenie's teasing demeanor faded. "Then you don't love her enough," she said. "Because if you did, you'd move heaven and earth to be with her."

His jaw tightened. "It's not that simple."

"It is," Eugenie countered. "But that's not for me to decide. Only you can."

"Eugenie—"

She held up a hand, silencing him with an elegant wave. "And don't tell me you're doing this for me. I'll be fine, Niles, whatever you decide. I think our family could weather a little scandal, especially if it meant your happiness."

"I'm sorry, but I will not yield on this. I can't."

"Then you do not deserve Elsbeth."

Niles turned his attention towards the window. He was bound by duty and responsibility, and he couldn't risk getting distracted by something so trivial and unpredictable as love.

The long clock in the corner chimed and Eugenie spoke up. "Why don't you go on a ride before you call upon Elsbeth? It might clear your head."

He turned, tugging at the cuffs of his sleeves. "I think I shall."

As he reached the door, Eugenie's voice stopped him. "Just so you are aware, you came alive again when you met Elsbeth."

He turned back, her words striking a chord he didn't want to acknowledge. "I know you mean well but I must think of our future. I cannot—no, I *will* not—allow myself to be distracted."

Eugenie offered a weak smile, but her disappointment was palpable. "Very well. I won't say anything more on the subject."

"Thank you," he said, already moving to leave, eager to escape the conversation that had begun to chip away at the walls he had carefully built around his heart.

"However..." Eugenie's voice stopped him mid-step.

He sighed, bracing himself before turning to face her. "What now?"

"I will say this—you deserve more than a marriage of convenience. You deserve love. Real love. And I want you to be happy. Truly happy."

"I thought you said you wouldn't say anything more on the subject."

She grinned, unabashed. "Now I am done. The lecture is officially over."

A wry smile tugged at his lips. "You are relentless."

"I am your sister," she quipped. "It is my duty."

The faint humor in her voice did little to ease the tension that consumed him. "I am unlikely to ever find what Mother and Father had," he said. "And even if I did, am I worthy of such a love?"

"Of course you are. You are more than worthy. But you have to believe that, too."

Her words struck something deep within him, and for a moment, he wanted to push back, to deny it all. But the sincerity in her voice left no room for argument. "I don't know what I believe," he admitted.

Eugenie's eyes held compassion. "And herein lies the problem, Brother." She picked up her book. "Now, go. I need to finish this chapter."

Her words hung in the air as she returned to reading as though their conversation hadn't just unraveled the tightly wound threads of resolve. He lingered for a moment longer, her words echoing in his mind before he finally turned and left the room.

A short time later, Niles was astride his horse, the brisk morning air biting against his face as he rode through the countryside. The fields were shrouded in a delicate haze, the faint white mist clinging to the ground. He urged his horse faster, seeking solace in the speed and the rhythmic pounding of hooves.

If only his father were still alive. This wasn't the first time he had wished for it. He longed for the wisdom and guidance that had once been a constant in his life. His father would have known precisely what to say, and how to navigate this tumultuous path. But his father was gone, and the burden of making the right choices fell squarely on his shoulders.

He couldn't afford a misstep. Not for Eugenie, whose future depended on him, and not for himself. Love was a distraction, an indulgence he couldn't afford. Not when so much was at stake. And yet, the ache in his chest whenever he thought of

Elsbeth refused to be ignored. She had changed something in him, unearthed a yearning for something more, something he couldn't quite name.

Why had he let her into his life, into his thoughts, into his heart? He should have been stronger, more disciplined.

In the distance, movement caught his eyes. Two riders were approaching, their figures becoming clearer as he closed the distance. One of them was unmistakable—Elsbeth, her dark blue riding habit a striking contrast against the pale morning light. Her dark hair was neatly tucked beneath her riding hat, and she sat tall and poised on her horse.

The second rider was Lord Bedford. Niles's jaw tightened. What was she doing with him? Despite the uneasy truce they had struck, Niles didn't entirely trust the man, and he doubted he ever would.

Urging his horse forward, he quickly caught up to them. Elsbeth turned her head, her expression shifting from surprise to something warmer. "Niles," she greeted, her voice holding a note of unexpected pleasure. "What are you doing up at this hour?"

"I am an early riser," he replied, though his gaze flicked to Lord Bedford. "Bedford."

"Westcott," he replied with a tip of his head.

Niles fell into pace beside them. "And what brings you both out so early?"

Elsbeth glanced between the two men, her smile faltering just slightly. "Charles invited me for a morning ride."

"Indeed," Bedford added. "A breath of fresh air does wonders for the nerves."

Niles's eyes narrowed, but he masked his suspicion with a polite nod. "Fresh air is good for many things." He looked to Elsbeth. "I trust you're taking care to avoid any... accidents."

Her smile faded. "Yes, of course."

Bedford's lips pressed into a thin, white line, his displeasure laid bare. "You worry too much, Westcott. Elsbeth is perfectly safe with me."

Niles didn't reply immediately, his gaze lingering on Bedford. He was too calm. Too collected. "I'm sure she is," he said finally, though his voice betrayed his lingering concern. "Perhaps I will join you both for the remainder of your ride. After all, the countryside is best enjoyed in good company."

"If you insist," Bedford said, his words curt.

Elsbeth glanced at Niles, a flicker of something unreadable in her eyes. Relief? Unease? Perhaps both. "It is a beautiful morning, is it not?"

Niles inclined his head. "It is," he agreed before he shifted his gaze back to Bedford. "I received word you spoke with the constable. Was anything decided?"

"Not precisely," Bedford admitted. "The constable was hesitant to label the incident as anything more than an unfortunate accident."

"You didn't tell me that," Elsbeth said, her grip tightening on the reins.

Bedford turned towards her. "I didn't want to upset you unnecessarily."

Elsbeth's back grew rigid. "I don't need to be coddled, Cousin. I have the right to know what's happening, especially when my life is involved."

Bedford offered a stiff nod. "You're right, of course. I should have told you."

"So, what now?" Elsbeth demanded, her voice tinged with frustration. "We just sit and wait for Alfred to make another attempt on my life?"

"We don't know for certain it was Alfred," Niles remarked.

Elsbeth turned to him, her expression incredulous. "Who else could it be?"

Niles flicked a glance at Bedford, considering an unspoken

possibility, but he kept the thought to himself. "It's too soon to make assumptions."

Elsbeth wasn't convinced. "I should confront Alfred directly," she said. "Ask him what he knows about my father's death."

"Absolutely not!" Niles exclaimed.

Elsbeth's chin lifted defiantly. "It's the only plausible solution. He knows something. We can't keep playing this waiting game, hoping for answers to fall into our laps."

Bedford shook his head vehemently. "I have to agree with Westcott on this. If Alfred was truly behind the attempt on your life, what makes you think he won't try again?"

Her lips thinned, but her determination didn't waver. "Then what's your plan? Do nothing? Let Alfred win?"

Niles hated to admit it, but she had a point. Their cautious approach wasn't working. They needed something bolder. "If you did speak to Alfred..." he began cautiously.

"*What*?!" Bedford cut in, his voice rising with disbelief.

Niles held up a hand to forestall further protests. "If Elsbeth insists on speaking with him, then you and I will be stationed outside the door the entire time. The moment Alfred tries anything, we'll intervene."

"I can agree to that," Elsbeth said.

Bedford, however, was less than pleased. He muttered under his breath, "This is madness."

Niles met his gaze. "Together, we can keep Elsbeth safe."

Bedford looked as though he wanted to argue further, but he let out a resigned sigh. "Fine. But the moment something feels off, I'm ending it."

"Agreed," Niles said.

This was a risky plan, but it was better than doing nothing.

16

With a purposeful stride, Elsbeth left the stables, her boots crunching against the gravel path as she headed towards the manor. The crisp morning air carried the scent of damp earth and pine, but she barely noticed it. Her mind was fixed on one thing: speaking to Alfred and uncovering the truth about her father's death.

But what if he was involved?

The thought tightened her chest, but she refused to waver. She had spent too long standing idle, waiting for answers that would never come on their own. If she was to find the truth, she had to seize it, even if it meant putting herself in harm's way.

As she reached the back entrance, she felt a firm yet gentle grip on her arm. Turning swiftly, she found herself face-to-face with Niles.

"Are you sure you want to do this?" he asked, concern etched on his features.

Elsbeth straightened her shoulders. "I do," she replied. "I need to know the truth."

His hand lingered for a moment before dropping to his side.

"Be careful," he urged. "I don't know what I would do if something happened to you."

Her lips parted, a reply hovering on the tip of her tongue. But before she could speak, Charles appeared beside them, his expression solemn.

"This is a terrible idea," Charles said, his voice clipped. "You're walking into a lion's den without even knowing if there's a lion inside."

"I need to do something, Cousin," Elsbeth retorted.

"I agree that action is necessary, but this is not the way," he insisted, his gaze darting towards Niles as if seeking an ally.

Elsbeth placed a hand on Charles's sleeve. "You must trust me. Besides, you and Niles will be right outside the door, ensuring I'm safe."

Charles's frown deepened as he turned his gaze to Niles. "You seem awfully familiar with Lord Westcott, calling him by his given name so freely."

Niles offered a faint smile. "I gave her leave to do so."

"That doesn't make it right," Charles muttered, shaking his head.

Elsbeth's voice grew determined. "I will be fine, Charles. You'll see."

"And if Alfred is behind the attempt on your life, as I suspect he is?" Charles pressed.

"Then you and Niles will keep me safe," she stated, her tone leaving no room for argument. "Shall we?"

A footman stepped forward and opened the door, and Elsbeth walked inside without hesitation, though her heart was pounding. Her steps echoed in the quiet corridors as she made her way to Alfred's study, each one a mixture of courage and fear.

Reaching the door, she peered inside and saw Alfred hunched over his desk, sifting through a stack of ledgers.

Elsbeth glanced back at Niles and nodded. She knocked lightly before stepping inside, leaving the door slightly ajar.

Alfred looked up from his work, a smile spreading across his face. "Good morning, Elsbeth," he greeted, his tone warm but tinged with something she couldn't quite place. "To what do I owe the pleasure?"

She forced a smile in return. "I was hoping to speak with you for a moment."

"Please, sit," he said, gesturing to the chair opposite his desk.

Elsbeth perched on the edge of the chair, her hands clasped tightly in her lap. She inhaled deeply, steadying her nerves. She could do this. She *had* to do this.

But before she could speak, Alfred rose and crossed the room, closing the door with an ominous click.

Her breath caught in her throat. She hadn't expected that. Now Niles and Charles wouldn't hear if something went wrong.

Returning to his desk, Alfred folded his hands and studied her with an unreadable expression. "Now, what is it you wish to discuss?"

Her mind wavered, caught between caution and determination. "I... I was wondering..." she began, faltering under the weight of his gaze.

"You can be honest with me, Elsbeth," Alfred encouraged.

The irony of his words almost made her laugh. Summoning her courage, she met his gaze. "I was wondering what you know about my father's death."

The smile faded from Alfred's face, replaced by a guarded expression. "And why, may I ask, are you curious about that?"

Her heart raced as she scrambled for a plausible response. "I've been thinking about him lately," she said, her voice steady despite the lie. "That's all."

"You shouldn't be asking such questions," Alfred replied, his tone carrying a subtle edge.

"Why not?" she challenged, her tone firmer now.

Alfred leaned back in his chair, studying her with an intensity that sent a shiver down her spine. "Your father's death was an unfortunate accident, nothing more."

"Is that what you believe?" she pressed, unwilling to let him dismiss her so easily.

"It doesn't matter what I believe," Alfred said. "It's what the coroner concluded."

Elsbeth's resolve wavered for a moment, but she refused to back down. "Sometimes coroners are wrong."

Alfred's eyes narrowed, his calm demeanor fracturing just slightly. "Be careful, Elsbeth. Curiosity can be a dangerous thing."

Her pulse quickened at his words, but she held his gaze, refusing to let him see her fear. "So can secrets."

Alfred studied her before finally breaking the silence. "Your father kept many secrets, secrets that nearly destroyed your family."

She shifted uncomfortably in her chair. "I am painfully aware of that fact."

"It would be best," Alfred continued, "if you let things lie as they are. It is much safer for you and for everyone if you stop asking questions."

"Safer for me?" she repeated, her voice laced with suspicion. "Why would my safety be at risk simply for asking questions?"

"You must trust me on this," Alfred replied.

A humorless laugh escaped her lips. "Trust you?" she echoed. "You cannot seriously expect me to do that."

His features softened, or perhaps they feigned softness, as if he were genuinely concerned. "I only want what is best for you and your mother," he offered.

Elsbeth felt a surge of anger rising within her, her hands tightening into fists on her lap. "Please don't insult my intelligence by pretending you care about me," she said, her words biting.

He blinked, clearly taken aback, though whether by her words or the truth of them, she couldn't tell. "Of course I care for you. You are my—" he hesitated before finishing awkwardly, "stepdaughter."

Her lips twitched with the urge to roll her eyes. The word sounded forced, as if it didn't sit comfortably in his mouth.

"I know we got off on the wrong foot," he started. "But I had hoped we might forge a cordial relationship, if not something more."

Her anger flared again, and she leaned forward, her voice trembling with restrained emotion. "You mean because you married my mother mere days after the mourning period for my father was over?"

Alfred's sigh was heavy, his shoulders sagging slightly. "We waited until the appropriate time for mourning."

"And what of the scandal it caused?" Elsbeth countered. "You think that was appropriate?"

Alfred arched a brow. "I daresay the scandal pales in comparison to what your father's secrets unleashed upon your family."

Her back went rigid. "Perhaps," she admitted, "but marrying my mother didn't improve anything. If anything, it only fanned the flames of gossip and judgment."

Alfred leaned back in his chair, his expression unreadable again. "I am merely a merchant, Elsbeth," he said, his tone quieter now. "But I do love your mother. You must believe that."

She regarded him with a mix of skepticism and weariness. "I don't know what to believe anymore," she admitted.

He rubbed his temple as if her words had struck a nerve. "I know what your mother sacrificed to be with me," he remarked. "And I pray every day that the good in our union outweighs the bad."

Elsbeth's chest tightened at his words. Was he being genuine? Or was this another carefully constructed act?

"You speak of love and sacrifice," she said slowly. "But what does that mean when shrouded in secrecy?"

Alfred's jaw tightened for a fraction of a second, a crack in his otherwise composed demeanor. "Some truths," he said carefully, "are more dangerous than lies."

A sharp knock echoed through the room, interrupting their conversation.

"Enter," Alfred ordered, his eyes locked firmly on hers, as if daring her to look away.

The door creaked open, and Charles stepped inside, his gaze immediately finding Elsbeth. "I came to inform Elsbeth that breakfast is ready to be served," he said.

Breakfast?

Was that the best excuse Charles could come up with?

Elsbeth rose gracefully from her chair, masking her irritation with a polite smile. "I do enjoy a good breakfast," she said. "Thank you for informing me."

Alfred stood as well, buttoning his waistcoat with measured movements. "Please inform your mother that I will be skipping breakfast this morning. I have pressing matters to attend to," he said, gesturing towards the desk.

Elsbeth tipped her head in acknowledgment. "Very well."

Alfred held her gaze as he added, "And Elsbeth... remember what we discussed."

"I won't forget," she replied.

"Good," he said curtly before retaking his seat and flipping open the ledger, his focus shifting as if dismissing her entirely.

As she stepped out of the study, she caught both Niles's and Charles's questioning gazes. Pressing a finger to her lips, she gestured towards the nearby parlor, her steps purposeful yet silent.

Once inside the parlor, she closed the door behind them

with deliberate care and turned to face the two men. "Alfred knows more about my father's death than he's letting on," she announced.

"What did he say?" Charles asked.

Elsbeth let out a groan. "Nothing substantial. He cautioned me to stop asking questions, but he didn't reveal anything useful."

Niles stepped closer, his concern evident in the way his eyes searched hers. "Did he threaten you?"

"Not directly. He only said he hopes we can have a 'cordial relationship,'" she replied.

Charles scoffed. "That is not likely to happen. He's more focused on keeping his secrets than forming any semblance of a family bond."

"We can't keep tiptoeing around this," Niles said. "The more he feels cornered, the more dangerous he might become."

"I understand the risk," she responded. "But I also can't stop now. If Alfred knows something about my father's death, I need to uncover the truth—no matter the cost."

Charles gave her an exasperated look. "And what happens if that cost is your life, Cousin?"

Her eyes flickered between Charles and Niles, her determination unshaken. "Then it's a price I'm willing to pay," she responded.

Both men exchanged a look, one filled with shared concern and frustration.

Niles broke the silence. "If we're going to proceed, we'll need a better plan. Furthermore, we will need to ensure you're never alone with Alfred again."

Elsbeth didn't argue, but her thoughts swirled with doubt and the relentless need for answers. Whatever Alfred was hiding, she would uncover it. She owed her father—and herself—that much.

Niles sat beside Elsbeth at the long, rectangular dining table, attempting to ignore the irritated glances that Bedford kept throwing his way. Despite the tension, his attention was drawn to Elsbeth. She sat silently, absentmindedly moving her food around with her fork, her brow slightly furrowed in thought.

Leaning closer, he lowered his voice so only she could hear. "Are you not hungry?"

Elsbeth placed her fork down and let out a soft sigh. "I will admit that I am not," she replied. "I suppose I can't stop thinking about my conversation with my stepfather."

Before Niles could press further, her mother's voice interrupted. "A word, Elsbeth," Lady Isabella said.

"Of course," Elsbeth replied, rising from her seat.

Niles immediately stood as well and offered his hand, a gesture that earned him a fleeting but appreciative smile from Elsbeth before she followed her mother out of the room.

As Niles returned to his seat, Bedford wasted no time, his words sharp. "Do you not have a home, Westcott?"

"I do," Niles replied, meeting Bedford's gaze with calm resolve. "But I think it's best if I remain here for Elsbeth's sake."

Bedford arched an eyebrow, his expression one of thinly veiled disdain. "And why, pray tell, is that necessary?"

"To ensure her safety," Niles said simply.

Bedford leaned back in his chair, his arms crossed over his chest. "I am more than capable of handling that myself."

Niles didn't miss the challenge in Bedford's tone. "Do you object to my presence here?"

"I do," Bedford replied. "I thought that much was obvious."

Niles allowed a small, knowing smile. "Then it seems I'm exactly where I should be."

Bedford's eyes narrowed. "Why do you care so much, West-cott? Elsbeth means nothing to you."

"That's not true," Niles shot back. "We're friends."

"Is that why you agreed to help her?" Bedford demanded, his tone mocking.

"At first," Niles admitted, leaning back slightly, "I agreed because I was intrigued."

Bedford scoffed. "Intrigued? So Elsbeth is nothing more than a diversion to you? Someone to occupy your time?"

"No, that's not—" Niles began, but his words faltered when a familiar voice came from the doorway.

"What would you say then, Lord Westcott?" Elsbeth demanded, her arms crossed tightly over her chest as she stepped into the room, her eyes blazing with anger.

Niles shot to his feet. "Elsbeth, please—"

"Save your breath," she cut him off. "I heard what you said. Do you even care about me at all, or am I just here to stave off your boredom?"

He took a tentative step towards her, his heart sinking as she took a step back. "Please, let me explain."

"I don't think anything you say will change what I heard," she replied, her voice cracking slightly despite her composed demeanor.

Before he could respond, Elsbeth spun on her heel and stormed out of the room, leaving an uneasy silence in her wake.

Bedford chuckled dryly from his seat. "Well done, Westcott. Let's see how you manage to talk your way out of this one."

Niles shot him a glare. "You're an arse," he muttered before hurrying after Elsbeth.

He followed her through the corridor and out onto the veranda, his boots echoing against the stone. Elsbeth was standing at the edge, her back to him, her hands gripping the iron railing as if it were the only thing grounding her.

"Elsbeth," he said softly.

She didn't turn around. "What do you want, Niles?"

"I want a chance to explain," he said, his tone earnest as he stepped closer.

Finally, she turned to face him, her eyes defiant. "I heard you. You find me 'intriguing', and I'm just here to amuse you."

He sighed, his heart aching at the hurt in her voice. "I do find you intriguing, Elsbeth. That much is true. How could I not? You're unlike anyone I've ever met." He paused, searching for the right words. "At first, I was curious—fascinated, even. You were a highwaywoman, after all."

"And that's the only reason you agreed to help me?" she challenged, her voice rising slightly.

"No," he said firmly, his gaze holding hers. "There were many reasons. One of them was to ensure you didn't get yourself killed."

"So, it was just a matter of honor for you?" she pressed.

"Perhaps at first," Niles admitted. "But things have changed between us. You can't deny that, can you?"

She looked away. "I don't know what to believe."

He stepped closer, closing the distance between them, and was pleased when she didn't move away. "You are stubborn. Maddening. Vexing..."

Her brow arched. "Is there a point to this?"

A grin tugged at his lips despite the tension between them. "Yes, there is a point," he replied. "You are all those things, Elsbeth. But you are also so much more. You have brought me to life in ways I didn't realize I needed. You've reminded me there's more to living than managing accounts and fulfilling duties. I can't stop thinking about you."

Her eyes searched his, uncertainty and hope mingling in her expression. "What are you saying, Niles?"

He took a steadying breath, his gaze never leaving hers. "I'm saying that no matter what happens—no matter where this leads—it's been worth it. Being with you, caring for you, has been worth everything."

Her lips trembled, and her voice cracked as she said, "It sounds like you're saying goodbye."

The words struck him, and he reached for her hand, holding it gently as though she might pull away at any moment. "I'm not leaving, Elsbeth. Not until I know you're safe. No matter how long that takes, I'll stay."

"But you *will* leave," she said, slipping her hand out of his grasp. Her tone was soft, but the pain in her voice cut through him.

He frowned. "I have responsibilities at my estate and the House of Lords in London. I never planned on staying here." He hesitated, his voice lowering. "I also never planned on meeting you."

She pressed her lips together. "I understand."

"Do you?" he asked gently, his voice tinged with regret. "Because I don't think I understand myself. Elsbeth, I care for you more than I should. More than I ever thought possible. You have made me a better man simply because you came into my life."

Her gaze dropped to the ground. "You are kind, Niles."

Niles reached out, his fingers brushing against her chin. Slowly, he tilted her face upward, forcing her to meet his gaze. "Your eyes," he murmured. "They are like windows to your soul, and I can't stop looking into them. Do you know why? Because what I see there is so very beautiful."

Lord Bedford's voice rang out from behind them, tinged with unmistakable amusement. "Oh, please say I'm interrupting something."

Niles let out an exasperated sigh, dropping his hand from Elsbeth's chin and taking a deliberate step back. "What do you want, Bedford?" he grumbled, turning to face him.

Bedford's lips curved into a self-satisfied smirk. "My aunt

requested that I ensure the two of you were properly chaperoned. She seemed rather concerned."

"Wonderful," Niles muttered under his breath.

Completely unbothered by Niles's tone, Bedford turned his attention to Elsbeth. "Your mother asked me to inform you that she is going to the village with Alfred this morning. She's also requested that you spend your time practicing your pianoforte piece for the soiree."

Elsbeth looked bothered. "Did she say why she's going to the village with Alfred?"

"She didn't, and I didn't ask," Bedford replied with a shrug, as though the matter held no significance.

Elsbeth shifted her gaze to Niles, determination lighting up her eyes. "We should follow them. Find out what they're up to."

"For what purpose?" Bedford asked, raising a skeptical brow. "They're probably shopping for ribbons at the haberdashery."

"And what if they're not?" Elsbeth countered.

Niles didn't like where this conversation was headed, and he didn't like the implication behind her words. "Do you really believe your mother could be involved in Alfred's secrets?"

"Yes... no... maybe? It would explain why she's dismissed my concerns so quickly. Why she always defends him," Elsbeth stated.

Bedford winced, visibly uncomfortable with the idea. "I don't think Aunt Isabella is capable of such deceit."

"I don't want to believe it either, but why else would she insist on accompanying him to the village today?" Elsbeth asked.

Niles saw the uncertainty and pain in Elsbeth's eyes. He stepped closer to her again, his voice laced with concern. "Elsbeth, are you certain this is a path you want to go down? Investigating your mother could open wounds you might not be ready to face."

Her eyes darted between Niles and Bedford before she squared her shoulders. "If there's even a chance she's involved, I need to know. For her sake and mine. I can't keep living with unanswered questions."

Bedford groaned as he rubbed his temples. "This is madness. I still think you're reading too much into this, Elsbeth."

"Perhaps I am, but is it not worth pursuing?" Elsbeth asked. "I was right about my stepfather keeping secrets."

"But this is not something you want to be right about," Bedford countered.

Niles saw the determination in Elsbeth's stance and knew she was not going to back down—not easily, and perhaps not at all. "I think we should travel to the village."

Bedford's head snapped towards him, his disbelief written clearly on his face. "Why are you encouraging this nonsense?"

"Because I believe in her," Niles replied.

Bedford looked heavenward. "Fine. We will all go together, if only to prove that Aunt Isabella has nothing to do with this," he said, already heading towards the stables. "Let's get this over with before I lose what little patience I have left."

As Niles took a step forward, Elsbeth placed a hand on his sleeve, stopping him. "Thank you," she said. "For believing in me."

Niles tipped his head slightly, a faint smile on his lips. "Always."

17

Elsbeth stared out of the coach window, the passing scenery blurring as her thoughts raced. Her heart felt heavy with doubt and fear. Could her mother truly be involved in Alfred's secrets? Worse yet, could she have had something to do with her father's death? The idea was unfathomable, but the questions gnawed at her.

No.

It couldn't be. Her mother loved Elsbeth's father. Didn't she?

Charles broke the silence beside her with a disgruntled sigh. "This is foolishness, Elsbeth. We should turn the coach around right now."

Elsbeth tore her gaze from the window and met his gaze. "I need to know what my mother is doing with Alfred in the village. I can't ignore this."

Charles frowned. "Why? For heaven's sake, this is your mother we're talking about. She doesn't have a single nefarious bone in her body."

Niles shifted in his seat, his calm voice cutting through the tension. "If that's true, then there's no harm in following them, is there?"

Elsbeth gave a small nod of agreement. "Exactly. If she has nothing to hide, then all we've wasted is a little time."

Charles threw up his hands in exasperation. "Fine! I see I'm outnumbered. But for the record, I think this is a terrible idea."

"Duly noted," Elsbeth said.

The coach came to a halt, and a footman stepped forward to open the door, offering his hand to assist Elsbeth. She descended gracefully onto the cobbled street and immediately spotted Alfred's coach parked farther ahead in front of the coaching inn.

"There," she said, pointing. "It seems Alfred has another meeting at the coaching inn."

"Or maybe they're just getting a drink," Charles muttered.

Elsbeth arched an eyebrow. "Do you really think my mother is sharing a pint with my stepfather?"

Charles shrugged, his frown deepening. "Perhaps not."

"Come on," she said, gesturing for them to follow her. She led the way to a narrow alley beside the inn, stopping at a grime-covered window. Peering inside, her eyes scanned the room until they landed on three figures: her mother, Alfred, and someone she instantly recognized as the blond-haired man who had met with her stepfather on two separate occasions.

Niles came to stand beside her. "What do you suppose they're discussing?"

Elsbeth's voice was tight as she answered, "I don't know, but it's clear my mother is aware of Alfred's secrets."

Charles, who had hung back, stepped closer, his tone grim. "I know that man."

Elsbeth turned to him. "How?"

"I saw him leaving the coroner's office when I went to speak about your father's death," Charles revealed. "I remember him because he had a pistol tucked into his waistband. It struck me as odd."

Niles's brow furrowed. "Do you think he's the one who threatened the coroner?"

"It seems likely," Charles replied. "But the real question is, why would Alfred go to such lengths to silence the coroner?"

Elsbeth felt her frustration mounting. "None of this makes sense. If my father's death was truly an accident, why investigate it? Why all these secrets?"

Niles's voice lowered, his words measured. "What if Alfred killed your father and is now covering it up? We overheard him telling that man that if Charles kept asking questions, it could get him killed. What if he's willing to silence anyone who gets too close to the truth?"

Elsbeth shook her head. "Alfred may have his faults, but I don't think he's a murderer. What would he gain from killing my father?"

Niles hesitated. "He could marry your mother."

"But if that's the case, then my mother is complicit in this. What could she possibly have to gain?" Elsbeth asked.

Charles spoke up, his tone tinged with sorrow. "Freedom, perhaps. Your father wasn't the man you thought he was, Elsbeth. He hurt your mother. Often."

Elsbeth's breath caught in her throat. "No. That's impossible. My father would never lay a hand on her."

Charles's expression was somber. "I wish it weren't true, but she confided in me. He made sure the bruises were hidden, but the pain was there. She even told me, at his funeral, that a part of her felt relieved that he was gone."

Tears stung Elsbeth's eyes. "Why didn't she tell me? I would have believed her."

"She wanted to shield you," Charles revealed. "She thought she was doing the honorable thing by preserving his memory."

Elsbeth's voice wavered. "Everything I thought I knew about my father... it was all a lie."

Niles placed a steadying hand on her arm. "Are you all right?"

"No," she whispered, her gaze locking with his. "I've been such a fool."

"You didn't know," Niles said softly. "It wasn't your fault."

"But I should have known," Elsbeth insisted. "I was so caught up in the comforts of London, the balls, the gowns, the endless distractions... I failed to see what was right in front of me. I failed to see my own mother's pain."

Charles stepped forward. "That's exactly what your mother wanted, Elsbeth. She wanted to shield you from his cruelty."

A tear slipped down her cheek, and she hastily wiped it away. "I could have protected her," she said, her voice trembling with regret. "I should have been there for her."

"There was nothing you could have done," Charles interjected, his tone resolute. "Your mother bore her pain alone because she didn't want you to carry that burden."

The walls of the narrow alley seemed to close in around her, the air thick and suffocating. Her chest tightened, and she struggled to draw a proper breath. Without saying another word, Elsbeth pushed past them, stepping out into the open street.

The crisp air hit her face as she stopped on the pavement, drawing in deep breaths to steady herself. She closed her eyes, ignoring the curious stares of passersby, and willed the tears to stop. But they came anyway, a reminder of her helplessness. When her mother had needed her most, she had been blind to her suffering. Blissfully unaware of the horrors her mother endured behind closed doors.

How could her father—her own father—have been so cruel? She had known he was distant, inattentive, even stern at times, but never had she imagined the monster lurking beneath his carefully curated façade.

And she had fallen for it.

The sound of footsteps behind her broke through her thoughts. She didn't need to look to know it was Niles. "We should get you home," he said, his hand brushing her arm with a tenderness that made her ache all the more.

"I think that's a good idea," she murmured, her voice barely audible as she fought to steady herself. The last thing she needed was to fall apart completely, especially not here in the open street where prying eyes could witness her vulnerability.

Niles stayed close as he guided her towards the waiting coach, his hand hovering near her arm in case she faltered. His presence was steady and reassuring, but his silence was what she appreciated most. She could feel his gaze, filled with a concern he wasn't voicing, and for that, she was grateful. Pity was the last thing she wanted—or needed—right now.

As she reached the coach and placed a hand on the door, a familiar voice cut through the air. "Elsbeth."

Her heart sank. She turned to see her mother descending the steps of the coaching inn, her hand resting lightly on Alfred's arm. Her expression was curious, but there was a glimmer of concern in her eyes.

"Whatever are you doing here?" her mother asked.

Panic surged through Elsbeth. She opened her mouth, scrambling for a believable lie, but her thoughts were a tangled mess. Before she could stammer out a response, Niles stepped forward, his voice calm and composed. "We were just doing a bit of shopping," he said smoothly, gesturing towards the general direction of the shops.

Her mother's expression softened, and a smile touched her lips. "How lovely," she said, clearly pleased by the explanation. "I shall see you at home, then."

"Yes, home," Elsbeth echoed.

Her mother's smile faltered, and her brow knitted with concern. "Are you feeling all right, my dear?"

Elsbeth forced herself to nod, her throat tight. "I am," she said quickly. Too quickly.

Her mother's frown deepened. "Perhaps we should send for the doctor. You look pale."

"There is no need," Elsbeth replied, her voice firmer this time, though her hands trembled slightly. She clasped them tightly to keep them still.

Alfred interrupted. "Leave poor Elsbeth be, my love. I'm sure she would tell you if something were amiss. Wouldn't you, Elsbeth?"

His gaze locked on hers. Elsbeth felt a chill run down her spine, but she forced herself to meet his stare, refusing to let him see her unease. "Yes, of course I would," she lied, her voice steady despite the turmoil churning inside her.

Her mother looked between them. "Very well," she said with a nod. "But do take care, Elsbeth. I shall see you at dinner."

Elsbeth watched as her mother and Alfred walked away, their heads close as they murmured to one another. She felt Niles's hand lightly brush her elbow, guiding her into the coach. Once inside, the door closed behind her, and the sound of the bustling street was muffled.

Niles's steady voice broke through her turmoil. "I don't believe for a moment that our explanation fooled Alfred."

She turned to meet his gaze. "I agree."

From across the coach, Charles groaned, rubbing his temples. "This entire ordeal is madness. We should forget the soiree and leave for my country estate at first light tomorrow."

"That's absurd—" Elsbeth began, but Niles interrupted her.

"I agree with your cousin," he said firmly.

Her brows shot up in surprise. "You do?"

Niles shifted slightly in his seat, his eyes holding compassion. "I don't believe it's safe for you here, Elsbeth. Whatever is happening, whatever Alfred is involved in, it's dangerous. Bedford's estate is the safer option. For now."

Charles folded his arms, smirking faintly. "Well, there's a first—Westcott agreeing with me."

Niles ignored the jab, his voice hardening as he turned towards Charles. "But let me be perfectly clear: I will ensure justice is served if anything happens to Elsbeth under your watch. No matter the cost."

Charles's smirk vanished. "And what, exactly, do you think is going to happen to her?"

Niles leaned forward, his expression stern. "You've already shot at her once, and let's not forget the possibility of poisoning her."

Charles's face twisted with indignation. "Good heavens, what are you even talking about?" he demanded.

Niles didn't back down. "The lozenges. She became gravely ill after accepting one from you. Care to explain that?"

Charles scoffed, shaking his head. "You're mistaken. I've been eating those lozenges for years, and I've never been sick from them."

"Convenient," Niles retorted. "But it doesn't change the fact that Elsbeth grew violently sick."

"I wouldn't hurt Elsbeth," Charles snapped, his face reddening. "She's my cousin."

Elsbeth raised her hand. "Enough, both of you. This bickering does nothing to address the real problem."

The men fell silent, their gazes shifting towards her. Elsbeth squared her shoulders. "I will not run. Not yet. There are still too many unanswered questions. But if I do decide to leave, it will be because I choose to, not because I'm being forced."

Charles sighed heavily and leaned back in his seat, clearly frustrated but unwilling to argue further. Niles, on the other hand, watched her closely, his expression softening just slightly.

"Very well," Niles said at last. "But you must promise to exercise caution. No unnecessary risks. You have your reputation to think about."

"I promise," Elsbeth said, though her gaze drifted back towards the window. She wasn't entirely sure she believed herself, but one thing was certain—whatever truths were lurking in the shadows, she was determined to uncover them.

Niles sat in the parlor of his aunt's grand manor, a half-empty glass of brandy clutched in his hand. The flickering candlelight cast restless shadows that danced along the richly paneled walls, their movement as agitated as his thoughts. It was late—far later than he should be awake—but sleep eluded him. His mind was filled with one thought, one person: Elsbeth.

He leaned back in the plush armchair, the cool leather creaking under his weight. He had stayed at Elsbeth's manor as long as he could, lingering far beyond what was polite. But he hadn't cared. Every fiber of his being wanted to ensure her safety, and even now, the distance between them felt insurmountable.

The line between his duty and desires was blurred, and the realization unnerved him. Could he simply walk away from her? Could he abandon the only person who had made him question what he truly wanted in life?

The soft click of the parlor door startled him from his musings. He glanced up to see Eugenie entering, her wrapper tied loosely around her waist and a candle in her hand. Her expression was curious and faintly amused.

"We missed you at dinner, Brother," she said, settling into the chair across from him.

"I dined with Elsbeth's family," he replied tersely, hoping she would take the hint and leave. He was in no mood for company, not even hers.

Eugenie, however, had never been one to ignore an opportunity to pry. "Why do you look like death?" she asked.

"I look like no such thing," Niles retorted, though even he knew his disheveled appearance betrayed him. His hair was unkempt, his cravat hung loosely around his neck, and his jacket was haphazardly draped over the armrest.

Eugenie gave him a knowing look. "You have the air of a man carrying the weight of the world on his shoulders."

Niles shifted uncomfortably in his seat, irritation creeping into his tone. "I do so enjoy our late-night talks, Sister."

"You must admit, I am right," Eugenie responded. "This is about Elsbeth, isn't it?"

He rubbed a hand across his face. "You aren't wrong, but I would prefer not to discuss it."

Eugenie leaned forward, undeterred. "Of course you don't want to talk about it. That's precisely why you should."

Setting his glass down with more force than necessary, Niles rose to his feet. "Goodnight, Eugenie. I think I shall retire."

She tilted her head. "You haven't come to terms with your feelings for Elsbeth, have you?"

He froze, his back to her, before slowly turning around. "And what if I haven't?"

"You're making a mistake," Eugenie said. "You're so consumed by your duty, your responsibilities, and what you think the world expects of you, that you're blind to the happiness standing right in front of you."

"I am happy," he insisted, though the words rang hollow.

Eugenie shook her head, her expression sympathetic. "Never be ashamed for loving the way your heart knows."

He frowned. "And what, pray tell, does that mean?"

Her voice softened, her words filled with quiet wisdom. "You can pretend you don't need or want love, Niles, but love is as essential as breathing. It doesn't always come when it's convenient or when you expect it, but that's what makes it so precious."

He sank back into his chair. "And what do you know of love, Eugenie?" he challenged.

A shadow passed over her face, and he instantly regretted his question. "I know enough to know I won't settle for anything less than love," she said quietly.

"And nor should you."

She lowered her gaze, her fingers tracing the edge of her candleholder. "I saw what Father and Mother had. That's what I want, but I also want to hold on to the freedoms I've been given. I don't want to trade one for the other."

Niles studied her for a moment before saying, "You deserve both, Eugenie. You deserve everything."

"And so do you, Brother," she said as she met his gaze. "The question is whether you'll let yourself have it."

"It isn't that simple," Niles responded, his tone clipped as he stared at the dying embers in the hearth.

"It can be," Eugenie countered.

He exhaled sharply. "I have you to consider first—"

His sister cut him off, her expression exasperated. "Not this again. I do not give a whit about Elsbeth's reputation, and neither should you. You're an earl, for heaven's sake. If you marry her, Society will fall all over itself to welcome her back with open arms."

He stiffened. "I never said anything about marriage."

"I know," she replied with a teasing lilt to her voice. "Just as you've said nothing about love, but it's obvious, Brother. Why is it that you are always the last to see it?"

"I care for Elsbeth," Niles admitted reluctantly, "but I need a wife with an impeccable reputation. That's what's best for my position."

Eugenie rolled her eyes dramatically. "Did you get hit on the head as a child?"

He scoffed. "You don't understand. It's the way things have to be." Even as he said the words, they felt inadequate. But he had to think about what was best for himself and for Eugenie.

"In the end, we all just want someone who chooses us. Over everyone else, under any circumstances. And I think Elsbeth is that person for you," she remarked.

Her words struck a chord deep in his chest, but he couldn't allow himself to yield. Not on this. "I daresay you've been reading too many fairy tales."

Eugenie rose gracefully from her seat. "Deny it all you want, but I can see how much you care for her. Now, I'll leave you to your brooding. Just think about what I said."

"Goodnight, Sister," he said stiffly.

She tipped her head. "Goodnight, Niles." With that, she left the room, leaving him alone with his thoughts.

Niles picked up his glass and took a long sip, the warmth of the brandy doing little to ease the cold knot in his chest. What was he to do? Marrying Elsbeth would undoubtedly change everything. His standing in Society. His carefully cultivated reputation. His future. But it would also keep her safe. It was the one thing he could give her, and yet he hesitated.

A sharp knock at the window shattered his reverie. He turned his head, startled, and saw Elsbeth's face illuminated by the pale moonlight.

Setting his glass down, he rose and crossed the room. He unlatched the window and opened it. "What in the blazes are you doing?" he asked in a low voice.

She didn't look the least bit repentant. "I came to say good-bye. Charles insists we leave after breakfast tomorrow."

Her words hit him like a blow to the chest. Elsbeth was leaving. Leaving him. There was so much he wanted to say, but the words tangled in his throat, heavy and unspoken.

Noticing how she pulled her wool cloak tighter around herself, he frowned. "Do come in," he said, stepping aside.

She hesitated, her uncertainty flickering across her face. "Are you sure?"

"It's far better than you catching cold," he asserted.

He extended a hand to help her through the window, and she placed her gloved hand in his. Once she was inside, she stood before him, her cheeks flushed pink from the cold and her dark curls escaping beneath her hood. She looked achingly beautiful, and he felt his resolve weakening under the weight of her gaze.

Her smile melted every last defense he had so carefully constructed, confirming what he had been denying for far too long. He loved her. Completely, irrevocably. The realization settled heavily over him, yet he knew he couldn't act on it. He couldn't risk her future or his own responsibilities for the sake of his feelings. Letting her go was the right thing to do. It had to be.

Elsbeth met his gaze. "I just wanted to thank you for everything you've done for me, Niles," she said. Her voice carried a vulnerability that made his heart ache.

"It was my pleasure," he replied, his words laden with sincerity. And it was the truth. He would do it all over again if it meant he could spend even one more moment with her.

She glanced at the window. "I should go," she murmured.

Yes.

She should go.

That was the sensible thing to do. But the thought of her leaving twisted something deep inside him. He wasn't ready to say goodbye. Not yet. Taking a step closer, he found himself standing so near that she had to tilt her head back to meet his gaze.

"How did Charles convince you to depart for his estate?" he asked.

She lowered her gaze, but not before he saw a sadness lurking within the depths of her eyes. "He promised he would hire a Bow Street Runner to look into my father's death if I left with him. I do believe that is our best chance to discover the truth."

"I think you are right," Niles said. "However, I would be remiss if I didn't tell you that coming here at this hour was foolish, especially under these circumstances."

"I know," she admitted, bringing her gaze up. "But I couldn't leave without saying goodbye."

His heart clenched. "I'm glad you did," he said, reaching into his waistcoat pocket. He pulled out his pocket watch and held it up between them. "I want you to have this."

She blinked, her brow furrowing as she stared at the watch. "I couldn't. It was your father's. It means so much to you."

"It does," he acknowledged, pressing the pocket watch into her palm. "But I want you to have something to remember me by."

Her fingers closed around the watch, her grip firm. "Thank you, Niles," she whispered. "I'll treasure it. Always."

He nodded, but the lump forming in his throat threatened to choke him. Before he could stop himself, the question tumbled out. "May I write to you?"

Her eyes widened for the briefest of moments before saying, "I would like that very much, but I'm not sure Charles would allow it."

"I don't care a whit about what Charles wants," Niles said, his tone firm. "I need to know you're well and being properly cared for."

"Charles will keep me safe," Elsbeth assured him.

Niles leaned closer. "That may be so, but you must promise me something."

"What?" she asked, her voice barely above a whisper.

"If you ever feel unsafe—if there's ever a moment when you need me—you must let me know," he said, his words almost a plea. "Promise me, Elsbeth."

"I promise," she said, her voice steady as she held his gaze.

He allowed himself a small, fleeting smile. "Then that's all I can ask."

"Goodbye, Niles," she replied.

Niles knew he should say more, that he should tell her everything weighing on his heart. That he loved her, and that he always would, no matter the consequences. The words were there, lodged in his throat, burning to be released. Yet, they stayed trapped, tethered by his fear, his duty, and the lingering thought that he might not be enough for her.

Coward.

The word echoed in his mind as he watched her carefully lift her skirts and step onto the windowsill. He should stop her. He should tell her how much she meant to him, how much she had changed his life, how the thought of letting her walk out of it was unbearable. But he didn't. He remained rooted in place, his hands clenching at his sides as she climbed through the window.

She turned back briefly, her eyes catching his one last time, shimmering with unshed tears. "Thank you," she murmured. "For everything."

And then she was gone, disappearing into the night like a shadow swallowed by the darkness.

Niles stood there, rooted in place, as the silence of the room pressed in around him. A sharp, relentless pain spread through his chest and stole his breath. Was this truly the end? Could he let it end like this?

The answer clawed at him, but he pushed it down. He couldn't follow her. Not now. Not when the life he had so carefully constructed was at risk of crumbling entirely. But as he returned to his chair and stared at the flickering candle, one thought consumed him: if this was truly goodbye, it would haunt him for the rest of his life.

A quiet rustling in the doorway pulled him from his thoughts. "I heard everything, Brother."

Eugenie's voice was soft but unwavering, laced with disappointment, maybe even pity. She stepped forward, her expression unreadable in the dim candlelight. "You can't let her go. Not now."

Niles let out a slow breath, shifting in his seat but refusing to meet her gaze. "She is leaving tomorrow with Lord Bedford. It is for the best."

"The best for whom?" Eugenie challenged, moving farther into the room. "For Elsbeth? Or for you?"

"It does not matter."

Eugenie huffed, folding her arms. "It matters to her. And whether you admit it or not, it matters to you."

He said nothing, the silence between them stretching long and taut.

She took another step closer. "You always tell me that I deserve love. That I should fight for it. But what of you, Niles? Do you not deserve it, too?"

His hands curled into fists. He did not want to have this conversation. Not with her. Not with anyone. He wanted the luxury of sitting here in his misery, drowning in the knowledge that he had just let the most remarkable woman he had ever known slip through his fingers.

"Goodnight, Eugenie," he said.

Eugenie, however, was not so easily dismissed. "You are a coward. You have a chance at real happiness, and you're letting it slip from your grasp. For what? For pride? For fear?"

"You know not what you speak of."

Eugenie let out a humorless laugh, tilting her head as she studied him. "No? Then answer me this—when you wake up tomorrow and realize she's gone, when you watch another man stand beside her, will you feel relief? Or will you feel regret?"

The words hit their mark. He knew it. She knew it.

He rose from his seat and came to a stop beside her. "She is gone. Let's leave it at that." His voice was quiet, edged with something almost resigned.

Eugenie said nothing more. She only watched as he turned and walked away, disappearing down the corridor toward his bedchamber—leaving behind only the echo of missed chances and the truth he wasn't yet ready to face.

18

As the soft rays of the morning sun crept into her bedchamber, Elsbeth fastened the latch on her final trunk and sighed, her heart heavy with indecision. "That should do," she murmured, more to herself than to anyone else.

Clara, busy tidying the dressing table, paused and looked over. "Are you certain you wish to leave after breakfast?"

Elsbeth sank onto the trunk. "I don't know what to think. Charles is insistent we leave, and I can't say he's wrong."

Clara tilted her head thoughtfully. "Have you told your mother yet?"

Elsbeth winced. "I haven't. I was hoping Charles would break the news."

A knowing look crossed Clara's face. "She will be quite upset that you're missing the soiree tonight."

"What am I supposed to do?" Elsbeth asked, her voice tinged with frustration. "Wait here until Alfred succeeds in whatever he's planning? I can't risk staying."

Clara approached and perched on the edge of the bed.

"You're certain it's Alfred? What if the falling planter was just an accident?"

Elsbeth shook her head. "No. It wasn't an accident. And if not Alfred, then who? I truly don't believe Charles means me harm. Which begs the question: who else would want me dead?"

Clara hesitated before asking, "And what of Lord Westcott? Can you truly leave him behind?"

"Lord Westcott and I are just friends," she said, her voice firm, though she couldn't even fathom her own lie. Whatever they were, it was certainly more than friendship. But he would eventually leave her.

Clara raised an eyebrow. "Yet you risked sneaking out last night just to see him?"

"It was to say goodbye," Elsbeth said defensively. "That's all it was. Nothing untoward happened."

Clara didn't look convinced. "You risked your reputation."

"My reputation is already in tatters," Elsbeth replied. "Lord Westcott would never be interested in someone who has fallen so far in Society."

"You're still the daughter of an earl, with an impressive dowry. You shouldn't discount yourself so easily."

Elsbeth wished it was that simple, but it wasn't. It was much more complicated than that. "It doesn't matter. We said our goodbyes. I'm leaving this village, and that's that."

"Are you truly giving up on Lord Westcott so easily?"

Pressing her lips together, Elsbeth rose and adjusted the folds of her traveling habit. "Clara, I would rather not talk about him."

Before Clara could respond, the door swung open to reveal her mother. She stepped into the room, her eyes sweeping over the packed trunks with a frown of confusion. "What is going on here? Why are your trunks packed?"

Drat. Charles hadn't spoken to her mother yet. In a voice

that she hoped sounded more confident than she felt, she revealed, "Charles and I are departing for his country estate after breakfast."

Her mother's eyebrows shot up in surprise. "When was this decided?"

"Last night," Elsbeth replied.

"And you're only telling me now?" her mother demanded. "What of the soiree tonight? Do you intend to embarrass me by abandoning your family's obligations?"

"It's not like that. Charles feels it's safer if we leave immediately."

Her mother crossed her arms, her posture as rigid as her expression. She turned to Clara. "Leave us."

Clara curtsied and quickly exited, shutting the door behind her.

Elsbeth's mother turned back to her, her eyes glinting with a mix of hurt and frustration. "And I don't get a say in any of this?"

"I'm sorry," Elsbeth murmured, lowering her gaze.

Her mother's voice rose. "Do you wish to humiliate me? What will people think when my own daughter is absent from the soiree?"

Elsbeth bit her lip, guilt gnawing at her. "It wasn't my intention to upset you."

"Then stay," her mother said. "Attend the soiree, at the very least."

Elsbeth nodded, knowing she had no desire to hurt her mother. "I'll speak with Charles."

Her mother exhaled, her shoulders relaxing slightly. "Thank you. I'm disappointed you're leaving, but I understand. Perhaps some time away will give you a new perspective."

Sitting on the edge of the bed, Elsbeth had a few questions that she needed to know the answers to. "Are you happy with Alfred?"

Her mother blinked, appearing surprised by the question. "Of course I'm happy with Alfred."

"But you weren't happy with Father?" Elsbeth pressed.

Her mother's face fell, sadness shadowing her features. "Your father was... a difficult man to love."

Elsbeth swallowed hard before saying, "I know he hurt you. Why didn't you tell me? I could have helped."

Her mother sat beside her, taking her hand gently. "You couldn't have done anything, my dear. I didn't want him to turn his anger on you. I endured it so you wouldn't have to."

Tears welled in Elsbeth's eyes as she listened to her mother's words. "I should have known. I should have done something."

Her mother squeezed her hand. "You were a child. It wasn't your burden to bear."

"So, you bore it alone?"

"That is a mother's job. To protect her child, no matter the cost." Her mother's voice was firm, the pain of past sacrifices evident in her tone.

A tear slipped down Elsbeth's cheek, and she hastily wiped it away, though it did nothing to stem the flood of emotions coursing through her. "I'm sorry," she murmured. "I was so consumed by my own pursuits, my own trivial concerns, that I failed to see what was right in front of me."

Her mother's lips curved into a bittersweet smile. "You did nothing wrong. Please know that. I wanted you to live a carefree life, untouched by the burdens I bore."

"I have been difficult since you married Alfred," Elsbeth admitted, turning to face her mother fully. "And I am so sorry for that. You deserve to be happy, and I should have supported you."

Her mother's expression was tinged with curiosity. "Where is this coming from?"

Elsbeth shifted uncomfortably, the words catching in her

throat before she pushed them out. "Because it's true. You deserve happiness, Mother. More than anyone."

"As do you, my darling. Which is why I cannot understand why you are leaving Lord Westcott."

The mention of Niles made Elsbeth's heart ache, but she forced herself to meet her mother's gaze. "It doesn't matter the reason, Mother. I have to leave."

Her mother's hand fell away, and she studied Elsbeth intently. "Did something happen between you and Lord Westcott?"

"No," Elsbeth replied quickly, not wishing to reveal the real reason as to why she had to leave. "We are merely friends, but he did ask permission to write to me. And I granted him leave to do so."

Her mother's lips pursed. "That is a dangerous path, Elsbeth. You are not betrothed, and allowing such correspondence could ruin what remains of your reputation."

"I no longer care about my reputation," Elsbeth stated. "It is already in tatters. What harm could come of it?"

"Much harm," her mother countered. "Lord Westcott may mean well, but the world will not look kindly upon such behavior, especially from the daughter of an earl."

Elsbeth felt the stirrings of anger rise within her, though she pushed it down. "I cannot deny him. He is the only one who has stood by me through all of this."

"Because he cares for you," her mother said. "And I think you care for him as well."

The words struck a chord deep within Elsbeth, and she felt tears prick at her eyes once more. "I don't know what I feel. I only know that leaving is the right thing to do."

Her mother studied her for a long moment, then reached out to brush a strand of hair from her face. "You are so much stronger than you give yourself credit for, Elsbeth. But strength does not mean running away from what scares you. Sometimes, it means staying and facing it."

Elsbeth bit her lip, her resolve wavering. "Perhaps," she whispered. "But I don't know if I'm brave enough for that."

Her mother's smile was warm. "You are brave enough for anything. You always have been."

Elsbeth was touched by her mother's words and thought it might be a good time to ask her a few more questions. This was the moment to press forward. "What do you know of Father's death?"

Her mother's smile vanished, replaced by a guarded look. "Why do you ask?"

"I have been thinking about it lately, and I wonder if it was truly an accident," Elsbeth replied, studying her mother closely.

Her mother abruptly rose. "Why would you ask such a thing? It *was* an accident," she snapped as she moved towards the door. "Nothing more. Now, let us go down for breakfast."

But Elsbeth wasn't willing to let the conversation end. She leaned forward, her hands gripping the edge of the bed. "If that's the case, then why is Alfred asking questions about Father's death?"

Her mother froze, her back stiffening. Slowly, she turned, her face paler than Elsbeth had ever seen it. "Why would you think that?" she asked, her voice strained.

This was her chance. Elsbeth took a deep breath, deciding to risk the truth. "Because I found newssheet clippings in his desk. Articles about Father's death."

Her mother's expression hardened, her lips thinning. "You broke into his desk?"

"Yes," Elsbeth admitted. "I knew Alfred was hiding something, and I needed to find out what it was."

"You shouldn't have done such a thing. You've no idea what you've meddled in," she chided.

"I had no choice," Elsbeth countered. "He's keeping secrets, and I need to know what they are. What else is Alfred hiding?"

"You don't understand," her mother said sharply. "You're chasing shadows, things that don't concern you."

"Then make me understand," Elsbeth demanded, rising to her feet. "Stop treating me like a child and tell me the truth."

Her mother's composure cracked, a flicker of panic crossing her face. "You *are* a child in this," she said, her voice trembling. "And we've been trying to protect you. You don't know the dangers of the answers you're seeking."

"I can handle the truth, whatever it is," she asserted.

Her mother placed a hand on the door handle. She didn't meet Elsbeth's gaze, her voice quiet but heavy with warning. "Stop asking questions, Elsbeth. It will not end well for you."

The ominous words sent a chill down Elsbeth's spine, but she couldn't relent now. "What do you mean by that? What won't end well?"

Her mother's hand tightened on the handle, her knuckles white. "Please, for once, do as you're told. Leave this alone. I cannot risk losing you."

Her voice cracked on the last word, and for a moment, Elsbeth saw the fear etched in her mother's features. "What will happen to me, Mother? What are you so afraid of?"

Her mother didn't respond. Instead, she opened the door and left, the sound of the door closing behind her echoing like a final warning. Elsbeth stood there, her mind racing with unanswered questions and a growing sense of dread. Something was very, very wrong, and she wouldn't rest until she uncovered the truth.

Niles hadn't slept a wink. The restless energy coursing

through him refused to let his mind settle, and by the time the morning light streamed through his windows, he'd made a decision. He loved Elsbeth. There was no point denying it anymore, not to himself, not to anyone. He had to act.

Pulling on his jacket with determined resolve, he stepped into the corridor. He rehearsed his thoughts as he walked, though it was less a polished speech and more a jumble of emotions clamoring to be voiced.

As he descended the grand staircase, he found his aunt waiting near the main door, a knowing smile playing on her lips.

"You're going after her, aren't you?" she asked, her tone filled with gentle encouragement.

"I am," Niles admitted.

Her smile broadened, her eyes glistening with pride. "I knew it. I've seen how you look at her, how she looks at you. You and Elsbeth are a perfect match, even if you're the last to see it."

"I only hope she sees it too," Niles said, pausing before her. "I've thought of a dozen ways to tell her, but what if it's not enough?"

His aunt placed a comforting hand on his arm. "You are enough, Niles. Speak from the heart, and she will see that."

"What if I can't convince her to marry me?" Niles asked.

"Why would she turn you down?"

Niles adjusted the cuff of his sleeves as he replied, "Elsbeth can be rather stubborn at times. Besides, she has given me no indication that she favors me."

Behind him, Eugenie's teasing voice chimed in. "Brother, you must be blind if you think Elsbeth doesn't already care for you."

He turned, frowning at her smug expression. "Has she said something to you?"

"She didn't have to," Eugenie said, crossing her arms. "The

way she looks at you is all the confirmation anyone would need. It is rather sickening if you ask me." She softened her words with a smile.

"Our family's reputation may suffer if I marry Elsbeth," Niles pointed out. "You must prepare yourself for that."

Eugenie rolled her eyes. "You're an earl. Marry her, and Society will welcome her back with open arms. Stop using reputation as an excuse."

"It's not that simple," Niles countered.

"Love rarely is," Eugenie replied. "But it's worth the complications, don't you think?"

Before he could respond, his aunt interjected. "Go, Niles. Don't let fear hold you back."

Taking a steadying breath, he nodded. "Wish me luck."

"You won't need it," Eugenie said confidently. "Just don't overthink it, and mess this up."

Niles exited the manor and stepped into the awaiting coach. By the time the coach reached Elsbeth's manor, he had abandoned any attempt to craft a perfect speech. Words could only go so far. It was his actions that would matter.

The coach came to a jerking stop and Niles stepped out. He headed up the stairs and knocked. The butler opened the door promptly, bowing slightly as he stepped aside. "Good morning, Lord Westcott. Please, come in."

Niles stepped into the entry hall, his gaze scanning the familiar surroundings. He had barely taken two steps inside when Bedford's unmistakably exasperated voice cut through the air.

"Good gads, Westcott, you're here again? Don't you have anywhere else you could be?" Bedford asked as he emerged from a side room.

Ignoring the jab, Niles replied evenly, "I'm here to see Elsbeth."

Bedford was clearly unimpressed. "Of course you are. As if last night's little escapade wasn't enough."

Niles stiffened slightly. "You knew about that?"

"Oh, who do you think followed her to make sure she didn't land herself in trouble?"

"I'm impressed she didn't spot you."

Bedford smirked. "Was that a compliment, Westcott?"

Niles gave a begrudging nod. "It may have been."

Bedford chuckled. "Well, wonders never cease," he said. "Come on, Elsbeth's in the dining room, taking breakfast."

As they entered the dining room, Niles's gaze immediately found Elsbeth. She was seated at the table, reading the Society pages, her hair catching the morning light in soft waves. When she looked up and saw him, her eyes brightened—just enough to make his heart ache with hope.

"Lord Westcott," Lady Isabella said with a welcoming smile. "Please, join us."

"I wouldn't want to intrude—"

"Nonsense," she interrupted, gesturing to the empty seat beside Elsbeth. "Sit. You're practically family already."

Ignoring Bedford's exaggerated groan, Niles took the offered seat. He turned to Elsbeth, smiling despite himself. "Dare I ask what has your attention this morning?"

She folded the newssheets and set it aside. "The Society pages. They're dreadfully dull, but sometimes I read them to remind myself of London."

"London is overrated," Niles teased. "Too many people. Too many rules."

"And yet, I miss it," Elsbeth countered. "The balls, the music, the freedom to be someone else for an evening."

"You could always return," Niles suggested. "With the right company, London might feel like home again."

Her eyes searched his, as though trying to decipher the deeper meaning in his words. But before she could respond,

Bedford cleared his throat loudly, reminding them that they were not alone.

The butler stepped into the dining room and offered a small bow, his gaze fixed on Lady Isabella. "Mr. Stockton has returned home, my lady."

"Wonderful," Lady Isabella replied, rising from her seat. "If you'll excuse me, I must speak with my husband."

As Lady Isabella left the room, Elsbeth pushed back her chair and stood abruptly. "We should follow her and see what she intends to discuss with Alfred."

"Now?" Niles asked.

"Yes, now," Elsbeth insisted, her voice quiet but urgent. "Come on, hurry up."

Niles sighed, rising to his feet. "Very well." He turned to Bedford. "Would you care to join us?"

Bedford waved his hand dismissively. "You two go on without me. I do believe this is a waste of time."

Niles offered his arm to Elsbeth and they moved silently through the corridors towards the rear of the manor. When they reached the open doorway of the study, Elsbeth pressed a finger to her lips, signaling for Niles to remain silent.

Inside the study, Lady Isabella's voice carried clearly into the corridor. "She's asking questions, Alfred," she said, her tone edged with concern. "I tried to warn her."

Alfred's exasperated sigh followed. "We can't have her asking questions."

"Maybe we should just tell her the truth and be done with it?" Lady Isabella suggested, her voice tinged with desperation.

Alfred's reply was sharp. "What is the truth? No. It's better if we say nothing."

"But keeping silent isn't working," Lady Isabella pressed. "She told me she snooped through your desk and found the newssheet clippings."

A tense silence followed, broken by a faint, familiar voice. "She needs to know the danger she's in."

"She's not ready," Alfred said firmly, his tone brooking no argument.

"But Alfred," her mother continued, "she is leaving with Charles at first light tomorrow. We can't let her go."

Elsbeth leaned closer to the doorway. But as she shifted her weight, the floorboard beneath her foot let out an audible creak that echoed down the corridor like a warning bell.

The voices inside the study stopped abruptly, and a moment later, Alfred appeared in the doorway. His expression was stern, his eyes narrowing as they landed on Elsbeth and Niles. "Eavesdropping, Elsbeth?" His tone was clipped and accusatory. "And Lord Westcott. What an unpleasant surprise."

Rather than shrink under Alfred's glare, Elsbeth tilted her chin defiantly. "I demand to know what you're speaking of."

Alfred's brows shot up, his expression a mix of amusement and irritation. "You demand?"

"Yes, I do," Elsbeth replied, though her voice wavered slightly. "It's only fair since you were talking about me."

Niles, standing just behind her, resisted the urge to smile at her boldness. That tenacity was one of the many qualities he admired about her.

Lady Isabella stepped into the doorway beside Alfred, her expression softer but no less strained. "I think it's only fair we tell her the truth," she said.

Alfred pressed his lips into a thin line, clearly torn. "She isn't ready."

Elsbeth stepped forward, her eyes flashing with determination. "I may not be ready, but I deserve to know. You're keeping secrets about my father's death, and if it involves me, I have every right to hear it."

Alfred studied her for a long moment before turning to

Lady Isabella with a sigh. "You had better handle this," he muttered, stepping aside.

Lady Isabella reached for Elsbeth's hand. "Come inside, my dear. There's much to explain."

Niles moved to follow, but Alfred held up a hand, blocking his path. "You can wait here, Lord Westcott. This is a family matter."

"I care for Elsbeth," Niles repeated, his voice steady but firm. "If it concerns her, it concerns me."

Alfred's eyes narrowed, his expression unreadable. But before he could respond, Elsbeth stepped in, her tone unwavering. "He stays. I want him here."

Alfred stepped to the side, gesturing for them to enter the room. "You might not feel that way after our talk."

Niles stepped inside, his posture tense as Alfred closed the door behind them. The study felt heavier than usual, the atmosphere thick with unspoken tension. Niles's gaze immediately landed on a man standing near the window. Recognition flickered in Niles's mind; this was the blond-haired man he and Elsbeth had seen speaking with Alfred before.

Alfred gestured towards the man. "Allow me to introduce you to Mr. John Glasker. He is a Bow Street Runner I've hired to investigate a rather delicate matter."

The man stepped forward, offering a polite bow. "My lord. My lady."

Elsbeth's brows furrowed as she gave Mr. Glasker a curious glance. "I thought all Bow Street Runners wore red waistcoats."

Mr. Glasker's lips twitched in a faint smile. "That is true if we wish to be easily identified. However, in this particular case, discretion is paramount."

Lady Isabella moved towards the settee, gently taking Elsbeth's hand and guiding her to sit beside her. "I have wanted to have this conversation with you so many times, Elsbeth, but I could never quite bring myself to do it. What we're about to discuss... it will be difficult to hear, and it must not leave this room."

"I understand," Elsbeth acknowledged.

Lady Isabella turned her gaze to Niles. "That applies to you as well, Lord Westcott."

Niles inclined his head and moved to sit beside Elsbeth. "You have my word, my lady."

Lady Isabella exchanged a glance with Alfred, who looked less sure of himself now. The tension in the room seemed to grow with every passing moment. Finally, Alfred broke the silence.

"This is about your father, Elsbeth," he began, his voice uncharacteristically subdued. "And the circumstances surrounding his death."

Elsbeth's breath hitched, but she remained still, her hands clenching the fabric of her skirt. "What about it?"

Alfred exchanged another glance with Mr. Glasker, who stepped forward, his voice calm but grave. "Your father's death, my lady, may not have been the accident it was believed to be," the Bow Street Runner said.

"What are you saying? Are you telling me my father was... murdered?" Elsbeth asked, her voice betraying her emotion.

Lady Isabella's hand tightened on Elsbeth's. "We don't know for certain, but there are things that have recently come to light."

Niles's jaw tightened. "And what, exactly, has come to light?"

Mr. Glasker looked to Alfred, who gave a curt nod before the Bow Street Runner continued. "There were discrepancies in the coroner's report. Paid witnesses. Threats made to individuals who tried to ask questions."

Elsbeth's face drained of color. "By whom?"

"That's what I've been trying to uncover," Mr. Glasker admitted. "Your stepfather brought me in to investigate quietly, to avoid drawing attention. What I can say is that someone went to great lengths to cover up the truth."

"Why would someone want my father dead?" Elsbeth whispered, her voice breaking.

Lady Isabella winced. "Because your father was not the man you believed him to be, my dear."

"What do you mean?" Elsbeth asked.

Alfred sighed heavily, pinching the bridge of his nose. "Your father had enemies, Elsbeth. Dangerous ones. And it seems one of them may have decided to take matters into their own hands."

The Bow Street Runner's expression was solemn as he added, "And we suspect that person was your cousin, Lord Bedford."

19

Elsbeth felt the air leave her chest as she considered Alfred's words. Charles? Could her own cousin truly be responsible for her father's death? It seemed impossible.

Alfred took a step closer, drawing her attention. "Think about it, Elsbeth. Your cousin had the most to gain from your father's death. He inherited the title and what remained of the estate."

"But the estate was practically bankrupt," Elsbeth countered, though her voice wavered. "My father left him nothing but debts."

"That's true," Alfred conceded. "But your father was a notorious gambler. Had he lived, he would have squandered every last piece of his estate. By dying when he did, your cousin retained the land and entailed properties. He can rebuild his fortune. It may take some time, but it is entirely possible."

Elsbeth turned to her mother. "Do you truly believe Charles is capable of murder?"

Her mother's face darkened with an expression Elsbeth rarely saw: doubt mixed with pain. "At first, no. But the more

I've thought about it... it makes sense. This is why you mustn't leave with him. We don't know what he is capable of."

"Yet you wanted me to marry him?" Elsbeth demanded.

"That was before certain things came to light," her mother replied.

"No," Elsbeth said, jumping up from her seat. "I don't believe it. I don't want to believe it."

Rising, Niles's eyes held compassion as he said, "Elsbeth, if Charles did harm your father, it would explain why he might want to harm you. You've been asking too many questions."

Lady Isabella's hand flew to her mouth. "He hasn't tried to hurt you, has he?" she asked, her voice cracking with fear.

Elsbeth hesitated, unsure how much she should reveal. Before she could answer, Niles spoke up. "Bedford did almost shoot Elsbeth and possibly poisoned her with a lozenge."

"You aren't helping," Elsbeth muttered.

Her mother's expression grew resolute. "I can't in good conscience allow you to go with Charles to his estate."

Alfred nodded in agreement. "Your mother's right. If something happens to you, your dowry reverts to the estate. It would go straight into Charles's hands."

Elsbeth's resolve faltered, her body sinking back onto the settee as the weight of everything pressed down on her. "Charles wouldn't do that. He wouldn't..."

But even as she spoke, doubt crept in, unsettling her more than she wanted to admit. "What am I supposed to do?" she murmured, her voice barely audible.

Niles sat beside her, his presence steadying. "I have an idea."

She turned to him, hope flickering faintly in her chest. "What is it?"

"Marry me," he said firmly, his eyes locking with hers. "I can take you far away from all of this. I'll keep you safe."

Her brows knitted together. "You cannot be serious."

"I've never been more serious," Niles insisted, reaching for her hand. "This isn't how I planned to offer for you, but it's the best solution. Don't you see?"

Her heart fluttered, but not in the way she hoped. "I... I don't know what to think," she stammered.

Lady Isabella interjected. "Perhaps you two should take this discussion to the gardens. Alone."

Niles stood, helping Elsbeth to her feet as well. "That's a wonderful idea," he agreed.

As they walked side by side through the corridor and onto the veranda, Elsbeth pulled her hands from his grasp, clasping them tightly in front of her. The silence between them was thick, laden with unspoken emotions.

"You're awfully quiet," Niles observed, glancing at her.

"Am I?" she replied. "Perhaps it has something to do with you blurting out an offer of marriage."

Niles stopped walking, turning her gently to face him. "I meant every word, Elsbeth. I want to marry you. I want to protect you—from Alfred, from Charles, from anyone who dares threaten you."

Her heart sank at his words. Not once had he mentioned love. "I appreciate your offer, truly, but it isn't necessary," she said, trying to mask her disappointment.

"But it is," he pressed, his voice rising with intensity. "I can't stand by and watch something happen to you."

She shook her head. "Thank you for your concern, Niles, but I must decline."

He stiffened, his expression one of disbelief. "You're refusing me?"

"I am," she said. "I want more than a marriage of convenience."

Niles ran a hand through his hair, leaving it endearingly disheveled. "Is that what you think this is?"

"Isn't it?"

Niles stepped closer, his voice low. "No, Elsbeth. You misunderstand me. If there's one thing I fear more than anything, it's losing you. I love—"

Charles's booming voice interrupted, shattering the moment. "I do hope I'm interrupting something," he said, his tone dripping with mockery.

Niles immediately moved in front of Elsbeth, shielding her from her cousin. "What do you want, Bedford?"

Charles smirked. "Oh, nothing much. Just wondering why you two are out here in the gardens... alone."

Elsbeth stepped out from behind Niles. "Mother gave us leave to talk."

Charles clicked his tongue, his smirk deepening. "Interesting," he muttered.

"There's nothing interesting about it," Niles shot back. "For your information, I was offering for Elsbeth."

Charles raised a brow. "Were you, now?" he drawled. "Well, this ought to be good. Please, proceed. Do not let me stop you."

Niles looked heavenward. "Do you mind giving us some privacy?"

"Oh, I do," Charles replied. "Because I do not think that Elsbeth should marry you."

"And why is that?" Niles asked, his jaw clenched.

Charles folded his arms. "You are not good enough for her," he replied bluntly.

Niles tilted his head slightly, acknowledging the insult without flinching. "I do not dispute that," he said calmly, "but I would be a good husband to her."

Charles scoffed. "Is that all you think Elsbeth deserves? Just a 'good' husband? She deserves so much more." He turned to Elsbeth. "Did he tell you, Cousin, that you are not the first woman he has offered for?"

Elsbeth briefly glanced at Niles before replying, "No, he did not."

Charles continued. "Westcott pursued the diamond of the Season and failed to secure her hand in marriage."

"That was for the best," Niles said.

"Are you sure you are not just settling for Elsbeth?" Charles asked. "Or, perhaps, you are more interested in her dowry than anything else?"

Niles's eyes flashed with anger. "How dare you!"

Charles shrugged nonchalantly. "I am merely asking questions—questions that should be considered."

Niles took a step closer to Charles, his movements slow and deliberate. "Perhaps you are the one interested in Elsbeth for her dowry," he retorted, his voice sharp with accusation.

Charles's eyes narrowed. "Pardon?"

"If I marry Elsbeth," Niles began, "then I control her dowry, and it will never revert to you. No matter what nefarious tactics you might attempt."

Charles's hands balled into fists at his sides. "I thought we settled this. I would never harm my cousin," he growled.

"What about Elsbeth's father?" Niles demanded.

Charles's face displayed a flicker of shock before he masked it. "You think I had something to do with my uncle's death?"

"If the shoe fits," Niles retorted.

"You pompous fool!" Charles spat. "Why would I investigate my uncle's death if I had something to do with it?"

"I don't know," Niles countered. "But you benefited the most from his death. That much is undeniable."

Charles moved forward, closing the remaining distance between them. "I had nothing to do with my uncle's death."

Watching the tension escalate, Elsbeth knew she had to intervene before they engaged in fisticuffs. She stepped between them, placing a hand on each of their chests and pushing them apart. "Stop this!"

Both men froze at her touch, their heated gazes flickering down to her before meeting each other's again.

"Enough!" she stated, her tone unwavering as she stared between the two men. "This isn't solving anything."

Charles turned his attention to her, his eyes clouded with both anger and hurt. "Do you believe any of this, Cousin?"

Elsbeth pressed her lips together before she admitted, "I don't know what to believe."

Charles's face contorted with disbelief. "You truly think I'm capable of hurting you? Of hurting your father?"

"I just need time to sort this out," Elsbeth said.

Charles took a step back. "Take all the time you need. But I am leaving for my country estate, with or without you."

"Wait, Charles..." she began, her words faltering as he turned on his heel and strode away, the echo of the door slamming behind him punctuating his departure.

Elsbeth turned to Niles. "What if we're wrong? About Charles, about Alfred, about all of it?"

Niles's eyes softened, and he took a step closer. "I don't have the answer to that," he admitted. "But I think it's better to err on the side of caution. Until we know for sure, you must focus on your safety."

Her thoughts remained rooted on Charles. This was her cousin, someone she had trusted all her life. She couldn't reconcile the Charles she knew with the one her stepfather accused. But what if her mother and Alfred were right?

Who was she supposed to believe?

As the weight of uncertainty pressed down on her, Niles stepped forward, pulling her into an embrace. She stiffened for a brief moment, being caught off guard. But as his warmth enveloped her, she felt herself relax into his arms. He held her firmly, yet gently. It was the kind of embrace that one needed when things have been falling apart for years. She hadn't realized how much she needed this, and for the first time in years, she felt at peace.

His chin rested lightly atop her head, his voice soft and comforting. "I thought you could use a hug."

"Thank you," she murmured, her voice muffled against his chest. For the first time since her father's death, she didn't feel entirely alone.

After a moment of silence, Niles asked, "What are you going to do about your cousin?"

Elsbeth tilted her head to meet his gaze, her eyes searching his for answers. "What do you think I should do?"

A small, knowing smile curved his lips, one that seemed to hold all the answers she didn't yet have. "I think you should marry me and we can ride off into the sunset. Just you and me."

For a fleeting moment, the idea was as tempting as it was improbable. But the memory of Charles—his dejected expression, the raw hurt in his eyes—came rushing back. His reaction to their accusations had seemed painfully genuine. "I'm not opposed to continuing this conversation," she said carefully, "but I need to speak to Charles first."

"That's the last thing you should be doing," he replied, a note of warning in his voice.

Elsbeth took a steadying breath. "In my heart, I don't believe Charles murdered my father," she said. She had no evidence to offer, only an instinct that refused to be silenced.

Niles studied her for a long moment, then sighed. "Then go," he encouraged, though he made no move to release her.

She laughed. "You'll need to let me go first."

His grip tightened ever so slightly. "I've waited a long time to hold you like this, Elsbeth. I'm not quite ready to let go."

A blush crept up her cheeks, and she leaned into him a little more. "Perhaps," she whispered, "we can stay like this for just a moment longer."

And so they stood there, wrapped in each other's arms, as the world beyond the gardens seemed to fade away. After a long moment, Elsbeth reluctantly took a step back. "I should go speak to my cousin."

"Very well," he replied. "May I walk you back inside?"

"That won't be necessary. I suspect Charles will be heading out to the stables. He tends to prefer riding when he's upset. It's his way of clearing his mind."

"Then I shall walk you to the stables," Niles said, his determination unwavering.

Elsbeth couldn't suppress a grin. "I think speaking with Charles will go much easier if you're not around. I don't think my cousin particularly cares for you."

Niles feigned shock, his hand flying to his chest in mock indignation. "*What*?! Impossible. I thought we were the best of friends."

A light laugh escaped her lips. "I shall see you soon," she responded before heading towards the stables.

"Be sure not to be left alone with Charles," Niles called out after her.

She spun back around. "Morton won't let anything happen to me," she replied, hoping to ease his worries. "And don't you think about following me. I can handle this on my own."

"Very well, but if you are not back shortly, I will come for you," he said. His words brooked no argument.

"I can agree to that."

As Elsbeth resumed walking down the gravel path, her lips hummed a faint melody, a habit she hadn't indulged in since childhood. It surprised her how content she felt. Perhaps a marriage to Niles wouldn't be so terrible after all. No, he might not love her, but in time, maybe he could come to care for her as deeply as she cared for him.

The sound of booted footsteps came behind her, but something struck her from behind before she could turn around. And everything went black.

Niles lingered in the gardens long after Elsbeth disappeared from view. A smile lingered on his lips. His proposal to Elsbeth had been interrupted, but he felt encouraged, considering she hadn't pulled away when he'd embraced her.

For the first time in years, he felt whole, as if her touch had mended the scars etched on his heart. She had brought light back into his life, and he was ready to fight for her, no matter the odds.

As he entered the manor, passing by the study, Lady Isabella's voice called out to him. "Lord Westcott," she began, a hopeful lilt in her tone. "Are congratulations in order?"

He stopped and turned towards the open door. "I'm afraid not," he replied, stepping inside. "My offer was interrupted by Lord Bedford."

Lady Isabella's face fell slightly, but her determination didn't waver. "But you do intend to marry my daughter?"

"I do," Niles said firmly. "Make no mistake about that."

A bright smile broke across her face. "Wonderful," she declared, her voice brimming with approval.

Alfred, who had been silently observing the conversation, stepped closer to his wife. "What did Charles want?"

Niles's expression grew serious. "He wasn't pleased that I was offering for Elsbeth. He made his objections quite clear."

Alfred's expression grew solemn. "If what we believe is true, then by you marrying her, he would lose access to her dowry," he said. "I never wanted to think Charles was capable of such things, but Mr. Strother's suspicions have made me rethink everything."

Niles's brow lifted. "Does Mr. Strother have proof?"

"He has been working with us to gather evidence," Alfred

explained. "Mr. Strother was a loyal ally to the late Lord Bedford and believes foul play was involved in his death."

Lady Isabella interjected. "Where is Elsbeth?"

"She went to the stables to speak to Charles," Niles informed her. "She was rather insistent on it."

"You let her go... *alone*?!" Alfred demanded.

Niles put his hand up. "She assured me that Morton would keep her safe while she spoke to Charles."

Alfred glanced at the window. "I do not think that is a good idea. She shouldn't be alone around Charles."

Before Niles could respond, a commotion erupted in the entry hall.

Lady Isabella turned her head sharply. "What on earth is going on now?" she asked.

"I'll find out," Niles said, excusing himself from the study.

When he reached the entry hall, Niles saw Lord Bedford directing the servants, his face a storm of frustration as they moved trunks towards the door.

"Good gads, you're here again?" Bedford said dryly. "Don't you have anywhere else to be?"

"I thought you were going riding," Niles replied.

Bedford scowled. "Are you daft? I told you I was leaving this manor, and I intend to make good on that promise."

Niles frowned. "Elsbeth went to the stables to find you. She thought you'd be riding to clear your head."

Bedford's expression shifted to disbelief. "Normally, I would. But today? After being accused of murder? I have no desire to linger where I'm not wanted," he said. "I am surprised you even allow Elsbeth to be around me, considering you think so poorly of me."

"It was Elsbeth's decision, not mine," Niles replied. "And I support her."

Bedford huffed. "Mr. Strother told me that it would be

nearly impossible to prove that Alfred was behind my uncle's murder. I just didn't want to believe that."

Niles pressed his lips together. "Mr. Strother told you that?"

"Didn't I just say that?" Bedford asked. "I do believe you get stupider every time we speak."

Niles's jaw tightened, but before he could formulate a response or retort, the manor's main door suddenly burst open with a resounding crash.

Morton, the white-haired groom, stumbled into the entry hall, his face pale and his wide eyes filled with panic. He clutched his cap in trembling hands as he scanned the room, his voice trembling as he cried out, "Lady Elsbeth! She's been taken!"

The words hit Niles like a blow to the chest, his breath catching. "*What*?!" he demanded, striding towards Morton. "Taken? What do you mean?"

Morton swallowed hard, stepping closer as his hands fidgeted with the brim of his cap. "I was at the stables, brushing down one of the horses. I saw Lady Elsbeth walking down the garden path. I—I looked down for just a moment, and when I looked up, I saw a man grab her. He carried her to a waiting coach. I shouted, but by the time I got there, the coach was already gone."

Bedford's face paled, his frustration and anger from moments ago replaced by pure alarm. "Did you see the man? Do you know who it was?"

Morton nodded shakily. "He was short, with thinning hair and spectacles. I've seen him before... it was Mr. Strother."

Niles's hands clenched into fists, his mind racing. "Mr. Strother," he said, his voice cold and steely. "Why would he—"

"It doesn't matter why," Bedford interrupted. "What matters is that Elsbeth is gone, and we need to act now."

"We need to notify the constable at once," Niles said, his voice steady despite the turmoil raging inside him.

Morton shook his head. "With all due respect, my lord, you must go after her now. By the time the constable arrives, it might be too late. The coach took the road leading out of the village."

Lady Isabella appeared in the corridor, her eyes darting between Morton and Bedford. "What is all this shouting about?"

Bedford turned to his aunt, his voice grim. "Mr. Strother has abducted Elsbeth."

Lady Isabella staggered back and Alfred appeared by her side, steadying her. "Please say it isn't true," she said, her voice trembling.

"I saw it myself, my lady," Morton confirmed.

Alfred's expression turned steely, a dangerous edge in his voice. "I'm going after her," he stated.

"I'm going, too," Niles said without hesitation.

"As am I," Bedford added.

Alfred nodded curtly. "We leave at once."

Morton spun on his heel. "I'll have the horses saddled immediately."

Alfred gestured towards the study. "Follow me. I have pistols for all of us. We'll make sure that Mr. Strother regrets ever laying a hand on Elsbeth."

The men exchanged resolute nods before heading towards the study, ready to do whatever it took to bring her home.

As they entered the study, Alfred strode purposefully to his desk. He unlocked a drawer and withdrew three pistols. "Here," he said, holding them out. "Be careful. These pistols are loaded."

Niles accepted a pistol, his gaze flicking to Alfred. "You keep loaded pistols in your desk?"

"I am a merchant, my lord," Alfred replied matter-of-factly. "One never knows when a disgruntled individual might decide to settle a score. And I would do anything to protect my family."

Bedford, standing slightly apart, examined the pistol before tucking it securely into the waistband of his trousers. "Enough talk. Let's get moving."

"Before we go," Alfred began, "I need to know that I can trust you both."

Bedford let out a dry chuckle. "Says the man who just handed me a loaded weapon."

Alfred's eyes locked onto Bedford's, his expression dark. "Mark my words: if you do anything to hurt Elsbeth, I will kill you myself."

Bedford's eyes narrowed. "The feeling is mutual," he growled.

The room grew heavy with tension as the two men glared at one another, their animosity tangible. Finally, Alfred seemed to deem Bedford's response sufficient and turned back to the matter at hand. "We need to figure out what the blazes Mr. Strother is after. Why did he abduct Elsbeth?"

Niles stepped forward, the pistol resting in his hand. "If I may," he said, his tone contemplative, "I believe Mr. Strother has been playing both sides. He's been stirring suspicion against both of you, but for what purpose?"

Alfred's brow furrowed as he glanced at Niles. "That may be, but I saw the ledgers. Bedford was stealing from the late Lord Bedford's estate."

Bedford's face contorted with anger. "Are you mad? I wasn't stealing anything! What could I possibly take from a nearly bankrupt estate?"

Alfred squared his shoulders. "The ledgers don't lie. Your uncle discovered your treachery, and that's why you killed him."

Bedford took a commanding step forward. "That is utter balderdash! You're projecting your own guilt on me, Alfred. You killed my uncle so you could marry my aunt."

Alfred's face reddened with fury. "How dare you! I did no such thing!"

The two men began shouting over each other, their accusations growing louder and more heated by the second. Niles, his patience snapping, stepped between them and raised his hand in a commanding gesture. "Enough!" he barked.

The room fell silent, and Niles fixed each of them with a stern gaze. "This infighting serves no purpose. While we argue, Elsbeth is out there, in danger. Whatever grievances you have with each other can wait. Right now, we focus on one thing—saving her."

Alfred and Bedford exchanged a tense look. After a long pause, Alfred gave a curt nod. "You're right. Elsbeth's safety comes first."

Bedford adjusted the pistol at his waistband and gave a firm nod. "Let's move. Every moment we delay only puts more distance between us and Elsbeth."

The three men exited the manor with purposeful strides. The sound of their boots on the gravel path was brisk and urgent as they made their way to the stables. Their determination hung in the air, thick and unyielding.

True to his word, Morton stood in the stable yard with three horses saddled and ready to ride. He hurried over as they approached, leading the first horse to Niles. "This is Elsbeth's mare," he explained, handing him the reins. "She is rather feisty, but I've no doubt you can handle her."

Niles accepted the reins. "Thank you, Morton," he said as he mounted the horse.

Beside him, Charles muttered, "The horse or Elsbeth? Which is feistier, do you think?"

Niles shot him a withering glance, his patience wearing thin. "Now isn't the time for jokes, Bedford."

Charles smirked but said nothing further as he mounted his own horse.

Morton stepped closer to the mare, his expression serious. "You'll need to move quickly," he urged. "Once the coach reaches the main road, Mr. Strother could take any number of routes. The longer you take, the harder it'll be to track them."

Niles turned his gaze towards the road that led out of the village. His jaw tightened as he considered the challenge ahead. "Then we'd best ride hard."

Morton stepped back, his weathered face lined with concern. "Ride safe. And bring Lady Elsbeth home."

With that, Niles spurred the mare into motion, leading the charge out of the stable yard and onto the road. The hooves of their horses pounded against the ground, kicking up dirt and pebbles as they raced against time.

The wind whipped past Niles's face, but his thoughts were singularly focused. Elsbeth. He had to reach her, had to save her. He couldn't fail. Not when her life—and his future—depended on it.

20

Elsbeth's head throbbed, and the rhythmic sway of the coach made her stomach churn. Where was she? Slowly, she opened her eyes, her vision blurring before settling on the figure sitting across from her. Mr. Strother. The solicitor was holding a pistol aimed directly at her, his expression unnervingly calm.

Panic surged as she brought a hand to her head, trying to steady her thoughts. "What is the meaning of this?" she demanded, though her voice sounded weak and shaky.

Mr. Strother's lips curled into an unsettling smile. "Good. You're awake. I was beginning to worry I'd struck you too hard."

The memory of being hit came rushing back to her. She straightened as much as she could in the cramped space. "You hit me? Why?"

He leaned back, the pistol never wavering. "It's much easier to abduct someone when they're unconscious. I would have thought that was rather obvious."

Her stomach twisted as his words settled. "I don't understand. What do you want?"

"Of course you don't," he said, his tone condescending. "But

I'll save you the guessing game. I've been trying to kill you for days now. You're remarkably resilient."

"You were the one behind the planter falling?"

He grinned. "Among other things. The barrel, the lozenges, and even the gunshot. All me. The arsenic in the lozenges should've worked, but I underestimated the dosage."

Her mind raced, connecting the pieces. "How did you even know Charles would offer me a lozenge?"

He shrugged dismissively. "It didn't matter who took it— him or you. I swapped one in, knowing that eventually, one of you would eat it."

Her voice rose in disbelief. "Why? Why would you do this?"

His expression hardened. "It's simple. You need to die for your dowry to revert back to the estate. That money is the only thing that can sustain the lifestyle I've grown accustomed to."

Her heart sank. "So Charles is behind this?"

Mr. Strother laughed, the sound cold and humorless. "Lord Bedford? He's just a clueless fool. I've been embezzling from the estate long before your cousin assumed his title. But now, the coffers are empty. Your dowry is the only way out."

Realization struck her like a blow. "You were stealing from my father, too, weren't you?"

He gave a slow, deliberate nod. "Indeed. But your father was much more clever than Charles. He began to notice discrepancies. That's why he had to die."

The air seemed to leave her lungs. "You killed my father?"

"I did," he replied, as if it were a mere inconvenience. "It wasn't difficult. Your father was a creature of habit and was predictable to the end."

Her fists clenched at her sides. "You're a monster."

He looked bored by her accusation. "Your father was no saint, my lady. He squandered fortunes on mistresses and debts. I simply took what I felt I deserved. And when he became a problem, I eliminated him. Just as I plan to eliminate you."

"It is only a matter of time before Charles figures out what you are doing," Elsbeth stated.

"I am counting on it," he replied. "Which is why Lord Bedford will have to die soon enough. Then, I will disappear with his money."

Elsbeth's mind scrambled for a way to stall. "I do believe you have underestimated Lord Westcott. He will come for me."

Mr. Strother's smile wavered for the first time. "Lord Westcott? He may have some affection for you, but he'll return to his estate soon enough. Important men like him don't waste their lives chasing lost causes."

Elsbeth held his gaze, attempting to sound more confident than she felt. "You don't know him as I do."

He leaned forward, his pistol gleaming ominously in the dim light. "It doesn't matter. You'll be dead before anyone can save you."

Desperation clawed at her, but she pressed on. "The gunshot—how did you manage that?"

Mr. Strother chuckled. "That was my favorite bit of ingenuity. I waited behind a tree for the right moment and timed it perfectly with Lord Bedford's shot. Everyone assumed it was an accident."

"And the barrel?" she pressed.

His eyes narrowed slightly. "I hired a shopkeeper to do the deed, but the fool failed. I had to silence him permanently after that."

"You killed him, too?"

"Of course," Mr. Strother replied, as though it were the most natural thing in the world. "Loose ends are a liability."

Elsbeth's mind raced, but her body remained frozen in place. She couldn't let this man win, couldn't let him snuff out her life so easily. Somewhere, somehow, she had to find a way to escape.

Her eyes darted to the coach door, calculating the distance to the ground. She could throw herself out, but she could be trampled by the iron wheels. The risk was too great. One misstep, and she'd trade one death for another.

Mr. Strother's sharp gaze followed her line of sight. "Thinking of making a dramatic exit, are we?" His smirk was smug. "Go ahead. I won't stop you. But let me assure you, if you somehow survive the fall, I'll put a bullet in you before you can take a single step."

His confidence, his arrogance, made her even more determined. She kept her expression guarded, not willing to give him the satisfaction of seeing her fear. Instead, she adjusted her position, feigning discomfort as she moved closer to the edge of the seat.

"What do you want from me?" she asked, her voice trembling just enough to sound genuine. If she could keep him talking, perhaps she could find an opening and a moment of distraction.

Mr. Strother leaned back against the cushioned seat, his grip on the pistol still firm. "I thought I made myself clear," he replied. "Your death is the key to my freedom. Once you're gone, your dowry reverts to the estate, and I can finally leave this miserable country behind."

"You're willing to kill for money?" she pressed, her tone incredulous. "Is that all you care about?"

"It's not just money," Mr. Strother snapped. "It's what the money represents. Power. Independence. The ability to live a life free of restrictions."

"And the lives you destroy along the way mean nothing to you?"

"Don't preach to me, Lady Elsbeth," he sneered. "Your father was no saint. He ruined lives with his reckless gambling and selfish pursuits. I'm merely playing the game he started."

Her heart ached at the cold reality of his words, but she refused to let his twisted reasoning deter her. "Just so you know, you are wrong about Niles," she said. "He won't stop looking for me."

"Lord Westcott is a practical man. He'll move on. Men like him always do."

Elsbeth allowed a flicker of defiance to creep into her voice. "You are wrong about him, and that will be your downfall."

Mr. Strother's lips curled into a snarl, but before he could reply, the coach hit a deep rut in the road, causing it to jolt violently. He grabbed for balance, his focus slipping momentarily.

It was all she needed.

Without thinking of the repercussions of her actions, Elsbeth lunged forward, her hands striking the wrist of the arm holding the pistol. Mr. Strother cursed, the weapon flying from his grasp and clattering to the floor of the coach. She lunged towards it, but he was quicker, grabbing her by the arm and hauling her back.

"You fool!" he spat out.

Elsbeth twisted and clawed at his hand. "I won't make it easy for you!"

Mr. Strother reached his hand back and slapped her, sending her flying back against the bench. "You little chit! You are not going to win this," he said as he retrieved the pistol.

She brought a hand up to her pounding cheek. "I am going to fight you. I won't stop until I am dead."

He pointed his pistol at her and cocked it. "That can be arranged, my lady."

As Elsbeth braced for the inevitable, her heart thundering in her chest, a shout cut through the tense air. "Highwaymen!" the voice bellowed from outside.

The coach jolted slightly as the driver reined in the horses, but Mr. Strother's reaction was immediate and furious. He struck the roof of the coach with the butt of his pistol, his movements frantic. "Don't stop! Keep going, you idiot!" he barked, his voice cracking under the weight of panic.

But the coach came to an abrupt, jerking halt despite his orders. The horses neighed loudly, their hooves stamping in protest against the rough stop. Then came the unmistakable sound of a commanding voice booming from outside: "Stand and deliver!"

Niles.

She would recognize that voice anywhere. Relief surged through her. He had come for her. A part of her knew that he always would.

Mr. Strother cursed under his breath as he yanked the curtain aside to peer out the window. "Well, it would indeed appear that I underestimated Lord Westcott. But that hardly matters." He opened the coach window, the pistol steady in his hand. "Stay back! I'll kill her if you come any closer."

From her limited view, Elsbeth saw Niles, Alfred, and Charles on horseback, each man armed and poised for action. Their faces were set with determination, and Niles's eyes burned with a fury she had never seen before.

"Strother," Niles's voice rang out, "you've lost. Step out of the coach, and no one needs to get hurt."

Mr. Strother's laugh was devoid of any humor. "Spare me the noble speeches, Lord Westcott. I hold all the cards here."

"Do you?" Alfred interjected. "You're outnumbered, outgunned, and surrounded. There's no way out of this for you."

Mr. Strother's hand tightened around the pistol, and he jabbed it towards Elsbeth. "That's where you're wrong. I have her, and I'm willing to use her to ensure my escape."

Inside the coach, Elsbeth's mind raced. She needed to buy

Niles and the others time, but every movement she made risked provoking Mr. Strother further. "You think you're clever, Mr. Strother," she said, "But you didn't quite think this through, did you?"

"Quiet!" Mr. Strother barked, but there was a flicker of uncertainty in his eyes. Elsbeth's words had struck a nerve.

Outside, Charles dismounted his horse and took a step closer to the coach. "Strother, listen to me. If you harm Elsbeth, there won't be a place on this earth where you can hide. You'll be hunted until your dying breath."

Mr. Strother sneered but glanced nervously between the window and Elsbeth. He was cornered, and he knew it. His confidence was fraying.

Taking a deep breath, Niles dismounted as well. "Let her go, Strother," he commanded. "You have nothing to gain by hurting her. Surrender now, and you might live to see another day."

Mr. Strother's grip faltered for the briefest moment, and Elsbeth seized the opportunity, knowing it was her only chance at saving herself. Summoning all her strength, she lunged forward, grabbing his wrist and wrenching the pistol upward. The weapon discharged with a deafening bang, the bullet lodging harmlessly in the roof of the coach.

"Elsbeth!" Niles shouted.

Mr. Strother shoved Elsbeth aside, scrambling to reload the pistol, but Niles reached the door and flung it open with a force that sent it slamming against the side of the coach. He grabbed Mr. Strother by his jacket and yanked him out, throwing him to the ground.

Charles and Alfred were quick to act, disarming Mr. Strother and pinning him to the dirt road. The once-arrogant man now looked small, his face pale and his eyes wide with fear.

Inside the coach, Elsbeth allowed herself to take deep breaths, knowing the nightmare was over. She felt a gentle hand on her arm and looked up to see Niles, his eyes searching hers.

"Are you hurt?" he asked, his voice soft but filled with urgency.

She shook her head, tears spilling over. "No, I'm all right," she whispered. "You came for me."

"Of course I did," he said, his voice breaking slightly. "I will always come for you. You must know that."

Niles helped her out of the coach, steadying her as her legs wobbled beneath her. Behind them, Charles and Alfred restrained Mr. Strother, binding his hands with a rope.

"It's over," Niles said, pulling her into a tight embrace. "You're safe now."

For the first time in days, Elsbeth allowed herself to believe it. She was safe; her home was in his arms.

As the afternoon sunlight cast golden streaks across the gardens, Niles led Elsbeth back towards the manor. His thoughts churned with all the things he wanted to say, the emotions he could no longer suppress. She had become the center of his world, and he knew he could not let another moment pass without speaking his heart.

He came to a stop, gently tugging her to pause as well. The manor loomed ahead, but they stood on the quiet path. Turning to face her, Niles took a deep breath. "May we speak for a moment?"

Elsbeth glanced ahead, where Alfred and Bedford were a few steps ahead of them. "I would like that."

Alfred stopped and turned back, his expression a mixture of impatience and curiosity. "Say what needs to be said but make it quick. Meet us in the study afterward."

Bedford opened his mouth, as though to protest, but instead, he sighed and followed Alfred into the house, leaving Niles and Elsbeth standing in the stillness of the gardens.

Niles turned back to her, his eyes locking with hers. "We are finally alone."

Elsbeth smiled, and he swore he had never seen anything more beautiful. "What is it you wish to say?"

Taking a step closer, Niles gently reached for her hand, clasping it. "I want to continue the conversation we started earlier. About marriage."

"There's no need anymore," Elsbeth replied. "I am safe now that Mr. Strother has been handed over to the Bow Street Runner. The constable will see to his arrest."

"I'm relieved that you're safe," Niles said, his tone earnest. "But that's not the only reason I wish to marry you." He stepped closer, his grip on her hand tightening slightly. "I want to marry you because I found a piece of my soul in your eyes and I don't want it back."

Elsbeth's gaze dropped, her cheeks flushing a delicate pink. "That is kind, but—"

"I love you," Niles interrupted firmly. His voice carried a depth that startled even himself. "You may deny it, and knowing you, you will. But it won't make it any less true. You've breathed life back into me, Elsbeth. You've shown me what it is to truly live."

Her gaze lifted to meet his, her eyes glistening with unshed tears. "What of my reputation?"

"I don't care about your reputation," he replied. "Not anymore. I only care about you. I just want you."

"But—"

He cupped her cheek in his hand, speaking over her. "No more 'buts.' Nothing you say will change my mind. I am so hopelessly in love with you that I cannot imagine a future without you."

Elsbeth leaned into his hand, her lips trembling as she whispered, "Then my answer is yes."

Relief and joy surged through Niles, and a wide smile spread across his face. "That was much easier than I expected," he said with a laugh. "I had prepared an entire speech to convince you."

"Perhaps you can save it for another time," she teased. "Though I do have some concerns on your earlier attempt at being a highwayman. You didn't even bother to steal anything from Mr. Strother. Not even a pocket watch."

Niles chuckled. "It seems to have worked out regardless."

"It did," she agreed. "But only because you came to save me. Thank you."

His finger caressed her cheek as he murmured, "I think it is only fair because you saved me from myself."

Her eyes filled with tears, one escaping to trail down her cheek. "I love you, Niles," she whispered, her voice breaking slightly.

Niles leaned in, his lips meeting hers in a kiss that was both tender and fierce, full of the promises he hadn't yet spoken aloud. Her lips were soft, her touch grounding him in a way he had never experienced before. In that moment, he knew he would never tire of her, of this, of them.

When they finally broke apart, their breaths mingling, Niles said, "We should probably share the good news with your family."

Elsbeth smiled mischievously. "We should, but I'd much rather kiss you a little longer."

"As would I," he replied with a grin, "but Bedford will likely come out and interrupt us again."

She laughed. "True. Let's tell them, and then we can plan for more uninterrupted kissing."

"I find that plan quite agreeable," he said, taking her hand once more as they resumed their walk towards the manor. "I suspect kissing you will be my favorite new pastime."

Once they arrived at the manor, they headed into the study, where Elsbeth's family was assembled.

Lady Isabella was the first to see them, and her face lit up. "Are congratulations in order?" she asked eagerly.

Elsbeth nodded. "Yes. Niles offered for me, and I accepted."

Lady Isabella squealed with delight, rushing forward to embrace her daughter. "Oh, my darling, I am so incredibly happy for you both!"

Bedford stepped forward next, extending his hand towards Niles. "Shall we let bygones be bygones now that we're about to be family?"

Niles shook his hand firmly. "I would like that."

Lady Isabella's gaze softened as she looked at her daughter. "I am so relieved you are safe, Elsbeth. Alfred told me how brave you were."

"I was brave because I had no choice," Elsbeth replied. Her gaze shifted to Niles, her voice softening. "And because I knew Niles would never let anything bad happen to me."

Bedford cleared his throat. "Need I remind you that Alfred and I played a part in rescuing you as well?"

Elsbeth smiled warmly at him. "No, and I am grateful to you both. And I am sorry for ever doubting either of you. I was wrong to do so."

Alfred spoke up from his place by the hearth. "What matters is that you're safe, my dear. And that you have found happiness."

"I have," Elsbeth said, glancing at Niles. "More than I ever thought possible."

Bedford tilted his head. "I am happy for you, Cousin."

"Thank you," Elsbeth acknowledged. She turned her attention to Alfred, her gaze unwavering. "There's something I need to say to you. I owe you an apology. I've been so unfair to you since you married my mother. I was angry and hurt, but I see now that the secrets you were keeping were only meant to protect me."

Alfred regarded her for a moment before tipping his head in a gesture of quiet acceptance. "You are forgiven," he said simply, though there was a trace of warmth in his voice that hadn't been there before.

Elsbeth continued. "Mr. Strother told me that he killed my father because he discovered he was embezzling from the estate. And he was behind all the attempts on my life. He wanted to kill me so my dowry would return back to the estate."

A heavy silence filled the room as her words sank in. Finally, Bedford spoke. "I had no idea that Mr. Strother was capable of such deceit," he admitted. "He fooled us all."

Elsbeth turned to face her cousin. "Charles, I owe you an apology as well. I'm sorry for believing, even for a moment, that you were capable of anything so nefarious."

Bedford stepped forward, placing a reassuring hand on her shoulder. "I don't fault you for that, Cousin," he said, his tone kind. "We were all deceived by Mr. Strother's manipulations. But if there's one thing we must learn from this, it's that we can't allow secrets to ever come between us again."

Alfred winced. "There is one more secret you need to know, Elsbeth," he said, his voice heavy with regret.

Lady Isabella gasped, her hand flying to her chest. "No, Alfred. She isn't ready for this."

"I want to start anew with Elsbeth and have no more secrets between us. Not anymore," Alfred said.

Lady Isabella stepped closer to her husband, her eyes pleading. "I don't think this is wise. Some secrets are meant to stay buried."

"I think Alfred is right," Elsbeth interjected. "If we're going to move forward, we need complete honesty."

"There must be another way," Lady Isabella said. "There has to be."

Alfred sighed. "There is no other way, my love. It's time."

Niles, sensing the gravity of the moment, reached for Elsbeth's hand, offering silent support. Whatever Alfred was about to reveal, Niles knew it would change everything.

Alfred straightened his shoulders and looked Elsbeth directly in the eyes. "There is no easy way to say this." He paused. "I am your father."

Elsbeth reared back. "That is impossible!"

Lady Isabella stepped forward. "It's true. I was pregnant with you before I married Stephen. He knew, but he was far more interested in my dowry than anything else."

"I wanted to marry your mother, Elsbeth, but her father forbade it. I was just a merchant, not someone he deemed worthy of his daughter," Alfred said. "When she married Stephen, it broke my heart. But you must understand, I devoted myself to building my business to prove that I was worthy of her. Of you."

Elsbeth slipped her hand out of Niles's grasp and pressed it against her forehead. "Did you ever stop loving each other?"

"No," Alfred replied without hesitation. "Not for a single moment."

Lady Isabella turned to her husband. "I tried to be a good wife to Stephen. I wanted to make it work, and a part of me did love him. But he was distant. Cold. He cared little for me."

Elsbeth's voice wavered as she asked the question, "So... I am not a lady?"

Lady Isabella reached for her daughter's hand. "You were born when I was married to Stephen," she explained. "As far as Society is concerned, you are the daughter of an earl."

"But I'm not," Elsbeth said, her tone sharpening. "I'm the daughter of a merchant."

Alfred's face fell. "I know this is a lot to take in—"

Elsbeth held up her hand, cutting him off. "No, you misunderstood me. You were there when it mattered, Alfred. That's more than my father... er, Stephen... ever managed to do. I've spent my entire life thinking there was something wrong with me. That I was somehow unworthy of my father's love. But now it makes sense."

Bedford, who had been quietly absorbing the exchange, stepped forward, his expression thoughtful. "So what do we do now?"

Elsbeth took a deep breath. "We move forward," she said. "As a family. But no more secrets."

Alfred nodded, his eyes moist. "No more secrets," he agreed.

Lady Isabella reached out, pulling Elsbeth into a warm embrace. "We'll figure it out," she whispered. "Together."

When her mother released her, Elsbeth turned to Niles as she bit her lower lip. "I know this changes everything," she began, "and I will not hold you to your offer—"

Niles cut her off before she could finish. "You're right," he said, his eyes never leaving hers. "This changes everything and, yet, nothing at all. I still want to marry you."

Her gaze searched his face for any trace of uncertainty. "Are you sure?" she asked. "If the truth ever came out, just think of the scandal that could unfold. Think of Eugenie..."

He reached for her hand and brought it up to his lips. "You stole my heart, and I don't want it back. Ever."

She knitted her brows together. "I need you to be sure, Niles."

"If I had to go through all of this, everything, just to arrive here with you—I can say with certainty, it was worth it."

"But—"

He didn't let her finish, leaning in to kiss her with a tenderness that spoke of all the words he couldn't find. She melted into him, the world around them fading away.

When he finally pulled back, a grin tugged at the corners of his mouth. "I think I've found my new favorite way to silence you."

Her laugh was soft, but it resonated deeply within him, filling a space he hadn't realized had been empty. Her smile, meant just for him, was more precious than any treasure. "I love you, Niles," she said.

No words had ever been more beautiful, and he couldn't help but grin. "And I love you, too, Elsbeth," he replied. "Although, I daresay that your voice is my favorite sound. I do not think I could ever tire of it."

Bedford leaned forward and joked, "Trust me, you will, especially when Elsbeth is arguing a point to death."

Elsbeth playfully narrowed her eyes at her cousin. "Was that truly necessary?"

"I just want Westcott to know what he is getting himself into," Bedford said, his lips twitching.

Niles slipped his arm around Elsbeth's waist. "I do believe I have finally met my match. The one who was brave enough to love me back. All of me." He smiled down at Elsbeth. "And I will love every part of her because of that."

Tears formed in Elsbeth's eyes. "I promise that I will love you, always and forever."

Lady Isabella clasped her hands together, drawing everyone's attention. "We will make the announcement of your engagement tonight at the soiree."

Bedford groaned. "Does this mean I have to attend the soiree?"

"Yes," Lady Isabella responded quickly.

"I don't mind," Niles admitted. "I do hope there will be dancing. I find that I very much want to dance with my betrothed."

"As do I," Elsbeth said.

Niles met Elsbeth's gaze. She smiled up at him, and in her

gaze, he saw not just a future—but *their* future. And he knew, with unwavering certainty, that this was only the beginning of their story.

EPILOGUE

Three weeks later...

Elsbeth stood in front of her dressing table mirror and admired her reflection. The silver gown shimmered faintly in the sunlight streaming through the window. It had once been her mother's, worn on her wedding day to Alfred. Now, knowing the truth about her father, the dress carried a deeper meaning, connecting her to both her past and the future she was about to embrace.

The revelation of her true parentage had been tumultuous, but it had brought healing. Over the past weeks, she had grown closer to Alfred, seeing firsthand the honor and quiet strength that had captivated her mother. He was not just a man who had helped rescue her from peril; he was a father who had loved her from afar, and now she was proud to call him her own.

She was happy now. Truly happy. She was about to marry the man she loved. A man who valued her. Understood her. The most beautiful part was she hadn't even been looking for love when she found Niles. But he completed her in a way that she never thought possible.

The door creaked open, and her mother stepped inside. Elsbeth's face lit up at the sight of her. "You look stunning!" her mother exclaimed, her voice warm with pride.

Elsbeth smoothed down the gown. "Thank you, Mother."

Her mother stepped closer, her eyes shimmering with emotion as she took in every detail. "This dress fits you perfectly. It's as if it were made for you." She reached out, taking Elsbeth's hands in her own. "I hope you find the kind of happiness I've found with Alfred."

Elsbeth smiled. "I have, Mother. Niles reminds me every day why I fell in love with him."

Her mother's expression softened further. "Good. You've been through so much, and you deserve every ounce of happiness."

"And so do you," Elsbeth said earnestly.

Her mother's lips trembled into a smile. "I love you, my darling," she murmured, drawing her into a gentle embrace. "Now, let's get you married."

As they exited the bedchamber, Elsbeth caught sight of Charles waiting in the corridor. His easy grin was already in place as he greeted them. "Good morning, ladies."

"Good morning," they replied in unison, their steps falling into rhythm with his as they made their way towards the staircase.

Charles glanced at her with a teasing glint in his eyes. "It's a fine day for a wedding, wouldn't you agree?"

"It is," Elsbeth agreed.

He leaned slightly towards her, lowering his voice in mock conspiracy. "Are you sure you want to marry Westcott? There's still time to change your mind, you know."

She laughed, shaking her head. "I do. With my whole heart."

"Well, I had to try one last time," he teased.

As they reached the bottom of the stairs, Alfred appeared in the entry hall. His expression was calm but purposeful. "Elsbeth, Charles," he called, gesturing towards the study. "May I have a word?"

"Of course," Elsbeth replied, glancing at Charles, who shrugged in response.

The three of them entered the study, and Alfred quietly closed the door behind them. His demeanor shifted, becoming more formal. "I wanted to speak to you both about something important," he began. "It concerns Elsbeth's dowry."

Charles raised an eyebrow, leaning casually against the edge of a desk. "And what's prompted this discussion?"

Alfred hesitated for a moment, his gaze softening as it fell on Elsbeth. "You look radiant, my dear."

"Thank you, Father," she replied.

His eyes grew moist, and he pulled a handkerchief from his pocket to dab at them. "Hearing you call me that means more than you could ever know. I waited so long to tell you the truth."

"And I'm glad you finally did," Elsbeth said.

Alfred took a deep breath. "I've spent weeks searching for the perfect wedding gift, and I believe I've found it."

"There's no need—" Elsbeth began, but Alfred raised a hand to gently silence her.

"It is my right as your father, and it involves both of you." Alfred's expression turned serious. "I know the truth about your parentage has complicated your feelings about your dowry, Elsbeth. But I believe I've found a solution. I intend to match your dowry with my own funds and gift it to Charles to help his estate."

Elsbeth's eyes widened. "Are you certain, Father?"

"Quite certain," Alfred replied. "Declining your dowry would only invite questions, and I refuse to let that happen. This way, we ensure discretion."

Elsbeth stepped forward, emotion spilling over. "Oh, Father, thank you. This means so much."

Alfred placed his hands on her shoulders. "All I've ever wanted is for you to be happy."

"I am happy, more so than I ever thought possible," Elsbeth admitted as tears flooded into her eyes. "How can I not be?"

As Charles stood quietly to the side, he looked stunned. "Thank you, Alfred," he said sincerely. "This will make all the difference."

"I wish you luck, I truly do. I know I am merely a merchant and can't possibly understand the pressures of your position in Society—" Alfred started.

Charles cut him off before he could finish. "You are one of the finest men I know, and you have accomplished more than most men could ever dream of. Do not think yourself any less because you were not born into gentry."

Alfred studied Charles for a long moment, his expression unreadable, before he finally tipped his head in quiet acknowledgment. "Shall we depart for the chapel?" he asked. "I suspect Lord Westcott is rather impatient to get this day started."

"I think that's a fine idea," Elsbeth agreed.

Alfred extended his arm, and Elsbeth placed her hand on it. The simple gesture carried an unspoken weight between them, a sign of their growing bond. As they made their way to the entry hall, the sound of Niles's voice reached her ears. Her heart quickened, as it always did when he was near. Would she ever grow used to this feeling? She hoped not.

Niles's face brightened as she approached. "Elsbeth," he greeted, closing the distance between them. Without hesitation, he leaned in and pressed a kiss to her lips.

"You cannot take such liberties," she teased, a light reprimand in her tone. "We are not married yet."

Niles, not looking the least bit repentant, said, "My apologies."

"Well, if you refuse to observe propriety, neither shall I," she quipped, and before he could respond, she kissed him back, letting herself melt into his embrace.

From behind them, Charles groaned loudly. "Good gads, could either of you show some restraint? Spare the rest of us."

Elsbeth broke the kiss with a laugh, stepping back but still holding Niles's hand. "Perhaps Charles has a point."

"Please don't say that again," Niles replied, placing a hand over his heart in mock distress. "It sounds dreadfully wrong."

Charles looked heavenward. "Why are you here, Westcott? Weren't you planning to meet us at the chapel?"

"I was," Niles admitted. "But I realized I wanted to be the one to escort Elsbeth to the chapel, assuming she doesn't object."

Elsbeth arched a brow playfully. "Will there be kissing involved?"

Niles's grin grew wider. "Always."

Feigning deliberation, Elsbeth nodded. "In that case, I most definitely want Niles to escort me."

"You two are insufferable," Charles muttered, though there was no mistaking the hint of amusement in his tone.

Her mother and Alfred stepped forward. "Go on," her mother urged. "We'll follow in the coach."

Niles extended his arm to Elsbeth with a flourish. She took it, and he led her outside to the awaiting carriage. "I've been counting down the moments till our wedding."

"Is that today?" she teased. "I hadn't realized."

Niles chuckled as he helped her onto the bench. "I was also thinking we could leave for our wedding tour right after the luncheon."

"Efficient and romantic," Elsbeth retorted. "I think I made an excellent choice."

Coming around the carriage, Niles stepped up to face her. "I have something for you," he said, reaching into his jacket pocket and pulling out a small, elegant box tied neatly with a red bow.

"You didn't need to get me anything," she said, though her hands eagerly reached for the box.

"It's just a small trinket."

Her fingers worked quickly to undo the bow, and she lifted the lid to reveal a stunning oval-shaped watch with a delicately engraved silver dial. "It is beautiful," she said as she lifted the watch from the box.

Niles leaned closer, pointing to the intricate design on the watch's face. "This piece was inspired by the one designed for Queen Caroline Murat of Naples," he explained. "It is meant to be worn around the wrist. The wristlet is made of gold thread and hair."

"I love it," she said. "But this is more than just a mere trinket."

"May I?" he asked, holding out his hand.

She offered him the watch, her heart swelling as she murmured, "Thank you."

Niles fastened the watch gently around her wrist, his fingers brushing against her skin. Once it was secure, he didn't move back. Instead, he stayed close, his face just inches from hers. "Rumor has it that a highwaywoman terrorizes this stretch of road," he said, a playful glint in his eyes. "Apparently, she has a particular fondness for pocket watches."

"At least I managed to steal something," she retorted. "Your attempt at being a highwayman was clumsy at best."

He smirked, his gaze never leaving hers. "I did save you, though, didn't I?"

"You did, my hero," she responded. "I'll never forget the day we met. I was completely unaware that you would mean so much to me."

"It felt like magic, the way you came into my life and made everything brighter."

Her smile widened as she reached up to cup his face. "I'm so glad I robbed your coach."

"And I'm so glad you did," he whispered before pressing his lips to hers.

The kiss was slow and deep and Elsbeth surrendered to his touch. How she loved this man. She had found the one person that made her think that forever didn't sound like enough time.

A loud groan shattered the moment. "You two didn't make it very far!" Charles's exasperated voice broke through the haze. "You're supposed to be on your way to the chapel to get married."

Reluctantly, Niles broke the kiss and leaned back with a sheepish grin. "Elsbeth distracted me," he joked.

Charles folded his arms, clearly unimpressed. "Well, can you try to manage a distraction-free journey? At least until after the ceremony?"

Elsbeth raised her wrist, flashing the watch. "Look at what Niles gave me!"

Charles inspected the intricate design with a nod of approval. "It's lovely, but it's still not an excuse for being late to your own wedding."

Niles chuckled as he grabbed the reins. "Shall we get married?"

"Why not?" she replied with a bright smile on her face. "I have nothing else to do at the moment."

"You are a minx," he quipped, flicking his wrist to urge the horses forward.

Elsbeth laughed, nestling close to him. He wrapped his arm around her shoulders, holding her tightly as they traveled down the road. She fit perfectly against him, as though he was born to hold her.

The End

NEXT BOOK IN THE SERIES...

She was determined to remain a spinster—until love gave her a new reason to dream.

Lady Eugenie Drayton is tired of being told what she can and cannot do. Bold, clever, and entirely too curious for Society's liking, she decides to take matters into her own hands by sneaking into an Oxford lecture disguised as a man. But her plan is swiftly upended when she is discovered by none other than Charles Ellsworth, Earl of Bedford—a man far too proper, far too persistent, and far too memorable, especially after the kiss they once shared.

Charles has spent the past few months trying to forget the infuriating and enchanting Lady Eugenie. He appreciates her desire to learn more than Society believes acceptable. But when he finds her where no lady should be, he's forced to intervene. Reluctantly, they strike a bargain—one that forces them into close proximity and threatens the fragile walls around both their hearts.

As their partnership teeters on the edge of scandal and something far more dangerous, Eugenie must decide if she truly desires a life of independence...or the kind of love that would change everything.

ABOUT THE AUTHOR

Laura Beers is an award-winning author. She attended Brigham Young University, earning a Bachelor of Science degree in Construction Management. She can't sing, doesn't dance and loves naps.

Laura lives in Utah with her husband, three kids and her dysfunctional dog. When not writing regency romance, she loves skiing, hiking and drinking Dr Pepper.

You can connect with Laura on Facebook, Instagram or on her site at www.authorlaurabeers.com.